Johnny Gone Down

Johnny Gone Down

KARAN BAJAJ

HarperCollins *Publishers* India
a joint venture with

THE
INDIA
TODAY
GROUP
New Delhi

First published in India in 2010 by
HarperCollins *Publishers* India
a joint venture with
The India Today Group

Copyright © Karan Bajaj 2010

ISBN: 978-81-7223-786-8

2 4 6 8 10 9 7 5 3 1

Karan Bajaj asserts the moral right to be identified
as the author of this book.

HarperCollins *Publishers*
A-53, Sector 57, NOIDA, Uttar Pradesh – 201301, India
77-85 Fulham Palace Road, London W6 8JB, United Kingdom
Hazelton Lanes, 55 Avenue Road, Suite 2900, Toronto, Ontario M5R 3L2
and 1995 Markham Road, Scarborough, Ontario M1B 5M8, Canada
25 Ryde Road, Pymble, Sydney, NSW 2073, Australia
31 View Road, Glenfield, Auckland 10, New Zealand
10 East 53rd Street, New York NY 10022, USA

Typeset in 10.5/15 Adobe Caslon Pro
Jojy Philip New Delhi 110 015

Printed and bound at
Thomson Press (India) Ltd.

To my parents
for always supporting Johnny and his friends

*So now, he is a legend when he would have
preferred to be a man.*

Prologue

'Stop staring,' said the woman through clenched teeth.

The little boy, presumably her son, looked away reluctantly. He fixed his attention outside the window as the train sped through the vast, arid plains of central India.

My son would look like him perhaps, I thought suddenly. If he were alive, that is. In the part of the world where he was growing up, infant mortality is as common as UFO sightings in America. The son I abandoned without seeing his face, feeling his breath, or touching his fingers – yet another life I had destroyed in my Faustian journey. It didn't hurt to think about it any more. Nothing hurt. I felt nothing, I thought nothing; just the moment now, the journey here. I would be crushed under the weight of my regrets if I allowed myself the luxury.

The boy, angelic face streaked with soot, soon began to tire of looking outside and started stealing glances at me once again.

'His left arm is missing,' he burst out finally. 'He is an amputee, Mama, isn't he? *Amputated.*' The boy, seven, maybe eight years old, had clearly learnt a new word and was beside himself with joy to see a live example in front of him.

His mother, a tall, young, big-boned lady with a firm, determined jaw and hard cheekbones, pounced on him, slapping him across his face.

'It's all right. Please,' I said. 'He's right. I don't have a left arm.' I took out my stump from my coat to show him.

It seemed strange to speak in Hindi after so many years. I had been gone far too long. I was back now, and it wasn't a triumphant return by any means, but this was home.

Everything had changed, yet nothing had changed.

'I'm really sorry,' said the mother as the boy escaped her grasp, staring at me in frank admiration.

'Not at all. He is very observant,' I said, managing to smile at the boy.

His face lit up. He now had the licence to stare openly at me, and his eyes darted from my stump to the punctured holes in my right wrist where they'd forced in the tubes.

'Are you going to Delhi?' asked the mother, still frowning at her boy.

I nodded.

'You live there?'

'I used to,' I replied. 'A while ago.'

'You live in Bombay now?' she asked.

I smiled. If I had missed anything in the twenty years I'd been gone, it was this uniquely Indian gift for immediate familiarity, the unabashed probing followed by a quick judgement on another's choices. In another life, I'd probably have warmed up to the interrogation. Now, every question unleashed an avalanche of memories – none of them pleasant.

'No,' I said shortly. 'I am coming from overseas.'

A sophisticated but defeated looking middle-aged man, the fourth occupant of our second-class Bombay–Delhi train compartment, buried in his newspaper all this while, perked up suddenly. He put down his newspaper, adjusted his thick spectacles and stared at me, his thick lips and dark moustache quivering, perhaps in anticipation of a debate which would ease the monotony of the twenty-four-hour journey in the hot Indian summer.

'What's the use of going abroad nowadays?' he said. 'Everything is in India.'

He picked up his newspaper again and pointed to the picture of a short, dark man on the front page. 'Look, Rahman is going to compose music on Broadway. Is he any less than Elton John? Is Shah Rukh Khan any less than Brad Pitt? All of Hollywood is coming to Bollywood now. India is going to be the next superpower. Why go anywhere else?'

I nodded noncommittally. None of these names sounded familiar. I had just risen from the dead. In the world I came from, there were no movies, no music, no life. Only time and darkness, boundless and pervasive, enough to last several lifetimes and then some more.

'How long were you abroad? Where were you?' the man asked; tall, erect body with just the beginnings of a paunch shifting as he spoke.

'Twenty-five years,' I said, wishing he would keep quiet. 'I've been in different places.'

'Twenty-five years!' he exclaimed. 'If I were to guess, you must be my age, forty or forty-five years old. That means you've been away since you were, what, fifteen or twenty.'

Unconsciously, he appraised me from top to bottom, glancing disdainfully at my worn-out shoes, frayed coat, unshaven face, amputated arm and long, matted hair streaked with grey.

'What did you get from it?' he asked.

Suddenly, I wanted to be alone in the darkness of my thoughts. I knew he didn't mean to offend; he was just a bored, curious man, intending to provoke, discuss, argue — it helped kill the time. But I had nothing to say, no desire for this conversation, or any other conversation for that matter.

'Arre,' said the woman, breaking in before I got the chance to mutter a response, 'not everything is about getting and giving, gaining and losing, victory and defeat. Imagine living twenty years in different countries! How much experience he has had; how many lives he has lived! Compared to him, we are like frogs in the well, jumping about in our tiny worlds without ever seeing the light outside.'

'The deer wandered restlessly from forest to forest, searching for the divine fragrance, not knowing that the musk rested in his own belly,' the man said smugly. 'The only light that needs to shine is the one in your own mind.'

'You are a strange one,' said the woman condescendingly. 'Not all who wander are lost. Besides, he must come back home to India almost every year. That's what my sister in the US does. She spends more time with my parents than I do, though I live in India.' She turned to me. 'Don't you?'

I shook my head.

'How often do you come back?' she asked.

'Never,' I said quietly.

'You didn't come to India even once in twenty-five years?' she said incredulously.

I shook my head again. 'I didn't get a chance.'

The man looked at her triumphantly.

'So what? He must have liked it there,' she said defensively. She pointed to another picture in the forgotten newspaper. 'Look at this woman. Would she ever want to come back? She is the CEO of the biggest company in the world. Like me, she is an MBA, but unlike me, she was smart enough to leave India. Women can't get anywhere in this country, but look at her.'

I looked at the picture out of curiosity – and

recognized her at once. She hadn't changed much: the hard, determined look in her bright eyes; the angular face; the short hair that was so unfashionable back then – but she hadn't cared.

'I march to my own drummer,' she used to say, and we would laugh because she played the drums in the college band, the only woman amidst the stoned grunge rockers.

Even her lovemaking was deliberate and measured and afterwards, when I would collapse on top of her, exhausted, she would methodically explain the latest positions she had read about in *The Joy of Sex* that she wanted to try next time. I had never seen her or spoken to her since that day in 1975 when we graduated. I never thought about how my life might have turned out if we had still been together. There had been too many wrong turns and missed opportunities for me to contemplate just one alternate universe.

'Why are you smiling?' asked the man, startling me a little.

'Nothing,' I replied, abashed by the sudden, clear memory.

'She isn't bad looking,' he conceded.

'She is the CEO of the biggest company in the world; *Fortune's* most powerful woman; the first woman to break the American glass ceiling – being an Indian, that too – and all you can talk about is how she looks. No wonder you are in a second-class compartment while she travels in her corporate jet,' said the woman in disgust.

The young boy, delighted that someone else was getting a lashing from his mother for a change, smiled conspiratorially at me.

'And what about you, madam?' the man said with a smirk. 'You say you are an MBA like her. Why aren't you travelling in your Gulfstream then? Some people are just lucky.'

'She was in my class at MIT. She deserves all her success,' I muttered, coming to the woman's rescue.

There was a sudden silence as they both looked at me with expressions of absolute contempt (him) and pity (her). It was so ridiculous a statement coming from an obviously broke, middle-aged loser, that it didn't even merit an acknowledgement or expression of disbelief. I bore them no ill-will; it sounded absurd even to me.

'Well,' said the man after a while. 'I guess I should go back to my newspaper.'

My unintended comment had spoilt his moment by sweeping the discussion into the ludicrous. What was the fun in engaging in a debate with a lunatic?

The man opened his newspaper, hemming and hawing from time to time. The woman leaned back in her seat, only, this time she held her child closer. I had proven to be as unreliable as I looked. She watched me from the corner of her eye, keeping another eye on the red emergency chain above, ready to pull it if I acted suspicious.

To make them feel comfortable, I got up and made my way towards the door. No one in the crowded passage gave me a second glance as I shuffled past. This was a second-class train compartment in India; every face hid a thousand tragedies, and it took more to surprise a person than an armless man with a large, ugly scar on his face. I opened the door and sat quietly on the steps, wondering whether this was – and secretly hoping it was – the last journey of my life. I was tired. I had been running far too long, though I had nothing to show for it. The train swept past the landscape, dry, hot wind blowing against my face. Dhaulagiri, Ratnagiri, Chopan, Chunar, Aurangabad: names from another lifetime when the past wasn't as desolate and the future still held hope. Twilight gave way to dusk and finally, the welcome blackness of night arrived as I continued to stare into the invisible landscape, devoid of thought, wondering only sparingly how I had ended up here on my fortieth birthday. It wasn't meant to be this way, I thought briefly as I closed my eyes, although I knew sleep was an impossible luxury. I had been an insomniac for years, unable to get rid of the images of a happier past with its unfinished stories, lost chances and wrong turns. I had everything, I thought, and I threw it all away.

⌐

'Oh my God! Are you crazy?'

Inadvertently, my hand reached for the Glock concealed in my coat pocket. It took me a second to recognize her as the woman from the compartment. I relaxed and took my hand out of my pocket.

She didn't seem to notice the movement.

'You will die here,' she said. 'This is summer in India, not California. Such a strong, hot Loo and you are sitting on the steps wearing this heavy overcoat. Shut the door and come inside!'

I stood up and pushed the door close.

She stared at me. 'How did you get up? You didn't even touch the floor with your hand. What are you? A kung fu master?'

Flashes from the past. Ten years in Rio de Janeiro, trained to fight like a dog – or a drug lord – by the best fighters in the business.

'I've had to learn,' I said.

'Ufff... Can't you close the door properly? I'm getting scalded. Aren't you human?' Another flash. Minnesota, homeless, sleeping under a bridge, shivering in my thin shirt and torn pants as the Arctic wind cut me in shreds. The body adapts, I had learnt.

'You adapt,' I told her.

She stared at me for a while. 'I like you,' she said

finally. 'I'm sorry I reacted that way inside. Did you really go to school with Lavanya Varma at the Massachusetts Institute of Technology, Boston?'

MIT. Placid, innocent, the lull before the angry storms that hadn't stopped raging since.

'It doesn't matter,' I replied.

She looked curiously at me. 'How did you lose your arm?'

Phnom Penh, Cambodia. The most dismal time of my life. Not because I hadn't seen worse after, but because I was young then. I was twenty-two. I was invincible. I wasn't supposed to get hurt. Once again, I felt that hollow, empty feeling in the pit of my stomach when I recalled the gangrene that ate up my hand.

'You ask too many questions,' I told her.

She laughed, the open, honest laughter of someone who has never known loss.

'What to do? I am the cliché of a bored housewife.' She smiled petulantly, no longer compelled to play the model parent now that her kid was tucked in for the night. 'I let go my job after Raja was born. My husband travels all the time, but he still doesn't make any money.'

Strangers on a train, I thought. She was desperate to reveal herself to any willing ear and drop every mask, secure in the knowledge that there would never be a next time.

She waited with an expectant look on her face, as

if wishing me to ask questions, to probe, or even to justify myself.

I didn't say a word. Don't ask, don't judge, just accept – the first lesson I had learnt in the monastery. Eight years wasted; no monk could have walked farther away from the Buddha's path than I had.

'Sometimes I feel caged by my circumstances,' she continued.

I shuddered as I recalled the small, dark cage where I had counted seconds, minutes, hours, days, months and years, chained to the wall.

'It's getting late,' I said.

She looked disappointed as I began to shuffle away from the train door.

'Stay for a while. What's early? What's late? Do you have any work tomorrow in Delhi?' She looked at me, half contemptuous, half teasing. *What work could someone like you have that can't wait?*

'Tomorrow is important,' I said with a mirthless smile as I limped my way back to the compartment. 'A matter of life and death.'

Another sleepless night staring into the darkness. I felt the train rumble beneath me, its motion elegant and rhythmic, a mockery of my own irregular journey. I had been running for twenty-five years, yet I was behind where I started. I closed my eyes and waited.

'Are you asleep?'

She was back in the compartment. A tall woman, the top of her head almost reached the upper berth where I lay, and her hair brushed lightly against my face. A sweet fragrance filled the air. A familiar fragrance, a whiff of patchouli and sandalwood.

Lara.

Her memory struck me with a crushing, almost physical force. A dull pain seemed to pass from my scrotum to the inside of my stomach.

'You are awake,' the woman whispered.

She bent down, possibly to check if her son was still asleep. Seemingly reassured, she looked up at me again.

'You aren't sleeping. Do you want to talk for a bit?' she asked.

I wished for her sake that loneliness would be the most serious problem she ever faced in her life.

'It's late,' I repeated.

'Not that late,' she answered.

'It's 2:20 a.m. Isn't that late for you?'

She checked her watch quickly and looked at me, a surprised expression in her narrowed eyes. '2:21,' she said. 'How did you know the time? You don't wear a watch, you don't have a cellphone, you… you don't even have a bag.'

I didn't say anything. I had counted every second in the years spent in captivity; old habits die hard.

'You don't even have a bag,' she repeated slowly.

'How can anyone travel from Delhi to Bombay without a bag?'

'Look,' I said. 'I don't mean to be rude, but I really need to sleep.'

I turned on my side and stared unblinking into the darkness. Forgive me, I said silently to her, but every word you say seems to bury me in an avalanche of regret – and after all these years, I have lost the will to claw my way out again.

The train arrived on time at the New Delhi railway station the next day, and I searched for the handler among the hundreds of bewildered travellers, deformed beggars and smiling urchins. I had no idea what he looked like but I spotted him at once. He looked as I had expected him to look: short, squat, inconspicuous, of indeterminate ethnicity – as likely to be South American as Indian. He blended into the crowd easily; his eyes, intent and sharp, took in everything like a chameleon ready to pounce on his prey. He was trained by the best, and I knew that beneath his bulky, baggy shirt lay hard, taut muscles trained in advanced hand-to-hand combat and sharp shooting. He spotted me simultaneously and raised his left eyebrow. I responded to his gesture and walked up to him.

'Good journey,' he said, more an assertion than a question.

In our world, any journey you came back from alive was a good journey. Expertly, he guided me through the crowds. A cut here, a turn there and we were out of the station and into the waiting car. The car, nondescript from the outside, was fitted with all the equipment an operative needs to perform successfully. He rolled up the dividing screen between the driver and us, made a quick phone call in an unknown language from the phone affixed to the door, punched a few keys into his custom palm pilot, and we were on our way.

'You've played before?' he asked, his voice raspy, guttural and laboured.

I looked at his neck closely and spotted the wound. The bullet had probably punctured his lungs.

I shook my head.

'It's just like in the movies, except there is no need for drama,' he said. 'Don't put on a performance. Just take the gun when it's your turn, pull the trigger and pass it back.'

I nodded.

'No drama,' he repeated. 'They've paid to see blood, they get blood. Nothing more, nothing less. This isn't a circus.'

'Okay,' I said, glancing out the window to see roads and highways, large, cold buildings, faceless cars and the absence of shantytowns under the bridges. Twenty-five years, I reminded myself, things change.

'Delhi has changed,' I said.

He didn't reply. Small talk wasn't a part of his job description.

'Two million rupees,' he said after a while.

'What?'

'The stakes,' he said. 'You take half a million, those who bet on you double their money; we take the remaining.'

'If I win, that is. If I lose, I get nothing except a bullet through my head.'

He shrugged. Life is tough, get over it.

They would pick up the money either way, I thought, though I suspected that the game was organized less for money and more for the entertainment of important clients – a morbid modern-day joust.

'The Donos says you are the first man he has met who is genuinely unafraid to die,' said the handler. 'Two million rupees isn't a joke in India. Do you know why the stakes are so high?'

I didn't know, nor did I care.

'Indians seem almost as afraid to die as Americans and Europeans. Elsewhere in south-east Asia – Vietnam, Cambodia, Indonesia, even Hong Kong – it's easy to organize. Here, we can't find two people we can trust to play the game till the end. Every time, one or both of them chickens out after the first shot, or they shiver so much that they can't even hold the revolver straight, or else they cry like babies. It's embarrassing. Why are Indians so afraid to die?' he asked rhetorically.

'Family ties, perhaps,' I said disinterestedly.

I didn't know. I didn't care. I had no ties in India or, for that matter, anywhere else. I was better dead than alive, and would have done the honour myself except for my irrational belief that suicide was morally wrong, a direct violation of the laws that the Buddha had taught me. Or maybe I was just a yellow hypocrite. I neither knew nor trusted myself any more.

'This time is going to be different, I know,' he said, studying me closely. 'Your eyes are steady.'

I didn't say anything. Blowing your brains out for money was cowardice, not courage.

'The other man is also a great find. He is dying of cancer but looks as healthy as an ox. It wouldn't work if he looked as if he were about to die.'

I didn't want to think about my opponent. It was best that he remained nameless and faceless.

'How's business?' I asked instead.

The thick muscles in his neck tightened. 'There are a lot of gang wars, especially with the big cartels from Colombia and Russia stepping in to get a piece of the action. I lost two men this month. You ran Marco's operations in India?'

I shook my head. 'I was with him in Brazil.'

'How did you get there? I heard you went to MIT or Harvard or somewhere. You don't meet too many of them in our line of work,' he said, his blank eyes showing a slight flicker of interest.

'Long story,' I said dismissively.

He shrugged. Whatever, your hell.

The car stopped in front of a furniture showroom on a busy street.

'Here?' I asked. It seemed an unlikely location for this diabolical duel. But where was I expecting him to take me anyway? India Gate or the Rashtrapati Bhavan, perhaps?

I followed him quietly as he scanned the road with a practised eye and made his way through the smoked glass doors to enter the main floor, which was filled with sparkling new cane furniture. The merchants in the showroom stood to attention. He ignored them and walked to the back of the shop. We went down a flight of stairs into a dark, stale basement where a small door opened into a surprisingly large, bare room with a wooden table in the centre and a chair on either side.

A man sat on one of the chairs, staring blankly at the light bulb above him, one of the two bulbs that lit the room.

'This is Dayaram, your opponent,' said the handler.

He looked about sixty, six foot plus, solidly built, with just a touch of grey in his thick black hair. The handler was right. God knows I had seen more dying men than anyone should see in a lifetime, and he didn't look like one. A little pale perhaps, but he might soon be blowing a hole through his temple, something that could make even the best of men lose colour. Dayaram got up from his chair and greeted me warmly.

'Nikhil,' I said, shaking his hand.

Or Jet. Or Monk Namche. Or Coke Buddha. Or Nick. Different aliases for each phase of my life. Take your pick, none had worked.

'I was worried they wouldn't be able to find an opponent,' Daya said in chaste Hindi. 'Thank you for doing this, sahib.'

I smiled slightly. He was thanking a man he was about to kill, or would be killed by in a few minutes. I liked him at once.

'You have your choice of revolvers, but you both have to use the same one of course,' said the handler, impatient to begin. 'Should I toss a coin to choose who picks? We need to hurry before the audience starts coming in.'

An array of revolvers lay on the table – .17 Remington, .416 Barrett, .25 WSSM, .35 Remington, .357 Magnum, .30 Carbine. It had been a while but I recognized all of them, I realized with some measure of pride.

'No need,' I said. 'He can pick.'

Dayaram looked bewildered at the range of options, just as I had been the first time Marco asked me to pick.

'Just pick the one that feels most comfortable in your hand. All of them are equally effective,' I said gently. 'Aiming right is more important.'

The handler seemed to like the advice. He picked up the Smith.

'You need to point here,' he said, placing the gun against his temple. 'Just move the barrel around a bit, like this, until you feel the slight bump, then press the trigger. Don't point anywhere else on the head. It will be slow and painful for you – and for us. Too much blood, too messy, and you know of course that going to a hospital isn't an option.'

To his credit, Dayaram seemed unfazed at the prospect of ending up in bits of bone and blood in a few minutes. He picked up the revolvers one by one, fingering each one gingerly, and finally chose the .35 Remington.

'Good choice,' I said approvingly. 'Let me unload the cartridges so you can practise.'

I took the pistol, unfastened the lock, removed the cartridges, and gave it back to him.

The handler looked at me appreciatively. I was quick despite my arm. We had obviously been trained in the same school.

'Can you help him out a bit?' the handler said. 'I need to check on a few other things. People should be arriving any moment now.'

He walked towards the door.

By the time Daya found the bump on the temple, he was sweating profusely, his hands clammy and unable to get a firm grip on the barrel. He looked down at himself in disgust.

'Don't worry,' I told him. 'You aren't scared. It's the heat in the room.'

He looked at me gratefully.

'They said you are from a big college like IIT, sahib,' Daya said, once he had practised a few times with a firmer grip. 'Is that true?'

I winced. My absent arm began to hurt again, the same throbbing, phantom pain that had plagued me for years now.

'MIT,' I replied shortly. 'It's outside India. I was there a long time ago, but it doesn't matter now.'

'I am honoured to do this with you, sahib.'

'Likewise,' I said.

'But I am no IIT graduate. I'm just a naukar in a big man's house. Now that I am dying, who is going to take care of my family? This money will be like a lottery for us if I win. If I lose, nothing lost, I'm dying anyway.' His face darkened. 'They assured me that they will give the money immediately if I win – can I trust them?'

I thought of Marco in the Jocinha favela of Rio de Janeiro, who had almost given up his life for me; good money thrown after bad.

'Yes,' I said. 'You can trust them with your life.'

The audience, all of them men, began to stream in and the small, airless room turned stuffier and sweatier. They eyed Daya and me curiously as they gathered around the table, sweat glistening on their temples, starched shirts darkened from being in an unsavoury part of town, their faces flushed, either from the stifling Delhi summer or with barely contained excitement.

That could have been me, I thought suddenly as I looked at the smartly-dressed, wealthy looking men. A few different turns and I could have been strolling in here on my way to a Bernard Shaw adaptation or a Beethoven rendition. But the old, naive me probably wouldn't have believed that such a game could take place in Delhi – or anywhere outside Hollywood. Now, nothing surprised me. I had seen the best of human nature and the worst of it. I believed in the evil of man as much as I trusted in the good.

A dark, well-dressed young man bumped against my chair. I looked up at him. Reflexively, he raised his right foot and rubbed it against his left pant sleeve. Polishing his shoes, I thought. What would he tell his young wife when he got back home? *Honey, I forgot the onions because I bet fifty thousand rupees on someone blowing his brains out.* What kind of emptiness made these men come here? How could you be so insulated from death that you had to seek it out? Our eyes met. I saw the gleam in his eyes and averted mine so he wouldn't see the pity in them.

The handler walked up to the table once the fifty-odd men in the audience had huddled around us.

'Thank you for being here,' he mumbled, looking uncomfortable at having to speak.

The room fell silent as the suits moved closer, breathing down hard on our necks, a few spare drops of sweat splashing onto the table.

'Move back, please,' said the handler authoritatively.

This was the kind of direction he was used to giving. The men complied immediately and shuffled back a few steps.

'As you know, we have been trying to arrange this for a while,' the handler continued. 'Finally, I present before you two fearless men.'

A smattering of applause broke out and seemed to unnerve the handler. The rest of his words came out in a jumbled heap. 'The rules are simple. The revolver has six rounds, but only one bullet. The other five are blanks. One shoots at himself, passes the gun to the other who shoots at himself, and so on, until one of them falls. Someone could die on the first shot or on the last shot. But one of them *will* die tonight. Those who bet on the winner will have their money doubled. I will rotate the barrel after every turn. Any questions?'

There seemed to be none.

'Let's begin the game. I will rotate the revolver to choose who goes first,' he said, obviously relieved at being done with the talking. He placed the revolver on the table.

'Do you want to call or spin?' he asked Dayaram.

Dayaram's hands began to tremble as he mumbled something. The reality had finally sunk in, I thought, he was probably thinking of the family he would never see again.

The handler looked disgusted. 'Are you going to call or spin?' he repeated impatiently.

'It's fine,' I said. 'We don't need the toss. I'll go first.'

A hush fell upon the room.

'Are you okay with that?' the handler asked Dayaram.

He nodded and looked at me gratefully. 'I'm sorry,' he muttered.

I shook my head dismissively. 'It doesn't matter. You will be fine.'

Every eye followed me hungrily as I picked up the revolver. I positioned the gun against my temple. They say your entire life flashes before your eyes when you are about to die. But no such thing happened to me, perhaps because I was no stranger to death, perhaps because my entire life had been a series of mistakes that I didn't care to recall in my last moments alive. As I placed the pistol to my temple and cocked the barrel, all I thought of was that beautiful garden where I had sat twenty-five years ago. When I placed my finger on the trigger, I swear I heard Sam laughing. And what was that sudden sweet fragrance? April cherry blossoms in Boston. The dark, cheerless room suddenly seemed to fill with sunlight and hope.

Karma Yogi

Therefore, o Arjuna, without being attached to the fruits of activities, one should act as a matter of duty, for by working without attachment the Karma Yogi attains the Supreme.

Lord Krishna in the *Bhagavad Gita*

15 April 1975, Massachusetts Institute of Technology, Boston, USA

'What about Cambodia?' Sameer asked.

'What about it?' I said.

'We go there tonight. What else?'

'Do I have to remind you that you're from Bhatinda, not Boston?'

He threw the fat *Lonely Planet* in my lap. 'Read this, you dumb fuck. Cambodia and Bhutan are the only two countries in the world where Indian citizens don't require a visa – apart from Nepal, of course. Let's choose one and go there.'

A Chinese woman turned around and glared at us.

'Sorry,' I said immediately.

'About the tickets…' whispered Sam.

'Can't we talk about this later?' I whispered back.

We were sitting in the last row of the massive student congregation that was MIT's graduating class of 1975, straining to listen to the keynote speaker. Or at least I was.

'I don't want to listen to this fat fucker,' said Sam after a few minutes of silence. 'He has nothing new to say. Work hard, take risks, learn from mistakes, be a people person, blah, blah, blah.'

I sighed and moved our chairs further back so

we wouldn't disturb the others, most of whom were listening in rapt attention as the head of America's biggest financial services firm dispensed advice on how to be successful in corporate America after graduating from MIT. The soft, pleasant Boston spring contributed to the upbeat mood. We are now MIT graduates, everyone's expression seemed to say, watch out, will ya?

'The thing is, I don't even want to end up like him,' Sam continued. 'Who wants to be a fat old turd peddling penny stocks and junk bonds and talking about how the best days of his life were spent at MIT?'

'I would, for one,' I said. 'Unlike you, I don't have any grandiose visions of happiness. I just want a simple life.'

'A simple life! See, that's what I'm talking about. That's what we are going to get in Cambodia,' he said, back on the subject of our yet unplanned vacation after graduation.

I wanted to do a road trip through the US. He, on the other hand, wanted 'something big', as usual.

Reluctantly, I stopped listening to the speaker and turned to Sameer (call me 'Sam'). The stocky, clumsy son of a poultry farmer from Bhatinda, pencil-thin moustache forming over red, cubby cheeks, now an MIT engineer with outsized ambitions to take over the world.

'Isn't there a civil war going on in Cambodia?' I asked him.

'There was a war going on in India as well, when we came here four years ago – the '71 Indo-Pak War,' he said. 'And I had barely heard about it in Bhatinda. Cambodia is as big as a whore's cunt; we can easily find some place where there is no fighting. Besides, who's going to harm two Indians? We are non-aligned like Chacha Nehru.'

His face was flush with enthusiasm and I suddenly realized that he was serious about this. We could actually end up on a flight to Cambodia tonight, as we had on a flight to Mexico after our sophomore year. Time to get practical, boy, I thought, else we might end up sleeping in a bus stand for a week like we did in Cancun.

'Do I have to remind you that we have no money?' I said. 'Zilch. Nada. I don't want this to be another Mexico.'

'This time it's taken care of,' he said triumphantly. He took out a cheque from his pocket with a flourish and waved it at me. 'Dad's graduation gift. No one in Bhatinda has ever graduated from an MIT before, not even from the Muzaffarpur Institute of Technology.' He stared into the distance dreamily, and for a second I thought he was listening to the speaker who was explaining the lessons he had learnt from a recent acquisition.

'The Angkor Vat is in Cambodia,' said Sam unexpectedly. 'The seventh wonder of the world.'

'Since when have you been interested in historical monuments? You haven't even seen the Taj Mahal, have you?'

He looked at me contemptuously. 'There it's all the same,' he said. 'The paagal-khaana is on the same road as the Taj Mahal.'

'And how does that make the Taj Mahal any less magnificent, fatso?' I said as we were rewarded with another look of disgust from the Chinese student sitting in front of us.

'So, are we on?' Sam asked.

'I don't know,' I said. 'Somehow, I don't have a good feeling about this. Why can't we just do a road trip like everyone else?'

He groaned and began to rock his chair. 'You realize this is our last chance, don't you? Three weeks from now, you will start pushing paper at NASA, and I will be sweeping factory floors at GE. It all goes downhill after that. Adulthood and responsibility; marriage, family, kids, finances, the works.'

'You've been saying that for a long time,' I said. 'And I haven't seen your downward journey begin yet.'

As if on cue, he tilted his chair back a little further than he probably intended, and landed on his back. A thunderous applause seemed to greet his fall. The speaker had just completed his speech.

A few folks in the last row tittered as Sam picked himself up.

'Bastard,' he muttered sheepishly like he always did when he stumbled, slipped, fell, or broke things – all of which happened with alarming frequency.

'Are you okay?' I asked him.

He nodded. 'Just got distracted thinking about the great time we're gonna have.'

'It's prophetic,' I said. 'A divine sign that we should stay put.'

'If I started seeing divinity every time I fell, I'd be Moses,' he said.

I couldn't contest that. His clumsiness was legendary at MIT.

'At least we should stop by the international affairs department to check on the political situation in Cambodia,' I said.

Sam waved his hand dismissively. 'Are you out of your mind? Final exams just ended, and you want to study political history in a crummy room to prepare for a vacation? America has turned you into a pussy.'

And so, later that evening, with tickets purchased at the counter and sparkling new degrees lodged in our backpacks, we were on a flight from Boston to Phnom Penh, the capital of Cambodia. Under Sam's able persuasion, I had omitted to gather any information about our destination and I found myself tense with excitement at the randomness of the journey. I knew nothing about Phnom Penh, but even the names of certain places – Phnom Penh, Bangkok, Istanbul, Marrakesh, Ulaan Bataar, Myanmar, the Amazon – gleam with the promise of hidden mysteries and undiscovered wonders.

Sam, despite his usual over-the-top enthusiasm, was right. Soon we would have rental leases, demanding bosses, nagging girlfriends (if we were lucky) and two-week vacations to cope with. Perhaps we'd never again have the luxury of making an impulse trip to another part of the world.

The airplane was empty sans a bunch of tough-looking marines in green berets and crew cuts, who eyed us curiously but didn't say much.

'I've planned it out,' said Sam, eyeing the air hostess as he fumbled with his seatbelt. I reached out and snapped it shut.

'Some mechanical engineer,' I muttered.

'We spend a few days in Phnom Penh, pick up some chicks and head to Angkor Vat. It's just a four- or five-hour boat ride. Picture it. Sitting atop a wooden ferry, a light breeze blowing in our faces, watching the picturesque Cambodian landscape pass by – all with a girl on each arm.' He grinned, his face flush with excitement.

He pointed to the guidebook. 'It says here that the Downtown Foreign Correspondents Club is a great place to meet expatriates and locals. We should find a hotel near it.'

'And leverage your significant success at picking up girls in the US, I assume?'

'Very funny, aren't you?' he said. 'Things are different now. We're MIT graduates.'

'And that matters in Phnom Penh when it didn't seem to have an impact in Boston?'

'American women don't like Indians. We don't have fair skin like the Caucasians, big dicks like the blacks, exotic accents like the South Americans, or even the sensitive femininity of the Chinese. But Cambodians are different. They love our spices.'

'I didn't see that written anywhere in the *Lonely Planet*,' I told him.

'What are *you* bitching about? You had your pick in Boston as well. Not that you made any use of it. If I was six feet tall and played basketball and soccer, I would be picking up a new girl every day,' he said. 'Anyway, girls or no girls, we need to smoke up in Phnom Penh with the Chinamen. I've heard gaanja is as abundant as air there.'

'Somehow, I don't think we have the same things in mind for this vacation,' I said.

'Yes, yes, I know you want to go and contemplate and philosophize and stuff. Lots of time for that there. It's quiet as hell. Nothing ever happens in Cambodia.'

'Looks like it. There isn't a soul on this flight

except those bomber types.' I glanced around at the empty seats.

'Oh, it's an undiscovered gem,' Sam said confidently. 'You know how tourists are. They'd rather push each other into canals in overcrowded Venice than see a place worth seeing. Anyway, what were the options? I'd rather sit in the MIT library looking at pictures of Cambodia than do a homo trip to Bhutan to watch mountains and sunrises with you.'

He piped down a little as the flight took off, and I stared out the window as the familiar landmarks came into view. The four years in Boston had done me good, mostly because I wasn't tormented by happy, cheerful images of the past every day. In India, every street reminded me of how life had been before Mom and Dad had expired within a few months of each other – she after a short but painful battle with cancer, he of a heart attack. The memories were everywhere, in our small, comfortable Army apartment on SP Marg, our sprawling ancestral home in Shimla, the bungalows of the aunts and uncles whom I subsequently stayed with. I had found peace nowhere, always harassed by the healthy ghosts of my parents pottering about the house, dropping me off to school, waiting for me when I returned. The sudden loss of everything I had taken for granted almost crippled me, and had it not been for Sam, I would probably never have summoned up the will to apply for undergraduate studies in the US. He was my best friend in school, a hostel mate in Delhi who, I half suspected, changed his IIT plans to MIT, sensing my need to escape from India.

I looked at him affectionately. His clumsy optimism had pulled me through, first in high school and then in MIT.

'All my life I dreamt of this, you know,' Sam said suddenly. 'Not Cambodia, I mean – just this absolute freedom to take a trip from nowhere to nowhere. That's why I wanted to get out of Bhatinda. Everyone around me had already planned the rest of my life without even asking me.'

I felt a sudden stab of regret at what I would never have. 'Like a Greek tragedy, one realizes the value of what one has only when one loses it,' I said softly.

'I guess that's why there aren't too many Greek heroes in Bhatinda's poultry farms,' said Sam with a grin. 'Nothing much to lose there.' He let out a gigantic yawn. 'Should we get some sleep, you think? So many empty seats, we have more room to sleep here than in the dorm.'

'Get up,' said Sam, shaking me violently. 'We're about to land. Just look outside, will you? Have you ever seen anything so beautiful?'

I opened one sleepy eye and looked blearily out the window to see a bunch of trees, some scrubs, a body of water, some buildings.

'It looks like any other place,' I mumbled.

'Your irrepressible enthusiasm after sixteen hours of sleep is very uplifting,' he said. 'I'm going to score here, you wait and see. You just see,' he repeated as the plane touched down bumpily.

I felt a surge of excitement as the plane skidded to a halt on the sparse runway. Phnom Penh, Siam Reap, Angkor Vat; all remote names from primary school history lessons that were suddenly becoming a reality. To top it all, we had no hotel reservations, no travel bookings, no maps and no fixed plans – the best way to travel. I felt myself sharing Sam's enthusiasm as we jumped up to take our backpacks from the overhead luggage compartment.

'You should try and get back on the next flight,' someone said.

Sam and I turned in surprise. One of the military dudes had walked up behind us.

'The civilian government was overthrown by the communist rebel army, the Khmer Rouge, in a coup yesterday,' he said. 'Things will get ugly very soon.'

Now what's all this, I thought. We were on a vacation. Where did coups, civilian governments and rebel armies fit in?

'Isn't the Khmer Rouge the people's army?' Sam

asked. 'Won't it be more peaceful now that they have replaced the unpopular government?'

The tall, middle-aged marine ran a hand through his, crew-cut blonde hair and shrugged. 'I don't know all that. This isn't a history lecture, son. Coups mean trouble, no matter who replaces whom.'

'When will things settle down?' I asked.

The marine laughed. 'A few decades, maybe; this is South Asia.' He began to walk away. 'I would go back if I were you.'

Backpacks in hand, Sam and I looked at each other.

'I thought nothing ever happened in Cambodia,' I said.

'Don't tell me you're going to listen to him. You know how paranoid Americans are,' he replied. 'Where we come from, there is a coup every day.'

'I don't know. This sounds serious. It's not worth getting shot at just to see a bunch of temples.'

The Cambodian air hostess looked at us expectantly.

'Anyway, we need to get out of the plane, I guess,' I said.

We began to move towards the exit.

'I think we should take the next flight back,' I told Sam as we walked towards the terminal.

'Maybe he was just a racist fucker getting off from scaring two brown curry boys,' Sam replied. 'He could be laughing with his buddies about how he scared us into running away as soon as we arrived.'

'Unlikely,' I said. 'He was a marine, not a hick cab driver.'

We reached the terminal – and realized immediately that something wasn't right. The small airport, barely a tenth the size of the Boston airport, was teeming with chaotic activity. Groups of westerners, mostly American and European hippies with matted blonde hair, grubby faces and dirt-streaked backpacks, were huddled in corners, talking in loud, agitated voices to nervous-looking Cambodian airport officials.

'This doesn't look good,' I muttered.

There was no one at the immigration counter to check our passports. A big white board hanging over the counter proclaimed 'All flights cancelled definitely' in English. They may have meant 'indefinitely', but 'definitely' had an ominous ring to it which seemed fitting given the dark looks on the faces of the hippies. The marines who had been on the flight with us were nowhere to be seen.

'How will we get out if all outgoing flights have been cancelled?' Sam asked fearfully.

'Why worry? Let's just pick up some of these hippie chicks and have a vacation right here,' I snapped, furious with myself for falling in with Sam's plans without doing any research of my own.

'Look, I'm sorry...' he began.

I cut him off. 'No, no, it's not your fault,' I said. 'Let's try to find a way out of this mess, shall we?'

We joined the thirty-odd hippies who were huddled together in the deserted baggage claim area.

'What's going on?' I asked a tall lean guy with shaggy blonde hair and vacant blue eyes, who was standing alone and looked more relaxed than the others. He smiled.

'We are fucked,' he said sweetly. His accent was unrecognizable, neither American nor European, the two accents we were most used to hearing at MIT.

'Why, what's wrong?' asked Sam in a rush.

'The Khmer Rouge has cut off all air, road, train and river routes. Who knows how long it will be before things get back to normal? A day, a month, a year, a decade?'

'We can't afford to wait that long. I start with GE in three weeks,' said Sam. He pointed at me. 'And he starts with NASA.'

The blonde guy just stared blankly at us.

'There may be bigger problems to worry about than not joining work on time,' I said. 'Just relax a bit, will you?'

I turned to the blonde guy. 'Is the government going to arrange for us to stay somewhere safe until then?'

He laughed, so incongruous a reaction in the circumstances that most of the hippies turned to stare at him. 'Here, take a look at the new government,' he said. He pulled us to a small window in one corner of the terminal.

I saw a carnival-like atmosphere on the clear stretch of road outside the airport. Three big, green armoured battle tanks, each one about fifty feet wide and fifteen feet tall, stood half a mile ahead at the entrance to the airport. Twenty or thirty young boys sat atop the tanks. They were maybe fifteen or sixteen years old, and were dressed in black with red bandanas tied around their heads. Hundreds of short, thin men and women dressed in bright, colourful clothes – presumably the Cambodian junta – danced on the road, around the tanks. Periodically, the black-clad boys pumped their rifles into the air, firing impromptu shots which were greeted with jubilant cheers from the junta. Sure, it was an unlikely sight – the crowds milling around the tanks were mostly middle-aged men and women who were cheering unruly, teenage boys – but it didn't seem sinister.

'Everyone seems quite happy,' said an American hippie with caked blonde hair and rings on her pierced cheeks. 'It doesn't seem all that bad. Why have they cancelled the flights?'

There was a general murmur of assent at this observation. Everyone began to crowd around the small window.

'I think we should talk to them and find out when they plan to resume normal services,' said a tall, muscular guy with a German accent.

'I wouldn't advise it,' said the shaggy blonde guy. 'These Khmer Rouge soldiers are illiterate village boys who've been taught to hate Americans all their lives. In effect, that means all foreigners, since they can't tell the difference between a Pakistani and a Texan.'

'How do you know that?' someone asked.

'I've been a PhD student at the University of Cambodia for a year,' he said. 'I saw this coming before even the government did, but I didn't get out in time. Now, it's over.'

'What's over?' asked the German guy. 'What did you see coming?'

The girl with the cheek piercings let out a sudden shriek and pointed outside. We followed her glance. The celebrations seemed to have gone silent all of a sudden. Everyone, except the hooting boys atop the tanks, seemed to be staring at something in front of one of the tanks. Although we were a few hundred metres away, we could make out the obviously dazed expressions on their faces.

'He shot him,' said the girl excitedly. 'I saw it.'

'Who? What?' asked the hippies huddled by the window.

'One of those guys in black,' she said, pointing outside. 'He just shot a man who bumped into him, he shot him right between the eyes. There was blood.'

Everyone stood in silence, staring at each other as the tanks began to roll forward towards the airport. The swirling crowds followed the tanks, though they seemed a bit subdued now.

'*This* is what I meant,' said the PhD guy. 'The Khmer Rouge are animals.'

A chorus of panicked voices broke out in the airport as the cavalcade approached.

'We need to run.'

'And go where?'

'We should reason with them.'

'And get shot?'

'Why would they shoot us?'

'They shot someone who just *bumped* into them!'

'Should we put up a white flag for peace? We don't even know if they are looking for us.'

'No use,' said the PhD student. Everyone turned to look at him. 'Do you know the motto of their revolution? *To keep you is no benefit; to destroy you is no loss.* They will gladly wrap you in your white flags if you give them half a chance,' he said, sounding quite calm despite the death sentence he was pronouncing for everyone in the room.

All flights were cancelled, the tanks were fast approaching the airport, and we had nowhere to go.

A petite woman began to whimper, which triggered a crying fit in the room.

'Can't we fight them off?' asked the muscular German. 'They are just a handful of boys, and the crowd doesn't seem to like them too much.'

He looked around the room for support. None of the hippies seemed enthusiastic about this course of action.

'And then what, we take over the city? Perhaps fight off thousands of boy soldiers in the country?' said a teenager with a French accent.

'Do you have a better idea?' asked the German.

'Any idea would be better than that,' said the Frenchman sarcastically.

The German moving threateningly towards him and caught him by the collar. 'If you can't help, don't speak, you bastard.'

'Okay, James Dean. Let's go Hollywood on the soldiers instead,' the Frenchman sneered.

The German struck him in the face. A babble of panicked voices broke out, although the Frenchman himself didn't react.

Thus far, I had been watching in a state of mild disbelief as the events unfolded. This was a vacation, I thought, no one got killed on a vacation, damn it. Everything would take care of itself. But the sudden eruption of violence in front of me brought back memories of a lifetime spent on basketball courts and soccer fields. My father, a colonel in the Indian Army, had ensured that I cut my sporting teeth playing rough ball with the jawaans in the army fields.

'Does anyone here have a map?' I asked, startling myself a little. I had had a sudden inspiration, quite like the ones I sometimes had when we were a three-pointer away from winning in the basketball league matches where I captained for MIT. And most of the time they didn't work, I reminded myself grimly.

Everyone stared at me.

'A map of the area? Come on, quick, somebody must have one.'

A young, sharp-looking brunette handed me a crumpled map.

'Sam, hand me the guidebook,' I said hurriedly.

'What?' he asked, looking dazed.

'Pull yourself together, will you?' I snapped. 'Get the Cambodian travel guide out of your backpack.'

He rummaged through his bag and handed me the guide with trembling hands. I thumbed through the pages quickly and found the address I was looking for. I tried to find it on the map, suddenly irritated with myself for refusing to go to the jungle reconnaissance training my father had wanted me to attend.

'I'm not even joining the army,' I had whined. 'Do I need a map to find my way around the school cafeteria?'

Despite being a strict disciplinarian, he had relented that once, although now I wished he had forced me as he had for the Himalayan mountain survival course and the marathon training.

'There is one way if we can figure it out, I think,' I said as I struggled with the map.

I looked up to see thirty pairs of petrified eyes fixed on me. 'We should head out to our respective embassies immediately. If we are lucky, there's still a chance they will be safe zones.'

They continued to stare at me with the same dazed expression, until the German spoke.

'That's an idea,' he said excitedly. 'Are the embassies close to where we are?'

'I can't read this map,' I said. I turned to Sam for help but one look at his white, petrified face, and I knew I would have to look elsewhere. 'Is anybody good with maps?'

No one moved for a while until the PhD student stepped forward.

'I can help,' he said, kneeling down beside me to study the map. 'I know Phnom Penh quite well.'

The German guy quickly broke away from the group. 'Let's divide into groups quickly, shall we?' he said authoritatively. He took the guidebook from my hand. 'I'm calling out the names of the countries that have embassies listed here. Just stand with your group, okay?'

Suddenly, I felt calm. We needed to treat this like a soccer match against a powerful opponent or like a tough mathematical regression problem. If we worked together and used our heads, we had a fighting chance to get out of this.

'USA,' the German called out.

Nearly three-fourths of the group raised their hands.

'Collect there,' he said, pointing to one corner of the airport. Folks huddled together, shivering despite the hot Cambodian summer, staring out the window at the rapidly advancing procession. They were barely a hundred metres away now, and the loud hoots of the boy soldiers outside could be heard as clearly as the subdued voices of the hippies inside the airport. The PhD student and I busied ourselves with the map as the German went through the list quickly.

'Britain.'

'France.'

'Germany.'

'Brazil.'

'Thailand.'

'Philippines.'

'Malaysia.'

Within seconds, he had exhausted the entire list of embassies that appeared in the guidebook, even as we managed to figure the route out. I looked up to see just one person unassigned: Sam.

The German checked the list again. No Indian embassy. I was an American citizen thanks to NASA's quick processing of my citizenship application, but General Electric hadn't processed Sam's application as yet. Sam turned a shade whiter, if that was at all possible.

'We'll go to the American embassy,' I told him gently as I joined him. 'We are students, so we should be good.'

He nodded, still looking dumbstruck as we walked over to the American group.

'Where are you from?' the German asked the PhD student.

'I am Ishmael from Estonia,' he said calmly.

The German looked at the list again. 'No Estonian embassy.'

Ishmael, I thought, wasn't that the narrator from *Moby Dick*? The name seemed eerily prophetic; and Estonia, well, I didn't know much but I would be surprised if there was an Estonian embassy anywhere in the world.

'You can pretty much choose any group to go with,' the German said.

'I will go with him,' said Ishmael, pointing at me.

I looked at him for a second, trying to ignore the rumble of the tanks crashing through the gates of the airport.

Then, hurriedly, Ishmael and I showed the German the map. It was a relatively straight route with the American embassy located right next to the king's palace, and all the other embassies clustered together on the other side of the diplomatic district bordering the airport.

'Let's move. The American group follows them,'

the German shouted, pointing at Ishmael and me. 'Others follow me.'

We ran out from the rear end of the terminal, jumped over the crumbling fencing surrounding the runway and split in different directions.

Ishmael and I ran at the head of the twenty-odd American hippies, glancing in every direction to check for signs of the black-clad Khmer soldiers. We didn't stand a chance if we ran into them. Despite knowing almost nothing about the Cambodian revolution, a lifetime spent playing rough sports had me convinced that any fifteen-year-old boy with a shiny black gun would pull the trigger, no matter how slight the provocation.

What a mess, I thought, as I ran faster to keep pace with Ishmael, and to think it started as a vacation.

The embassy was three miles away as per my estimation; a good thirty minute run, maybe longer. We would be very lucky if we didn't encounter any soldiers en route. And what if the embassy had already been evacuated, I thought suddenly. If the coup had taken place the previous day, like the marines on the flight had said, the Americans wouldn't be hanging around, would they? Where would we go then?

'Have you been to Thailand?' I puffed to Ishmael,

who was running calmly in front, not breaking into much of a sweat despite his shaggy, emaciated look.

He nodded. 'It's safe there,' he said.

'The map indicated that there is a forest bordering Cambodia and Thailand. Do you think we can get there if we manage to slip inside the forest?' I asked.

'The forest is strewn with land mines to keep out the Thai. Besides, the border is a hundred miles from here. How will we get there?'

'What do we do if the embassy has already been evacuated?'

He shrugged. 'Shit happens.'

Indeed, I thought. A five minute trip to the MIT international affairs department would have given us the latest on the crisis. Instead, we had taken a twenty-five hour journey to arrive in the middle of it. I had no one to blame but myself.

Two miles in and the road became less bumpy. Dirt tracks gave way to narrow, pebbled streets, and the deserted countryside was replaced with colonial buildings. There was still not a soul in sight, neither soldiers, nor the ordinary junta. I prayed Ishmael had read the map right.

'What is the Khmer Rouge after?' I asked him. 'Why don't they just take over the government and be done with it? Why the violence?'

'They are extreme communists. By "they", I mean the top lieutenants, not these boy-soldiers of course.

The soldiers are just village kids looking to kill for kicks. The leader of the Khmer Rouge is a crazed communist despot called Pol Pot, who hates the "bourgeoisie", a word he uses for just about everyone who isn't a farmer – teachers, doctors, industrialists, factory workers, city dwellers, foreigners, even the Red Cross. His personal ideology is less Marx, more Hitler on steroids. He wants to exterminate all bourgeoisie, partly to make this a nation of farmers, partly because he is a psycho.'

'Would they attack the embassy?' I asked.

He shrugged. 'Who knows? I don't trust them one bit. They are all crazy motherfuckers.' He laughed. 'Believe me, it's going to be brutal.'

'And you don't care because?'

'Because I am a karma yogi,' he said, mispronouncing and mangling the words. 'I learnt it in *your* country, atop the Himalayas. All I have control over is my actions, my karma; the results are beyond my control. Que sera sera.'

I stared at him in incomprehension, but I was too breathless to ask anything more. I looked around to check on Sam. Finding him all right, although still lagging behind the others, I began to run faster.

We spotted the embassy at the end of a deserted Parisian street with empty colonial bungalows and abandoned cafés on either side. My heart leapt when I saw the American flag still flying high atop the building, and I felt even better when I saw no sign of the Khmer soldiers anywhere on the street.

We raced up to the spiral embassy gates at the end of the street, panting, and joined a large group of Cambodians, all dressed in plain clothes, standing outside the closed gates and shouting in their dialect. We pressed ourselves against the gates, begging to be let in.

'American citizens only,' said the two crew-cut marines guarding the gate.

A howl of protest broke out from the Americans who were safely on the other side of the gate. Apparently, they were trying to get their Cambodian friends evacuated too.

'He is my cameraman,' said an agitated, red-faced giant on the other side of the gate, pointing to a thin young Cambodian who was clutching the bars of the gate tightly. 'The *New York Times* cameraman, goddamn it.'

The marines remained impassive to this and similar shouts:

'He is a Red Cross worker who saved American lives.'

'A hospital nurse.'

'She is the Ambassador's nanny.'

'Citizens only,' the marines repeated.

'We are Americans,' shouted someone from our group excitedly.

The Cambodians holding onto the gates moved aside to give our group space. They looked at us longingly. I felt bad for them for a moment, but shrugged away the thought. My own life was at stake here; the drowning couldn't save the drowning.

'Take out your passports,' said the marine.

We began to fumble through pockets and backpacks to get our passports out amidst the growing din.

I glanced quickly at Ishmael as the rest of our group began to queue up in front of the gates.

'Why don't you run to the French embassy or some other European embassy?' I said desperately. 'Maybe there is a chance there.'

'If the Americans don't let me in, it's unlikely anyone else will,' he said.

'What will you do?' I asked.

Before he could respond, there were shouts from the crowd. A large tank had arrived at the far end of the street, about half a mile from where we stood. The crowd began to scatter, afraid perhaps of being seen at the gates of the enemy. Our group moved forward and began to push their way inside. I rushed over to Sam, who was at the end of the queue, and stood behind him.

'Get your student ID out,' I said.

He fumbled in the back pocket of his cargo pants, still looking a bit dazed.

'You need to focus, Sam,' I said. 'We are almost out of this, okay?'

His hands were shaking as he produced his MIT student identity card.

'Don't show them your Indian passport,' I said. 'Show this. Do you understand?'

He nodded.

'Take this map,' I told Ishmael, who was standing behind me, staring vacantly at the tank. 'And this.' I emptied my pockets of money.

He accepted the map and the money without question. 'Good luck,' he said.

He sauntered casually to the sidewalk and began studying the map while he sized up the street.

The rest of us shouldered our way in through the gates – to freedom. It had worked, I exulted; we had pulled it off.

☞

'You can't enter with this,' said the marine at the gate when Sam showed him his student identity card. 'Show me your passport.'

My fear had abated; now it returned with a numbing force.

'Are you a citizen of the US?' the marine repeated. 'Where is your passport?'

Sam stared at him nervously. 'I…I…'

'We are both students of MIT,' I said forcefully. 'The Massachusetts Institute of Technology in

Boston.' The Ivy League namedrop didn't have an impact.

'American citizens only,' said the marine flatly.

'His citizenship is being processed by General Electric,' I said in a rush as the street shuddered with the rumbling of the approaching tank.

'Please,' I said. 'We came in with a group of marines from Boston just this morning. They must be inside. You can check with them.'

'American citizens only,' he repeated impatiently. 'Is there anyone else with an American passport?'

No one came forward.

'Okay, we are all in,' he shouted to someone inside. He began to move the Americans away from the gate, perhaps to board the helicopters that would shepherd them to safety.

'Wait,' I said, rushing up to show him my passport and escape to safety.

I glanced at Sam quickly as the marine came up to us. Sam's baby-face had contorted in fear.

I don't know what came over me. 'Here is his passport,' I said quietly.

The marine looked at the passport reluctantly, then looked at Sam.

Our grainy photos would pass for each other's, I knew, at least to an eye unaccustomed to Indians. Besides, all he cared about was matching the number of passports to the number of people; if somebody wanted to be stupid, that was their choice.

What was I thinking? For a second, I almost wished he would catch the bluff.

'Okay,' he said. Sam looked confused as the marine pulled him inside.

'Do you have an American passport?' He looked at me.

I shook my head and turned away from the gate.

I walked with heavy steps to join Ishmael. Fuck, I thought with a sudden, sinking feeling, what had I done? What would happen now? So far, escape had felt like a certainty. Now I was caught in the middle of raging lunatics who were likely to shoot me on sight. I was about to *die*, I thought. It felt surreal.

'Holy fucking fuck, you gave him your passport, didn't you?' said Ishmael amidst the roar of the departing helicopters.

'Can we get to Thailand? How far is the border?' I asked, my eyes stinging with tears.

I wasn't a hero. I didn't want to be a hero. My life mattered more to me than anyone else's, but did I have an option after seeing the way pale, petrified, clumsy Sam had floundered along since we landed in Phnom Penh? I at least had a sliver of a chance of making it alive; Sam had none.

'How could you do that? How could anyone do that?' Ishmael said.

Sam had pulled me out of the darkest phase of

my life. I couldn't turn my back on him now. Or could I? Was anything more important than your own life?

'We need to get out of here,' I said.

Gunshots and hoots filled the air as the tank began to roll our way. From that distance, they couldn't make out that we were foreigners, but that would change very quickly.

'Get out where?' he asked.

'Thailand?'

'I told you, the border is a hundred, maybe hundred and fifty miles from here.'

My heart sank. 'Let's at least get started, shall we?' I told him.

He shrugged. 'Sure.'

We began running in the general direction of the border, knowing we wouldn't even get close.

'I can't believe you did that,' he repeated.

'Enough of that now,' I said sharply. 'There are things you don't understand.'

But did I really understand any better? What had made me behave like a hero in a cheap Hollywood flick?

Another tank with soldiers entered the street from the other side and we ducked into an alley, which led us smack into what looked like the city centre.

I stared disbelievingly at the sight in front of me. Like a scene from a low-budget zombie horror flick, hundreds, maybe thousands of Cambodians were on the street – men, women, young, old – crying, begging, pleading with the black-clad Khmer soldiers in their midst. Shops and houses stood abandoned as everyone walked reluctantly in one direction, shepherded by the Khmer boy-soldiers who coaxed them along with sticks and rifles.

'They are evacuating the city,' said Ishmael. 'Everyone will be moved to the villages to work on farms. We are dead.'

'Why?'

'They are going to make it a Utopian communist society. You eat what you produce; everyone works equally, everyone eats equally. Great in theory, but in practice, these idiots don't know a thing about farming except how to produce rice. Soon, everyone will die of starvation.'

I didn't care about macro-economic socio-political issues. I just wanted to get out of here alive, to go back to the security of my dorm in Boston. Once there, I promised myself I would gladly embark on the downward journey that Sam kept referring to. I would lock myself in the room and never leave, not to buy groceries, not even to watch films – if I managed to get out just this once.

'Keep your head down and try to merge with the crowd,' I said. 'If we can make it to a village without being spotted, perhaps we can find a way from there.'

'You aren't going to give up, are you?' He smiled. 'Works for me.'

A heavily pregnant woman fell down a hundred yards in front of us. One of the soldiers walked up to her and struck her on the head with the butt of his rifle, while shouting at her to get up. She resisted. He seemed to go ballistic. Again and again, he hit her on the head with the rifle until all I could see was a pulpy mass of blood and skin. Still dissatisfied, he sliced a bayonet through her stomach and the traditional white Cambodian dress she was wearing turned crimson. She stopped moving and he walked away, satisfied. I watched silently, then continued to walk with my head bowed. No one's life matters more than my own, I repeated to myself.

Soon though, it became increasingly difficult to be inconspicuous as more and more people became victim to sudden eruptions of violence from the boy-soldiers. An old man had his legs broken with a staff because he had stopped to rest; a baby was thrown into a ditch because it was wailing; a young man's head was burst open with a rod because he was drinking water from a ditch. The crowd began to thin alarmingly.

'How far is the closest village?' I asked Ishmael.

'Two, maybe three days walk,' said Ishmael. 'It's going to be fun in the sun then. Harvest rice twenty hours a day so that Pol Pot can measure his dick against Mao's and Lenin's.'

He was a funny guy, I thought, completely unperturbed by what was happening, almost enjoying himself.

'What if…'

An intense light blinded me as someone struck me on the back of my head. I turned around in reflex and another blow on my side seemed to shatter every bone. I felt my face hitting asphalt, heard gravel crunching – and then there was silence.

I tasted blood. Every part of my body hurt. My eyes refused to open. I drifted out of consciousness.

I awoke again with a throbbing pain in my head. I tried to move but something weighed me down. My throat was parched. I moved my tongue over my lips and tasted more blood. I coughed and it felt as if someone was dropping massive piles of bricks on my ribs.

'My name is Nikhil Arya. I'm from Delhi. I study at MIT,' I told myself silently.

I was alive.

But where was I? I tried to wiggle my toes and felt them move. I moved my fingers and they touched a hard surface. I was lying on a cement floor. A sudden thought struck me. Why was everything black? Had I lost my eyesight? Not my eyes, I thought, anything but that, please.

I tried to speak but only a whimper escaped my lips.

'Are you awake?' A steady voice pierced the darkness.

The Khmer Rouge. Ishmael. The city centre.

'Yes,' I said.

My throat hurt. A rush of blood filled my mouth. I coughed, and again felt the shooting pain in my ribs as if a bus had run over me.

'Don't worry. You aren't going blind. It's pitch dark,' said Ishmael.

I felt a sharp relief despite the situation.

'Where are we?' I asked through gritted teeth. It hurt to speak, but I resisted the urge to cough up blood again. I tried to use my arms to sit up, but something restrained my wrist. I pushed again, and a heavy mist seemed to surround me. I drifted away again.

☞

'Eat it,' said a voice.

I woke up again. My face touched something cold; iron or steel, perhaps. A tumbler of some sort, maybe it contained water. I tried to lift myself up. Again, something dragged me down.

'Don't try to get up,' said Ishmael. 'We are tied to the wall.'

'Where are we?' I asked.

'I don't know,' he said. 'Someone hit us on the

head in the city centre. You fell face down. I thought you had died.'

I felt dead. I needed water. My throat felt rough, as if someone was rubbing sandpaper on my tonsils.

'Water,' I said hoarsely.

'They've mixed some rice and water in the bowl,' he said. 'Lap it up. This is the only thing we'll get to eat today.'

I tried to sit up again. Every inch of my body throbbed with pain, and I felt cold metal against my wrist.

'Don't get up. One of your wrists is tied to the wall with a chain,' he repeated. 'Try to lap it up.'

I moved to my side and collapsed from the effort.

Focus.

Slowly, carefully, I managed to move little by little, until my face reached the bowl. My tongue touched a liquid that smelt like rotten fish and I began lapping greedily. Blood mixed with rice and water, the best meal I had ever had in my life. I lapped until my tongue scraped the bottom, and then I licked the sides until every drop was gone. Exhausted, I lay down on my side and drifted out again.

Finally, some light. I looked around. My left wrist was in a manacle tied to a crumbling cement wall. Ishmael was tied to the opposite end of the tiny cell

we were caged in. We faced another cell like ours
with a dark, unlit corridor in between. Somewhere
behind us there was probably a door from which the
tiny rays of sunlight trickled in.

'Are you okay?' Ishmael asked.

'No,' I said, tasting the mucus and blood in my
mouth. But I was alive, my mind was working. They
hadn't killed us. We could still find a way out.

'I'm hungry,' I said, looking at him in the faint
light. Two angry cuts stretched from his eyes down
to his heavily bearded cheeks, and his face was
bruised and swollen like a balloon.

'The chef serves his gourmet meal only once a
day.' He smiled, revealing two missing teeth in the
front.

I ran my tongue over my own teeth. I tasted more
blood, but my teeth seemed intact. 'How long has
it been?' I asked. It hurt to speak, and my stomach
growled, roared, with hunger.

'A week; maybe less, maybe more. You've settled
well into your routine. You sleep the whole day, lap
up the food, and sleep again. A good way to pass
time.'

'Why have they...'

A sudden noise. I heard footsteps approaching
our cell. A short, nondescript Cambodian man
with a scar on his face entered the cell. He was in
plain clothes, not the dreaded black dress with red
bandana.

He wasn't a Khmer solider, I thought cautiously. Maybe the old government was back.

The man stood in front of us and screamed out something in Khmer. Then suddenly, without provocation, he slapped me. I held up my free left arm to ward him off. He rolled his fist and hit me, again and again, until the familiar taste of blood filled my mouth. The pain was so excruciating, I was surprised I didn't pass out. It was Ishmael's turn next, and he took his beating with a passive, almost cheerful expression, his shaggy blonde mane now caked with dirt and blood.

The man left as suddenly as he had entered. I glanced at Ishmael. He looked like a pale, frayed, worn-out ghost of the guy I had seen at the airport.

I opened my mouth.

Ishmael looked at me and signalled frantically with his eyes.

'What are you saying?' I mumbled through broken teeth. 'What did he want?'

'He wanted us to keep quiet.' He laughed as the man came back again.

This time the man hit me until I fainted.

There was blood all over the cold floor when I awoke next. A bowl was kept next to me and I lapped up the rice and water hungrily. Ishmael was staring blankly at the bars. He smiled at me, but this time we didn't exchange a word. I didn't know how many hours or days it had been since the beating. I forced myself to think about escape, but the pain made it impossible to concentrate. I don't know when I passed out again.

Someone kicked me awake. Three short, thin men were standing over me. Ishmael indicated that I needed to get up. The threat of being hit again gave me new life, and I followed Ishmael's movements as he dragged himself up and kneeled down, pushing his free arm against the ground for support. They hosed us with water, and the cold water hit me like an electric shock. I nearly cried out in pain, but silenced myself in time.

The bath did me good, and with the blood, dirt and excrement washed away from my body, my wounds began to hurt less. I looked around once the men had left. Ishmael had shrunk to half his size. His bones stuck out of his shrivelled frame, and ugly red wounds covered every inch of his torso. His belly had swollen enormously, and I felt mine and saw that the same had happened to me. Perhaps starvation did that to you; perhaps it was some disease which had struck us both. I didn't know. I wasn't supposed to know. This wasn't taught in the mechanical engineering course at MIT; this wasn't what NASA expected me to know when I was selected to join their graduate engineering trainee programme; this wasn't written in the Cambodian *Lonely Planet* guide. I broke into sudden, convulsive sobs.

The door swung open behind us, and the same man who had beaten us to pulp days, maybe weeks ago, entered. I shrunk against the wall but he didn't spare me a glance. Quietly, he untied Ishmael and pulled him to his feet. Then he dragged Ishmael outside the cell, holding him by his tattered T-shirt.

Alone in the cell, I drifted in and out of consciousness. I worried intermittently about Ishmael, but mostly, I just thought about food. My throat burnt like it was on fire but I felt no thirst, just gnawing, overpowering hunger. When would they bring the rice? I licked the floor; maybe a morsel had fallen there. Nothing. I tried to imagine food. That made it worse. I tried to stop thinking about food. It felt even worse. I tried to shut my swollen eyelids but felt hungrier from the effort.

I couldn't hold out any longer. I was dying.

Suddenly, there was the welcome sound of footsteps as a faceless man threw two bowls down on the floor. I threw myself at one of the bowls immediately and lapped up the gruel in a second, my tongue scraping against the steel again and again until it bled.

The only effect it had was to make me hungrier than I had been before.

I eyed the second bowl and was about to attack it

– but stopped. Ishmael. Wherever he was, he would come back hungry. But would he come back? For one long apocalyptic moment, I wished he wouldn't so I could eat his rice in peace. But what was stopping me now? I lunged for the bowl, tugging at the manacle around my wrist – and stopped again. I couldn't get his face out of my mind. The seconds ticked by. I continued to eye his bowl hungrily. Just a taste, I told myself, or even just the smell. Just once, please. I tried to keep my eyes shut. It was agonizing to sit so close to the bowl, to see its curvature, to feel its texture in my mind, to smell the wafts of wondrous fragrance that seemed to come from it.

Just as I reached for the bowl once again, I heard the sound of the door opening. Two men dragged Ishmael into the cell, threw him on the floor, and left. A tiny puddle of blood began to form around his body as he lay motionless, face down on the floor. I tried to reach him with my untied arm, but he was too far away. I pulled with all my strength at the manacle. It didn't budge an inch.

'Ishmael,' I shouted.

I didn't care any more if they came and beat me to death.

'Ishmael. Ishmael. Ishmael.'

He didn't stir.

He was losing blood. If he wasn't dead already, he would die soon unless he woke up and tried to close his wounds. I picked up my empty bowl and hurled it at him with all my strength. The sound of metal grinding against bone resonated through the cell. Ishmael moved a little.

I pushed his rice bowl towards him. 'Eat,' I said.

He looked at me. His eyes seemed to have been pushed back against their sockets; his nose, lips, chin had all been reduced to a bloody pulp. He opened his mouth to say something and tried to lift himself from the floor, but collapsed. He mumbled something; his voice was strained, his words unrecognizable.

He opened his mouth again. He stopped. And then, as if mustering up all his energy, 'Just tell them something,' he said. And collapsed.

He never rose again. Every day I envied him, and wished my release would come sooner.

They removed his body after a few weeks, maybe months, when the smell must have reached outside the cell and bothered them.

I felt no sadness when he was taken away. No one replaced him. I was alone in the cell but I felt no need for companionship. I felt nothing at all, just silent acceptance.

At first, I had been consumed with regret for giving Sam my passport. He belonged here, I thought, not me – it had been his idea to come to this wretched place. I held an irrational grievance against the hippies, whom Ishmael and I had helped escape from the airport – they should have been here with me, I thought, instead of sharing their story at cocktail parties as they must be doing now. I had raged against the madness of the Khmer Rouge, who had locked us up for no reason at all – we weren't enemies of the revolution, we didn't care whether it was good or bad, we didn't even know anything about it. Most of all, I blamed myself for the wrong choices that had led me here – abandoning India to study at MIT, agreeing to Sam's Cambodian vacation, and holding on to life when it was so much easier to slip away.

Now, I thought nothing, I felt nothing. If Ishmael had learned to accept, so would I.

Months passed, maybe years. Time meant nothing in that small, dark cell where I lay, tied by my hand to a wall. I slipped in and out of consciousness, my thoughts coherent for only brief periods of time after I drank my bowl of rice gruel. When awake, I would try to imbue my day with some meaning by remembering equations from fluid mechanics or reciting passages from Milton's poems. I tried to make myself indifferent to the pain, although sometimes when a sudden movement made the manacle press harder against the gash on my wrist or my decaying teeth began to slowly break away from my gums, I would give in to the impulse of screaming silently until I collapsed. For the most part though, I waited, either for death or for a chance to escape, both options equally appealing – and unattainable.

☞

After an eternity, they came for me. Two men, perhaps the same ones who had taken Ishmael – though I wasn't conscious enough either then or now to be sure – untied the manacle that had bound me for months. They lifted me to my feet and dragged me out of my cell. I was escorted through the darkness, past a row of small box-like cells similar to mine, and out of a door which I had often heard opening and closing. It brought in flickers of light into my cell in the mornings and shadows in the evenings.

The sharp glare of daylight hit me like a lightning bolt, and I stumbled. They caught me, not unkindly, and I glanced gratefully at their blank faces. I took in a breath of fresh air and felt suddenly, irrationally elated. Down a flight of stairs we went, into a small but well-lit room with crumbling walls.

A thin man sat on a chair in the centre of the room with a desk full of files, papers and journals in front of him. He looked up on seeing me enter, and squinted.

He said something to me in Khmer.

I tried to decipher if it was a greeting, a command or a question but his tone was flat and expressionless.

I bowed my head to indicate my respect. He walked over to me, and I tried not to look down at him – which wasn't difficult as I seemed to have shrunk to half my size.

He said something again.

'English?' I said tentatively.

'Confession,' he said in a sharp, high-pitched tone, and rattled off a string of Khmer.

'What confession?' I said, confused.

He raised his eyebrows and one of the men stepped in front of me. Before I could react, he hit me in the face – not hard, a mere tap – but I was so weak that I crashed to the floor. I heard bone crushing against bone but felt no pain.

'Confession,' he screamed again, followed by another string of Khmer.

I tried to sit up. For the first time in months, I saw my body in daylight. I had been reduced to a skeleton, the skin hanging from my bones like a loose coat on a hanger. Scabs, bruises and cuts covered every inch.

'What should I confess to?' I cried out.

He raised his eyebrows again, and the second man kicked me in the ribs. This time I felt a hollow pain spread through my body, magnifying as it went up, and almost exploding in my chest. I took a second to catch my breath. I knew I wouldn't last much longer if this continued.

I was about to plead with them to stop when

Ishmael's words flashed through my mind. 'Just tell them something.'

This was what he had meant.

Like me, he must have been asked to confess and had been beaten to death because he didn't know what to confess to.

'I'm a spy,' I said suddenly. 'American spy,' I added.

If I was a foreigner, I was probably expected to have plotted against the Khmer Rouge, I reasoned quite astutely for someone as fucked up as I was. Ishmael had said they hated Americans, so being an American spy was probably the most shocking confession I could make.

I looked tentatively at my interrogator, wondering if I had overstepped my boundaries.

He went back to his chair and the men came towards me.

I cowered in fear, but they picked me up and placed me on the chair opposite him.

'Confession,' he said again with a new gleam in his eyes.

'I work for the CIA,' I said with renewed confidence. 'CIA,' I emphasized.

His eyes widened. With luck, I thought, I could convince him I was the biggest traitor Cambodia had ever seen. And then what? He would probably execute me swiftly, without torture. I cheered silently at the prospect. He probably knew only a few words of English, so I decided to choose the ones with the maximum impact.

'Kill Cambodian farmers,' I said. 'End communism. Kill them all.'

His face lit up. Perhaps this was the first confession he had heard; the other hapless prisoners must have denied their involvement vehemently, as I too, would have done if I hadn't been warned by Ishmael.

'Fuck Pol Pot,' I said.

His eyes widened.

'Fuck Pol Pot,' I repeated, feeling faint from the exertion of speaking after so long. 'Kill that bastard.'

I had run out of things to say, given my limited knowledge of Cambodian history and the dizziness that had overcome me.

'Down with the Khmer Rouge. Motherfucking dog fuckers,' I said with all my remnant energy.

I seemed to have done my job. He barked out an order to his men.

Finally, I thought, escape to a hopefully kinder afterworld.

I prayed for it to be swift. A shot in the back of the head, perhaps, or a sudden twist of the neck.

Instead, they grabbed me by my arms and dragged me outside.

I blinked in the harsh daylight as they took me through an open courtyard and into a jeep with logs of wood piled high in the back.

They gestured for me to get in.

I knew better than to ask, and slowly clambered into the back. My swollen belly hit against the edge of a log, and I sprawled face down on the pile. They tied my wounded left wrist to the partition between the driver's side and the back of the jeep. The steel scraped against my wound, still raw from the manacle, and I moaned. As the jeep began to move, I forced myself to stay conscious to take in the first view of the place where I had spent the last several months – or years. It looked like a… a school. Yes, it was a school, I realized. The garden was actually a playground with the remnants of a soccer goalpost. The classrooms in the yellow brick building had been converted into holding cells, one of which had been my home, and the man who had just interrogated me sat in what was probably the principal's office. They had converted a school into a torture chamber for the educated bourgeoisie – did they even see the irony of this wonderfully symbolic gesture? I chuckled, and realized that I was slowly going insane. Ravaged by starvation, a wrist that had been all but sawed off, crippled by pain as the wood struck against my brittle bones, and on my way to certain execution – yet, I was tickled by the unintended irony.

We began crawling through the city of Phnom Penh. Abandoned cafés on the roadside, factories that had closed down, deserted buildings, damaged vehicles, rubble, tires and skeletons; no living being in sight, not even a dog, except a few vultures that hovered around the decaying bodies strewn along the sides of the road. The jeep continued its bumpy ride through the debris-strewn dirt tracks, and soon the city gave way to the vast, empty countryside. I remembered Ishmael talking about the forced movement of people to the villages. Perhaps I was being taken there, I thought, and felt a little cheerful. I would prefer to die in the open than in that airless cell, wallowing in my own shit. The steady rumble of the jeep lulled me out of consciousness.

I woke with a sharp pain in my side. Daylight had given way to dusk and the jeep had entered a forested area with deep valleys on both sides of the road. The road became less bumpy but the turns became sharper. We swerved dangerously with every turn; again and again, I was thrown about on the wooden logs.

The jeep took a sudden, sharp turn as we entered an even thicker forest. I was thrown to the other end and banged my head against the opaque front partition. Painfully, I tried to adjust my body and realized that the manacle which tied my wrist to the partition had come loose. I didn't plan what I did next, I didn't even actively think about it; I just did it.

Scrambling to the edge of the logs, I jumped out

of the speeding jeep as it navigated its next sharp turn. Down I fell, maybe twenty feet, and landed with a deafening splash in a shallow stream. For a second, I just lay face down in the cold water in disbelief. The water rose up my mouth and nose, and sputtering, I raised my head and looked around. I couldn't see anyone in the stream, or in the forests on either side. I looked up at the road. The jeep didn't seem to have stopped. If they hadn't heard me, it would take a while for them to notice my absence. The logs were piled high and they could neither see nor hear me, nor had they shown any inclination to stop during the journey.

I was free. *I am free*, I repeated to myself, still in shock. A sudden thought struck me. There was only one forest indicated in the Cambodian map, which meant that this was the forest that bordered Thailand. After months of darkness, I could see a tantalizing ray of light in the distance – elusive, but suddenly attainable. I could escape, I thought with sudden resolve. But first, I needed to get out of sight. Slowly, I picked myself up and began to wade towards the bank – and fell in the water.

Come on, Nick, you can do this.

I picked myself up again – and fell. Again and again, I tried and kept falling. I began to cry in frustration. Just months ago, I used to run ten miles a day at soccer practice; now, I couldn't even muster the energy to walk three feet.

Those bastards could come back any moment.

Think, boy, think, I told myself. *Mens et Manus*, Mind and Hand – the MIT slogan. Use your mind if the body doesn't listen. I summoned all my energy to get up again, and collapsed once more. This wasn't working. I tried to drag myself out of the stream. Slowly, painfully, stumbling on the sharp-edged stones, I began to crawl my way to the bank, almost willing the Khmer Rouge lackeys to retrace their steps and put me out of my misery. With a last burst of effort, I dragged myself to the edge of the stream. I slipped out of consciousness when I reached the bushes.

I woke after an eternity, delirious and uncomprehending. I had missed the final examination at MIT because of soccer practice, I thought with a sinking sensation. Why were these dark, angry mosquitoes feasting on me in the soccer field? Coach, coach, I shouted, these plants are eating me. I tried to push the branches away, but there were so many of them, just so many of them… I slipped away again.

When I woke up next, the sun had risen.

Where was I?

You are in a forest in Cambodia trying to escape to Thailand, someone said.

What? I'm running late for an examination.

Remember the Khmer Rouge? Remember Cambodia? Boy, you need to get it together, don't you?

Eat. Remember what Sam said? 'I eat anything that moves.' Look around. Find something that's moving.

I spotted a crab in the thick undergrowth and threw a stone at it. It scuttled away.

Easy, boy. Focus. Wait for the kill. Impatience has always been your downfall.

This time I waited for a crab to come near me, and picked up a larger stone. Crash. There, killed the bastard, I said triumphantly.

Now, light a fire.

I looked around for two stones and realized that my left wrist was hanging from my arm like a loose thread. How could I build a fire with one arm?

No problem. Just eat it raw.

Raw?

Yes. No seven-course meal awaits you here.

I retched, but slowly tore the poor sucker to pieces. I ate all the soft bits.

Good, now remember your father's stories from his NDA days? Eat some grass to digest it.

Now, drag yourself to the stream and drink as much water as you can. Idiot, don't stand like that. First, fasten your legs with those fallen branches for support. Good. Make them tight.

Get your bearings. Remember where the jeep came from? Remember the map from the time you first arrived?

Now boy, don't get sad. Think of Ishmael, the Karma Yogi. Pleasure and pain. Joy and sorrow. Triumph and disaster. You control nothing, your only duty is to escape.

Okay, now rest and then start walking west.

Yours is not to question, boy. Just walk. Avoid the dirt tracks, just walk through the brambles and the bushes, not much left of you to be torn to pieces. Change course only when you smell decomposing flesh, because that means the Khmer Rouge are killing some villagers nearby.

Stop walking like that, will you? Be careful of the land mines Ishmael said are planted in the forest — stop whenever you see an aberration on the ground and change course.

Eat, drink, rest, walk, and stay out of trouble. How difficult is that, you spoilt son of a brave army officer?

I heard voices as I edged closer to a clearing with small huts, a herd of cattle, and a few men and women dressed in plain clothes walking around in what appeared to be a state of normalcy.

Who are they? I asked. Are we close to the Thai border?

I didn't receive an answer.

I looked around frantically.

For five days and five nights, we had stumbled through the dense, bracketed forests together.

Together, we endured the small, pointy bamboo plants that pierced the soles of our feet, and the angry mosquitoes that feasted on us at night. We stayed awake to beat away the snakes slithering in the bushes, and avoided the herds of trampling elephants in the distance. If it weren't for him, I would still be sitting on the bank, cursing my fate, staring at the pieces of bone that were now my left wrist and obsessively rubbing away the dried, caked blood that stuck to my body like another layer of skin.

The voices grew louder as I approached the clearing cautiously, hiding behind bushes and tall grass.

They were speaking in Khmer, I suddenly realized. Why were they speaking in Khmer when this was the Thai border? The realization, when it struck, almost knocked me to the ground.

I had completely misjudged the coordinates. I had always been bad at reading maps.

Instead of walking to Thailand, I had probably walked in the opposite direction, to the northern end of Cambodia. I was probably back where I had started. I felt every bit of hope and life drain away from me.

The voices became louder and I saw three healthy looking men approaching the bush behind which I stood.

I didn't try to hide. I didn't try to run. I had

nothing left to fight for any more. It was over. I had tried my best, but it wasn't good enough.

The men spotted me and shouted in angry voices.

Maybe it was for the best, I thought. Who knew what horrors awaited me in Thailand?

They came running towards me.

Peaceful, unresisting, I allowed myself to fall, glad that it was finally over.

Monochromatic, multi-hued colours, lights going in and out, an array of bald men parading in orange robes, no hunger pangs, no overpowering thirst. This is heaven, I thought – except for the excruciating pain in my arm. I drifted away, peaceful despite the pain.

More colours, the sweet smell of incense, a reassuring, low-pitched chant, cool and calm, no hunger, no thirst. Just the pain, no longer throbbing, but dull, aching, and grey. Please make it go away, God, and I will be completely at peace.

'Can you hear me?'

I woke up with a start. A bald white angel with golden eyebrows dressed in splendid orange-brown robes was sitting next to me. God, the Almighty. Deliverance.

His calm face broke into a smile. 'Are you feeling better?' he asked in English with a strong American accent.

I was alive, I thought abstractly. This wasn't heaven but it would do just fine. 'Where am I?' I asked, my head still throbbing.

'You are in a monastery in Thailand,' he said kindly.

But I wasn't supposed to be here, I thought. My guide had led me back to Cambodia.

'Where is he?' I asked.

'Who?'

'The man who was with me.'

'They found you alone.'

I drifted away again.

'Where am I?'

I was alive and conscious, lying on a wooden bed in a small, well-lit room with light blue walls. The bald American in orange robes was sitting next to me.

'You are in a Buddhist monastery in the Rong Glua village on the Thai side of the border,' he said.

I was trying to process this information when a sudden pain shot through my left arm. I reached out to grab it with my right hand. My hand hit the wooden bed.

'The doctors had to amputate your arm,' he

said gently. 'Gangrene had set in from the elbow down.'

I stared at him in disbelief. Just how long would this nightmare last, I wondered. It was a bloody vacation, goddamit. I knew I had made a mistake. But how long would I have to pay for it? My arm, I thought, my arm. No basketball, no soccer, no NASA. I was a cripple. Tears stung my eyes.

'I can't even begin to imagine how terrible you feel.' He leaned forward and held my right hand. 'But if it makes you feel any better, you are lucky to be alive.'

I looked at him, tall, broad-shouldered and erect in his flowing monk's robes, both arms intact – and hated him.

'We weren't confident that you'd make it when the villagers at the border brought you here a month ago. You had lost a lot of blood, your body was badly bruised and cut, and you looked like a skeleton. They thought you were dead until you started mumbling. They brought you here because you spoke English and didn't look Cambodian. The refugee camps on the border are well-intentioned, but so busy that individual attention is impossible.'

It came back to me. The villagers who I'd thought were Cambodians were probably Thai, and Khmer must be spoken at the border in the same way that Hindi is spoken at the Indo-Nepalese border. When we were in high school, Sam and I had once run away to Nepal to get stoned. Suddenly, I wished I hadn't been found by the villagers. I would rather be dead than be a cripple.

'I am from Texas,' he said. 'I came here as a Red Cross worker, but became a Buddhist monk instead.' He shook my right hand. 'I am David, now Monk Dechen.'

'I am Nikhil,' I said. 'I came from Boston on a vacation.'

It sounded unreal.

He patted my head, and I cried shamelessly against his arm.

'Where is the man who helped me?' I asked after a while, trying to pull myself together.

'Who?' he said with a puzzled expression.

'There was someone in the forest who guided me to the border, otherwise I'd never have made it.'

'They found you alone.'

How could he die in the forest when he seemed so confident? Why couldn't I remember his name or his face?

'Was it a voice that spoke to you?' David asked.

I nodded, although I didn't like the implication of his words. I wasn't a lunatic. I didn't have visions of God speaking to me.

'You aren't going crazy,' said David kindly. 'Many crisis survivors experience this third presence. I am not a psychologist, but from what I understand, the mind divorces itself from the body in situations of extreme duress when the physical systems shut down.'

It made sense. I was too fatigued to move even a step, yet I had managed to walk for five days without stopping or treading on a mine. For what, though? I wished I had known it would end like this. I would have allowed myself to slip into eternity.

'Do you know the date today?' said David.

I shook my head.

'5 June, 1977,' he said.

Sam and I had arrived in Phnom Penh on 17 April 1975, just after our convocation at MIT. I had spent more than two years in that cell. What was my fault? What was Ishmael's crime? What had she done, the pregnant woman who had been hacked to death in front of our eyes?

'You are a survivor. A brave, brave man,' said David. 'The Red Cross estimates that nearly six million people have been killed since the Khmer Rouge took over two years ago. That's a third of the Cambodian population. Can you believe that? A third of the population eliminated using methods that are nowhere as sophisticated as the Nazis', as you well know.'

I recalled the shrivelled corpses of children in the countryside with vultures feeding on them. Madness, I thought, stark, raving madness.

'Isn't someone doing anything about it?' I asked.

'They have cut off all international ties completely, and frankly, no one cares. America is busy fighting a war with Vietnam, and Cambodia is too small an economy to matter to anyone else. Besides, there is just a handful of survivors who've escaped to tell their stories; most of the country is dying slowly of either starvation or the not-so-random acts of brutal violence in the fields.'

But it's their country, I wanted to shout. They had something to do with it, or at least they were born there. What about me? What did I have to do with anything? Suddenly, I was reminded of Ishmael, smiling and dignified even in death, accepting his destiny with grace. He had helped me escape. He wouldn't be complaining right now if he were me, I thought. He had given me a chance to live; if nothing else, I owed it to him to make something of it.

'When can I get back to the US?' I asked, my mind a confused jumble of thoughts.

'As early as tomorrow, if you feel up to it,' he replied. 'There are flights every night from Bangkok to New York. We could arrange for you to leave for Bangkok tomorrow with someone from the monastery. The American embassy has a standing record of missing Americans and is likely to process your paperwork immediately. You could be on a flight late tomorrow or the day after.'

'Yes, I feel fine,' I said sharply. 'I would like to leave as soon as possible.'

He nodded understandingly and I felt like a jerk. He had saved my life. He owed me nothing, yet I was speaking to him as if my foolishness in coming to Cambodia was his fault.

'I'm sorry,' I said. 'Thank you for saving my life.'

He smiled broadly. 'No apologies required. You have taken this extraordinarily well. As I said, you are a very courageous man to have made it out of there alive.'

My missing arm began to hurt again. I looked at it in surprise.

'It's called a phantom pain,' he said, noticing my reaction. 'Soon it will get better as you... err... get used to it.'

As soon as I got used to being a cripple, I thought bitterly.

He stared at me. 'You are at the right place to get the answers you are seeking,' he said after a while. 'Would you be willing to come with me for a discourse by the Maha-thera, the head monk of the monastery? You are lucky. We are inducting a few new monks today so he will give an overview of the Buddha's teachings.'

Great, lucky again, luckiest bastard in the world, wasn't I? Lucky to get a chance to hear a cheerful, well-fed monk in the pink of health tell me what an ennobling experience my suffering was. I didn't want to be a noble person, I thought. I just wanted my arm back.

'Like you, I could never understand why the innocent had to suffer. That's why I left the Red

Cross,' David said as he helped me get out of bed and walk a few hesitant steps. The soles of my feet seemed to burn, and I grimaced in pain. Some suffering, I thought. Look at me. I didn't even have an arm to balance my movements any more; if I fell, I fell.

'Whatever your questions, the Buddha has the answers,' he told me.

Sure, I thought, who better to understand my pain than a thirty-something prince in the throes of a mid-life crisis who abandoned his family so he could 'find himself'. Today's junkie was yesterday's Buddha.

David laughed. 'You don't do a very good job of hiding your emotions. If you prefer to rest before your trip to Bangkok, please don't feel obliged to come.'

'No, no. I want to come,' I said, suddenly ashamed of myself.

So later that day, I limped my way through the silent, well-lit corridors to the common room.

'The first noble truth is this: All life is dukha.'

Despite my vow to keep an open mind, I felt a surge of irritation. What was I doing here, in the middle of these orange-robed, bald, stoned looking monks with impassive, content faces, listening to a phony Chink godman who had probably never seen the outside of a secluded monastery spout paternal homilies on the nature of existence?

Get me a man with an amputated arm or a man who sat for two years in his own faeces smelling his friend's decomposing body – and I will hear him speak all day. But spare me this, I said silently to the fat, cheerful teacher, who looked ageless and radiant, nowhere near the eighty years of age David had said he was. I already know all life is suffering, in a way you will never know.

The forty-odd monks in the small room were listening in rapt attention. Despite the location of the border village, most were westerners. Red Cross dropouts or trust fund hippies, I thought uncharitably. Crest cleans your teeth in ten days; the Buddha gives you nirvana in ten days. Salvation or the Buddha will give your money back. Try next door at Walmart.

'Contrary to popular perception, dukha is not just suffering,' the teacher continued. I focused my attention on him again. Unlike the pastors at church, he stated his position untheatrically and calmly, without trying to convince or provoke.

'Dukha in Pali also means uneasiness, disquietude, restlessness, a vague feeling of incompleteness that characterizes all life.'

I found myself getting just a little interested. A lifetime ago, when my troubles weren't as concrete as a missing arm, I had occasionally felt that sense of vague, inexplicable dissatisfaction. It surprised me to hear it being articulated as such.

'The origin of dukha is attachment – craving and clinging to emotions and experiences whose fundamental nature is to change, to be in flux. This is the second noble truth. We crave a simpler past, or a brighter future, without realizing that the loss of that past is inevitable, that the self which is seeking the future is itself changing.'

I had a sudden, surreal sensation that there was no one else in the room. He seemed to be speaking directly to me. He was right, I was clinging to my past. I was craving the happiness of a better time. What was that better time, though? When I was at MIT, I would think about the time Mom and Dad were alive; here, I was craving my time at MIT. If I ended up losing both arms, I would probably be pining for the time I had one arm. I know life changes, I thought. I understand it's always in flux. But how do I rid myself of the burden of the past?

'I don't teach anything here,' he continued. 'I am not a godman, I don't fly on carpets, I don't walk on water. I can only be a guide on your journey to free yourself from the craving that binds us to this ultimately unfulfilling cycle of life and death. But this journey is yours and you have to walk the path alone.'

He was addressing weighty topics – birth, death, rebirth, bondage, enlightenment – but his tone wasn't patronizing. Every bone in his body screamed sincerity, his face radiated truth. He wasn't a quack – as I had half hoped he would be.

'Make no mistake, it's a tough journey. Through intense meditation, you will annihilate the self, destroy the ego, and lose the "I" that craves. I haven't reached this goal myself. I am not the Buddha, the enlightened one. I am just rowing the ferry that separates this world from the other, but the peace in my heart tells me I am paddling in the right direction. You can choose to follow my imperfect path and perhaps waste a lifetime or maybe more getting there – or you can choose to return to the life you know. Whatever you choose, I wish you peace.'

For the rest of the discourse, I stared at him in a daze, watching his calm face mouth words which sometimes made sense but mostly sounded esoteric and obscure. But all of it sounded sincere. Was there really a chance that the body was just a shell? That losing an arm wasn't a tragedy, but not taking steps to achieve nirvana – the union of the individual soul with the universal soul – was? I looked around the room full of impassive faces deep in concentration. There were monks as young as ten or twelve, and they were ready to devote their lives to this important but ultimately elusive quest, unsure of the outcome but trusting in the path paved by someone thousands of years ago, who had left no written record of his existence. If they could have faith, couldn't I believe once more?

There was a sudden buzz of activity in the small room as the discourse drew to a close.

'I hope that wasn't too boring.'

I was taken aback for a moment. I had forgotten that David was sitting next to me.

'Let me introduce you to the monk who will take you to Bangkok tomorrow,' he said as he helped me up.

I would soon take a flight from Bangkok to New York, I thought, and hopefully still be able to join NASA in some capacity. If I was lucky, I would help build equipment to transport people to a distant, perhaps kinder world. And one day I would be married to someone who wouldn't care that I was a cripple. Maybe we would have two children and live in a quiet suburban home, and I would never understand the madness of these last two years, I would never be able to explain to my children why there was evil in the world and whether it would ever cease.

'We don't have a phone here, but as soon as you reach Bangkok, you should give your family a call.' He smiled. 'They won't be able to believe their ears, will they? How absolutely delighted they will be!'

No one was waiting for me. A few spare friends, a couple of professors perhaps, but I was a footnote in their lives, at best an interesting subject for cocktail

parties, forgotten as the complexities of their own
lives took a grip on them. Someday, I would matter
less than a missed promotion or a failed relationship,
if that hadn't already happened. Sam would care, yes,
but he must think me dead by now, which was better
for both of us. I wasn't big enough not to grudge
him his health and happiness and he, in turn, would
be obligated to me in a way that would threaten our
friendship. No, my going back would help no one
at all. I was better off away from the memories of
happier times.

'The bus leaves early morning. Try to get a good
night's sleep.'

Would I ever be able to have a good night's sleep
again, I wondered. I would probably continue to be
scared of the dark, terrified of every footfall I heard
in the corridor, tormented by the nightmares of the
past.

'Come, let's go back to your room,' he said.

I didn't move.

'Is something wrong?'

'David, I want to stay here,' I said in a rush. 'I
don't want to go to Bangkok or New York. I want
to stay in the monastery. I want to try and walk the
Buddha's path. Will you give me a chance?'

Space and silence, breathing and concentration,
hearing without judgment, listening without

speaking. In the stillness of the hall with its solid, wooden columns and the rhythmic rotation of the prayer drums, days passed, then months, then years. Time lost all relevance. Instead of moving from space scientist to senior space engineer to explorations project leader in NASA, I climbed the monastic hierarchy and went from the novice monk samanera, to the middle-ranked majjhima to the more senior thera. But even that meant nothing. I didn't want to get anywhere. All I wanted was not to feel the wrench every time I saw the empty sleeve dangling by my side, not to feel regret on seeing the impish grins on the faces of the young monks shuffling through the large, silent hall. Peace was too lofty a goal; acceptance would do just fine.

'Are you okay? Nick? Nikhil? Buddha?'

Someone was shaking me vigorously.

'Haanh?' I said.

I looked up to see the handler hovering over me, looking irritated.

I shook myself out of my reverie. He hadn't brought me here to think about my past.

'Yes, yes,' I said hurriedly. 'I just got distracted.'

Distracted, thinking about how life would have turned out had I gone back to the US immediately. It would certainly have been better than this; anything would have been better than this.

Get on with it, the handler's expression said. Blow your brains out quickly. People are waiting. Unlike you, they have things to do and places to go.

The room went silent as I positioned the gun against my temple. The crowd around me clapped tentatively and egged me on in muted tones. Dayaram peered at me anxiously.

Slowly, deliberately, I squeezed the trigger.

Click. I drew a blank.

A collective sigh went through the room. I passed the revolver to Dayaram. His hand trembled as he took the gun. I don't know who was more disappointed that I hadn't managed to kill myself – he or I.

With shaking hands, he picked up the revolver.

'Don't wait, just do it,' I whispered. 'It's always better that way. Just hold steady.'

He looked at me gratefully and managed to point the gun at his temple. He seemed to lose his nerve when he looked around at the sweaty, expectant faces in the room.

'Don't look at those fuckers,' I said. 'Look straight into my eyes.'

He did as I asked, his hands steady again.

'Go,' I said.

Click.

Another blank. I sighed with relief. His eyes filled with tears as he handed me the revolver.

Everyone tensed again. I held the gun to my temple as they shuffled closer to the table.

Finally, I thought, a chance to end what should have ended in Cambodia twenty years ago. So many people could have been spared the grief I caused in the years that followed.

The Donos

Don't say it's a fine morning or I will shoot you.
John Wayne

17 April 1985, Flight from Phnom Penh, Cambodia to Rio de Janeiro, Brazil

'Is Rio de Janeiro your final destination?' the air hostess asked.

I smiled. My final destination was nirvana, liberation from the cycle of birth and death that binds us humans, and the cessation of all suffering. For now, Rio de Janeiro would do just fine though.

I nodded.

She smiled at me. 'Have a pleasant flight.'

The last time I heard those words, I lost my arm. But that was a distant memory now, a mere event that took place almost ten years ago and which I now looked back on quite dispassionately – with some degree of success. The Buddha taught me that all that happened to me was the fruit of my karma, and that I was in fact lucky to be given a chance to pay off the debts of my past lives so I could strive for the ultimate goal in this life. On most days, immersed in the ten hours of mandatory meditation in the quiet, peaceful monastery with its clanging prayer bells and deep, resonant chants, I believed this explanation. But on some days, when a phantom pain seared through my absent left arm and the smell of Ishmael's decomposing body pervaded my senses, despite the omnipresent incense, the words seemed empty and unfulfilling.

But the hours of constant meditation and the weighty spiritual discourses had had an extraordinary impact on my wellbeing. It had taken eight years of living an intense, disciplined life secluded within the four walls of the monastery, protected by the singha, the mythical lion-head, but I had finally made a grudging, fragile peace with the past. Now, I could sleep at night with both the nightmares and the images of a happier, uncomplicated past gradually beginning to recede. And I wanted nothing to upset my silent, if sometimes uneasy, calm, which is why I had deeply resisted David's – Monk Dechen's – suggestion that I travel with him to set up Brazil's first Vipassana meditation monastery in Rio de Janeiro.

It was the Buddhist dhamma to spread the message of acceptance and inner peace, and Rio de Janeiro, the most violent city in Brazil, was a natural first stop for Vipassana's South American pollination. We were lucky that the new civilian government in Brazil had allowed us this opportunity, David said.

I hadn't yet progressed from the lowest form of personal fulfillment to the noble task of spreading joy in the world. I had sacrificed myself for someone once, and I hadn't become sanguine enough not to regret that decision – especially when I struggled with the hundred basic tasks that I had taken for granted all my life.

But David persisted, and I eventually acquiesced, considering it small repayment for the gift of life that the monastery had given me. Besides, I knew that his request for help was actually a desire to help me. For the past few years, he had been urging me to break the wall of silence that I had carefully constructed around myself. But I felt neither the inclination nor the need. Meditating for hours, staring vacantly at the statue of the smiling Buddha in the courtyard, ruminating on the discourses, disengaged from the small talk and petty politics of the monastery, and just being by myself made me happy – or perhaps I didn't know what being 'happy' meant any more. I was living without fear, anger or hatred. Did that qualify?

'Are you a monk?'

I shook myself out of my reverie. I was sitting next to a fashionably dressed olive-skinned woman about my age, with bright, curious eyes, high cheekbones, long, flowing hair, and a regal air. I had been taught to practise non-judgment – to be unmoved by any person, word, action, or event, to just *be* – but I liked the way her smile reached her eyes. 'Not technically,' I said as the flight took off. 'Monasteries have rigid hierarchies. I am a thera, one step below a maha-thera, which is full monkhood. It will take me a few more years to become a monk.'

She laughed and said in thickly accented English. 'You don't talk like a monk. You don't even look like one, except for your bald head and your robes. Aren't monks supposed to be round and clumsy? You look like First Blood Rambo!'

'Who?' I said absentmindedly, glancing out the window. We were flying steadily over the green forests along the Thai-Cambodian border. There were too many memories associated with those forests, none of them pleasant. I turned away and found myself staring into her curious brown eyes.

'Never mind.' She laughed. 'You exercise a lot in the monastery? Is it like Shaolin, with martial arts and kung fu?'

'No,' I said. 'Shaolin is a Chinese interpretation of Buddhism. We practise Vipassana meditation, which doesn't propagate martial arts at all. In fact, it forbids any form of intense physical exercise because the artificial high from such exertion distracts from true dhyana. But I still exercise for different reasons.'

Unmentionable reasons like a deep-rooted fear of being caught off-guard again. Despite the Buddhist belief in the unity of the soul, I was unable to trust mankind any more. Every day, I ran like a madman through the dark streets of Rong Glua, did hundreds of push-ups with my remaining arm, used bricks as weights and the thick, concrete walls of the monastery as a punching bag – all surreptitiously, in the dead of the night, breaking every monastic rule.

Next time, I had vowed, I wouldn't be a victim.

'Quite fascinating. I didn't realize there were sects within Buddhism,' she said and stretched out her hand. 'My name is Lara.'

'Monk Namche,' I said and we shook hands.

I felt a vague stirring. Despite myself, images I'd spent the last eight years banishing from memory flashed through my mind – making love to Lavanya by the warm fireplace in our cold Alaskan camp, walking hand in hand through the New England autumn, hidden kisses in the MIT corridors. Immediately, I reminded myself of the second tenet in the Buddha's Noble Eightfold Path. Right intention, it said, the intent of renunciation and resisting the pull of desire. This craving was maya, an illusion, which ultimately causes suffering.

'I am in the entertainment business,' she said.

'I figured,' I said involuntarily.

'What do you mean?'

'Nothing,' I said, ashamed to be behaving like a schoolboy. 'I mean, you look very, well, accomplished.'

'Why, thank you,' she said, looking a little surprised. 'That might just be the most honest compliment I've ever received. Are you interested in movies?'

I paused.

'Once upon a time,' I said, remembering the nights spent with Sam, discussing Guru Dutt and avant-garde French films over unending cups of tea in our MIT dorm. 'Now, I get very little time.'

'Really?' she said curiously. 'What do monks do all day?'

I smiled. 'You don't think much of monks, do you?'

'I didn't mean it that way,' she said, looking flustered. 'Not at all.'

'I know.' I smiled. 'I actually have a pretty busy day. We start by begging for food. Then…'

'You beg! Why? A person like you – you could do anything!'

Not a mention of my arm, not even a glance at it.

'Begging for alms is mandatory for a monk because it destroys his ego, the root cause of all craving, which leads to dukha or anguish,' I told her.

She listened quietly.

'Then we meditate for ten hours with a small break for lunch,' I continued. 'After a rest period in the evening, we listen to a discourse by the oldest and wisest monk in the monastery.'

'That's a lot of meditation!' she said. 'What do you meditate on?'

'The impermanence of existence,' I said. 'Buddhists believe that all human suffering originates from our craving for sensory pleasure, whether physical or emotional. Sustained meditation rids you of such attachment by destroying the self that craves these pleasures.'

'But why would you do that?'

'Do what?'

'Stop seeking these pleasures.'

'It is this craving that leads to a vicious cycle of disquietude,' I replied. 'You seek pleasure and feel disappointed if you don't attain it. And if you do, you seek even more. You are always restless, unhappy, looking for the next high like a drug addict. Then you get tired of the kick and start looking for a new one – and so it goes.'

'So?' she said. 'Isn't that life? Joy and sorrow, pleasure and pain, gaining and losing, ambition and failure – that's what makes it interesting, surely? If there isn't any darkness, how do you appreciate the light?'

'There is a higher spiritual plane where there is only light,' I said. 'No amount of joy in the material plane can substitute for that.'

'How do you know?' she demanded.

'Well,' I said hesitantly. 'That's what Buddhists believe.'

'But you haven't experienced it yourself, have you?' she said with interest.

'In flashes,' I said, recalling the sudden, electric joy that filled me sometimes after meditation. A sense of utter, indescribable joy, an eternal peace that enveloped me for a few brief moments before vanishing.

'How is it permanent if you've only experienced it in flashes?' she asked.

'It takes a lifetime of practice to achieve that

light permanently and, well, it's hard to define it in words.'

'You are prepared to spend a lifetime meditating for an end you can't even define!' she said incredulously. 'Isn't it better to live a full, interesting life now – even if it has a measure of suffering – rather than chase an elusive goal that others have talked about? Anyway, why were we sent into this world if we weren't supposed to experience it?'

Her hazel eyes bore into mine, demanding an answer.

'Just what *kind* of entertainment business are you in?' I asked.

She burst out laughing and woke up David, who was sleeping across the aisle with his mouth open. He eyed me curiously.

'I'm sorry, I didn't mean to pry,' she said. 'I don't usually have such conversations with anyone. Something you said triggered off a memory.'

What memory, I wondered. I found myself drawn to her despite my efforts to remain detached.

'No offence taken. I've asked pretty much the same questions myself over the years.' I paused. 'But sometimes meditation helps make sense of the world. It helps explain suffering and loss in ways that the rational mind can't. It allows you to accept, even to make peace with the past.'

She looked at my crippled arm for the first time. 'How old are you?' she asked.

I hadn't thought about my age in a while. Once upon a time, being young and successful had seemed like the most important thing in the world; now I didn't even know how to define success. Like Rip Van Winkle, I had unknowingly checked out of the world I knew.

'Thirty,' I said, mentally calculating the years and overcome again by the same creeping sense of failure that had haunted me in the monastery recently.

'You are young. You have your whole life ahead of you,' she said. 'I am a year younger, by the way.' She smiled at me.

I felt my face flush.

'I could show you around Rio,' she said. 'How long will you be there?'

'I don't know,' I said. 'We are opening our first Vipassana centre, so I will be there as long as it takes to establish it.'

'So you will travel around converting people?'

'That isn't the way it works,' I said, feeling an inexplicable urge to defend the Buddha. 'We'll just do our thing. Maybe one person will come out of curiosity; maybe no one will turn up. Ultimately, if there is truth in the message, it will spread of its own accord. There is no ceremony or conversion, or any "ism" involved. If it helps you, stick with it; if it doesn't, you are free to go.'

'I might just give it a try then, Monk Namche.

Maybe I could be your first student,' she said teasingly.

'You can call me Nick or Nikhil,' I said and we shook hands again.

'Nikhil.' She repeated the name a few times. I watched her lips move as if of their own volition. 'That's a beautiful name.'

I was suddenly concerned for everything I'd been taught.

'I need to sleep now,' I said.

She looked disappointed but didn't say anything.

I stole a final, hesitant glance at her as I covered myself with the blanket and leaned against the window. Despite the steady hum of the airplane, I had trouble falling asleep for the first time in years.

I found myself thinking about her at odd times of the day and night. As I hammered planks together to make wooden beds for the dormitory, I remembered the glances I stole at her as she slept in the airplane seat. When speaking of the Buddha's teachings to the small class, I thought of her expressive face as she listened to my arguments in favour of Buddhism. While buying groceries in the local shops, I would recall the way she delicately held the spoon to her lips as she ate her airline meal.

Was I in love? I didn't know, nor particularly cared. I knew that the explanation for what I felt was simpler and much less exotic. I had been in a bubble for ten years; she was the first woman I'd come within touching distance of – a model or a movie star at that. I was merely mooning over her like any thirty-year-old full-blooded male would. Besides, I thought as I remembered my MIT days, she was way out of my league. Intangible spiritual progress aside, at thirty, I was broke, had lost an arm but gained no new perspective, was unemployed for all intents and purposes – and would soon be homeless.

A year after arriving in Rio de Janeiro, I could no longer ignore the tumult in my mind. I finally decided to speak to David. We had worked hard to get the monastery running in the small farm that the government had allotted us just outside the city. Bit by bit, we had transformed the rocky land into a functioning monastery with a cemented meditation hall, utilitarian sleeping quarters with wooden beds, a common dining area and a sparse vegetable garden. David and I had taught ourselves basic Portuguese by using translation books and practising on each other, and soon we knew enough to spread the word.

The first few inductees had been second-generation Japanese immigrants in Brazil, a significant population in Rio, who had perhaps heard of Buddhism from their ancestors. But word spread fast and now the monastery boasted a diverse gathering of thirty-odd monks. I knew David was proud of what we had accomplished – which made it even more difficult for me when I hailed him in the garden that day.

He stopped mulching the lawn and looked at me quizzically, his face ageless and unwrinkled, just the way it had been eight years ago when we first met. I felt a sudden, overwhelming rush of affection for him. How could I do this to the man who had saved my life when everyone had given up on me, including myself?

'David,' I began. 'I…' I stumbled, then stopped.

He sighed, and I realized he knew.

'You want to leave, don't you?'

I nodded. 'I can't renounce until I know what I am renouncing; I can't abstain unless I know what I am abstaining from.' My carefully practised words came out in a rush. 'I haven't lived enough to forsake life. I want to…'

He placed his hands on my shoulders. 'You don't have to explain,' he said gently. 'I've known for a while.'

I hung my head in shame. What was I doing? I had no idea what I wanted to do or where I would go next. A blurry image of Lara haunted me, but I wasn't stupid enough to leave to chase a mirage. I wasn't suffering any crisis of faith either, because I still believed in the Buddha's path. Nor did I crave material achievement or sexual conquest. All I knew was that I felt a gnawing sense of unease – a sinking feeling of losing time and wasting opportunities – and neither meditation nor reading Buddhist texts was helping to quell that one bit.

'I'm sorry. I'm really, really sorry,' I said. 'I don't think I'm doing justice to anyone by being here. If I can't internalize the words I preach to the novice monks every day, it's not fair to them – or to you.'

'You are young,' said David. 'Don't be hard on yourself. You will return stronger from the experience.'

'I've let you down,' I said, my head still bowed.

'Look at what you have accomplished.' He swept his hand around the monastery compound. 'I haven't been prouder of anyone in my life.'

I held his hand and cried disconsolately.

He touched my head with gentle fingers. 'I know you will come back stronger,' he repeated. 'You didn't know, but I saw you all these years, exercising, running at night, convincing yourself that you weren't a cripple, shying away from everyone's pity. You meditated longer and more intently than any of the other monks, struggling to accept and push the doubts away from your mind.'

I looked up at him, surprised. He hadn't stopped me from breaking the rules of the monastery despite being a maha-thera.

'There is a fire inside you I wouldn't want you to lose. Will you go to the US or return to India?'

'I don't know,' I said. No one was waiting for me anywhere. I was leaving the only person who cared whether I was dead or alive.

'Whatever you decide, my only advice to you is to just let go. You have been in a cocoon for too long – break free and fly; you will emerge majestic, like a butterfly.'

I nodded.

'I have no money of my own, as you know,' he continued. 'But I will give you money from the monastery's funds, which should be enough to buy you a flight ticket at least.'

'I can't take any money from the monastery.'

'Think of it as a loan, or maybe a payment for your services. We owe you that.'

'No,' I said firmly. 'Don't worry about me. You know I've survived on less.'

'But…' He stopped, perhaps sensing that I wouldn't change my mind. 'The doors here are always open to you,' he said. 'Don't ever hesitate to come back. After all, you are the one who built it all.'

I looked around at the small world we had created together and an aching sense of loss gripped me again. If I waited any longer, I wouldn't be able to gather the courage to leave.

'If I have your permission, I'll leave now,' I said.

'Now?' he said. 'I can't let you go now. It's getting dark and this is the most violent city in the world.'

'I'll survive,' I told him. 'I've been in worse situations.'

His brow creased.

I touched his arm. 'I'll be safe. Please take care of yourself.'

Reluctantly, I turned away and walked along the dirt track that led outside the farm, never looking back for fear of breaking down on seeing the unconditional affection in his eyes.

Aimless and penniless, barefoot and still clad in my monk's robes, I walked until I lost all sense of place, direction and time. The quiet streets adjoining the farm gave way to wide, busy roads with motors whizzing past, then to a large rocky cliff with jagged edges and finally to crowded beaches full of revellers – the vista seemed to change with every turn, and even in my confused, disorganized state of mind, I wondered at how much Rio had managed to pack into a few miles.

Then the ocean front suddenly veered away towards a rugged shantytown where young boys drove mopeds at breakneck speed and small, busy shops appeared crowded with beautiful, dark-skinned men and women with an easy swing in their step. A narrow, potholed road with broken brick steps on either side wound its way up to what looked like the main centre of the small slum-like township.

I had no money, so a slum looked like a good place to catch my breath. I made my way through the throngs of people. No one gave me a second glance. A barefoot, crippled monk seemed to fit right in with the assortment of quirky characters on the street – urchins toting big black rifles, groups of young boys and girls carrying large stereos on their shoulders and belting out songs, cheerful, boisterous men and women sauntering to the beach in cheap swimwear, groups of hawkers peddling unhygienic but delicious-looking food. Rows of shacks stood tightly packed together on both sides of the road with unearthed wires dangling from a few electric poles outside.

With a pang, I thought of myself twenty, maybe twenty-five-years ago: a schoolboy dressed in a smart uniform, listening avidly to our class teacher explaining the plight of 'those slum-dwellers' on a school trip with other similarly privileged children to the Dharavi slum in Mumbai. Now I was 'them'. Only, worse – without a dime to my name or a shack to call my own. Yet, I wasn't particularly unhappy, perhaps due to the vibrant, joyful music that seemed to be playing in every corner of the shantytown.

I spotted a few urchins milling around what looked like a café, and decided to rest there for a while. A group of shaggy-haired black men sat on broken chairs, playing a board game that looked like carrom. They looked at me curiously for a moment. Then one of them pushed a chair towards me and they returned to their game. I rolled up the sleeves of my thick robe and wiped the perspiration from my head as I sat down.

I could rebuild my life, I thought with a sudden burst of optimism as I looked at the playful shadows caused by the mild March evening sun and the vibrant crowds. If I managed to get work somewhere – any kind of work – I could soon save enough money to take a flight to the US. There would be a problem with the paperwork – I would be classified as dead by now – but my past could be verified and I trusted the American system. Of course, the NASA offer wouldn't be waiting for me, but being an MIT graduate would probably get me an entry-level job somewhere. Soon, I could restart the life I had left behind and in time, it would come to have some semblance of order. I could do this, I thought, yes, I could get back on my feet again.

A few women dressed in simple T-shirts and low-cut denim shorts sauntered into the café and Lara's image flashed through my mind. No time for fantasies, I told myself sternly. I had wasted ten years chasing mirages, I couldn't afford to waste a minute now.

'You want a beer?' A short, plump, dark-haired woman, probably the patron of the café, stood in front of me.

'I don't have money,' I said in halting Portuguese.

She gave me a curious glance and went in.

She came back with a beer and a deep-fried snack.

'Have beer,' she said. 'It's hot outside.'

'I don't have money,' I repeated.

'No matter.'

I didn't have the will to send it back. I gulped down the beer and took gigantic bites of the snack filled with meat, probably beef. How fickle I was. In a single moment, I had forgotten eight years of learning: to avoid alcohol, fried food and meat. The beer seemed to soothe the weariness in my feet and I stared vacantly at the people strolling past. Women with shopping baskets, children in school uniforms, young men and women holding hands. I had missed this sense of normalcy, perhaps that's what I had come chasing after. Just as I was drifting into a soporific lull, a sudden movement caught my attention.

'Duck!' I shouted, my hand moving instinctively to push down the head of one of the carom players. The other players scattered immediately.

We both fell crashing down from our chairs as a bullet whizzed past his head. Reflexively, I pulled up the board with my right hand, and a volley of bullets struck against the flat, wooden board and went through it, narrowly missing us. The man who I had pulled down took out a revolver from his pocket and began shooting in front of him while I held up the board awkwardly. Suddenly, without warning, he threw aside the revolver and tugged me forcefully into the café, shutting the tin door behind us.

A scream rent the air as a few more shots ricocheted against the door. I cowered against the far wall while the café owner and the tall, powerfully built black man who had just pulled me in leaned against the opposite wall. I began to feel suffocated in the tiny, airless café, uncomfortably reminded of Cambodia.

I covered my right ear with my hand and pressed the left tightly against the wall as the bullets continued to pound against the door, and tried to calm myself with slow breathing. Not again, please, not again. *I will go back to the monastery, I will serve the Buddha's cause, I will…*

Suddenly, the bullets stopped.

I stayed where I was. The man sat down on his haunches after a while, his muscular body tense with anticipation as he crouched against the door. He peered through a crack and then turned to us, his brow creased.

'The dogs have gone,' he said, running his hand through his closely cropped curly hair.

He walked over to the woman who had served me the beer. She was sitting against the wall.

'Lucia, bitch,' he growled at her. 'You told them I was here, didn't you, men?'

She shook her head fiercely and opened her mouth as if to say no.

He shot her twice, in the soles of her outstretched feet. In the spaghetti Westerns I'd seen, the victim took the gunshots silently – and heroically. But Lucia probably didn't share my taste in films because she let out a piercing scream.

He pointed the gun at her forehead.

'Did you tell Baz?' he asked.

'No, you bastard,' she shrieked. 'I didn't tell anyone.'

He lowered the gun, apparently satisfied with her response.

'Get out,' he said, and she limped to the door, howling in agony. She let out what seemed like a stream of expletives, though my Portuguese wasn't sophisticated enough to understand any of it. I stared at her receding figure as she opened the door of the café and limped out into the setting sun.

He had shot her for no reason, I thought, yet he showed not a bit of remorse. What would he do to me?

He turned and pointed the gun at me. The muscles in his tattooed arms tensed, beads of sweat forming on them. He was about my age, but his easy familiarity with the gun made him appear formidable.

I felt nothing. There was just the vague thought that my soles already hurt from walking, so it would be better if he shot elsewhere.

'Who are you?' he asked.

A tough question for me to answer at any time, more so at gunpoint.

'Nick.'

He looked me up and down. 'Why are you dressed like a bobo, men?'

'I don't understand bobo,' I said.

'Idiota. Joker.'

'I am not an idiot. I'm a monk,' I replied.

He stared at me in incomprehension, and came closer. 'I could shoot you, you know,' he said, pointing the gun at my forehead.

'I saved your life,' I said softly.

He guffawed so hard that he doubled up.

'You are right, men,' he said, flashing a smile. 'I forgot.'

He acted like a man who was used to shooting someone every day.

Just then, three or four men with large black guns came running into the café. I stiffened.

'Behind you,' I shouted and he turned around immediately.

I expected them to shoot him. Instead, they aimed their guns at me.

'Stop, don't shoot, you bastards,' he told the men. 'While you midget fuckers were busy chasing women, he saved my life.'

He looked at me. 'Bom,' he said, 'you are a good man. I'm Marco.'

'Nick,' I said again as he shook my hand.

The others put down their guns and shook my hand one by one.

'Alex.'

'Re.'

'Jesse.'

'Maki.'

They seemed like a walking advertisement for Brazilian diversity. One was blonde, one was brown, one was Oriental, one was black. No one looked at my arm.

'You speak Portuguese like a foreigner but you don't look like a tourist. Didn't anyone warn you about the favelas of Rio? If you go around dressed like a joker, someone will mug you or shoot you sooner or later, men,' said Marco.

'I've been in worse spots,' I told him.

He stared at me. 'Why are you here?'

I hesitated for a moment. 'I need a job,' I replied.

'But why in this favela?'

'It's a long story.'

He laughed. 'Let's hear it back home, men. You don't have any place to go, right?'

I shook my head. He put his arm around me and began to lead me out.

'Donos, should we go after Baz?' Alex asked.

'Another time,' said Marco. 'Today is for new friends.'

I hesitated. Although the gang had an easy frat boy air about them, the significance of the big guns in their hands, the attempt on his life, and the casual ease with which Marco had shot the café owner weren't lost on me.

'Come on, men,' Marco said. 'You aren't afraid of us, are you?'

I shook my head. Fear was the last thing on my mind. But it just didn't seem right to join a street gang on the day I left the monastery.

'You don't understand, men,' he said, patting his revolver lovingly. 'Out here, this is a necessity.'

The Buddha had taught me not to judge people and situations. If he could accept Angulimal, the serial killer who wore a garland of human fingers, who was I to judge a man who had almost been killed?

We began walking through the narrow streets, Marco and I, followed by four men openly toting guns. No one seemed to pay much attention to our odd procession as we made our way through a maze of streets and alleys. People went about their business despite the noisy shootout, as though encounters like this occurred every day. But everyone greeted Marco with a tone of hushed deference and I finally understood the meaning of 'Donos'.

Unwittingly, I had saved the life of a Brazilian slumlord, a smalltime Don. My only exposure to the mafia thus far had been the *Godfather* movies, but this setup didn't seem as majestic. Instead of protecting the defenceless damsel-in-distress Lucia,

Marco had shot her in the feet; the expensive suits of the movie Don's henchmen had given way to tattoos, crosses and chains; and Marlon Brando's meaningful pauses had been replaced with Marco's wild laughter. The only thing I was sure of was that if I tried to escape, they would make me an 'offer I couldn't refuse', and I didn't particularly feel the desire to negotiate terms just now.

We stopped in front of a large brick building that stood incongruously amidst several small wooden huts. The building's façade was covered with colourful, arresting images of crying children, pregnant women and young men snorting drugs.

'All done by the local favela artists,' said Marco with a measure of pride.

We entered the two-storied house and I was immediately struck by its contrast to the world outside. Fully air-conditioned, with elegant furniture, a variety of electronics, and tasteful art lining the walls.

'You live here alone?' I asked.

Marco nodded. 'Yes, but this whole street is ours. You don't have a place, right?'

I shook my head.

'Many strange creatures come here but I don't think I've seen a stranger one,' he said, more to himself than to me. 'What work do you do, men?'

'Nothing,' I said. 'I told you, I don't have a job.'

He laughed. 'You have no house, no job, no shoes,

no suitcase, not even an arm, men. Yet, you don't look broke. You seem like a guy who should be living in an expensive apartment facing the Copacabana beach, but you wander around barefoot in Rio's most feared favela, wearing circus clothes. You are not from Brazil yet I can't recognize the accent, though I deal with all kinds of foreigners. Did you just drop off another planet, men?'

'Something like that,' I said.

At this, he laughed even more and sprayed the beer he was drinking on the carefully upholstered wall. I noticed he had no pictures on the wall, neither of himself nor his family, and I felt a certain kinship with him.

'What are you good at?' he asked me.

I was good at staring at walls, especially those covered with blood, I could sit in my faeces smelling decomposing bodies in airless rooms for years without going insane, I was something of a pro at escaping from jungles, I could survive without food or water for extended periods of time, and I could meditate without speaking to a soul for hours on end. Quite a skill set to have, wouldn't you say? Even if it was completely, utterly useless.

'I'm good at numbers,' I said, suddenly reminded of my time at MIT.

'You are not serious, men!' he said. 'I have enough thugs, what I don't have is a good contador.'

I looked at him blankly.

'What do you call it in English... yes, an accountant,' he said.

The Buddha forbade me from working in any profession that hurt others – robbery and arms, for instance. A Brazilian Donos was likely to deal *only* in things that hurt others, yet I had somehow taken a liking to him despite everything I had seen. Or perhaps I was just too tired of moving from place to place rudderless, without an anchor.

'What business are you in?' I asked.

'Is this your interview or mine?' He laughed, the chains around his neck jiggling. Then, more seriously, he added, 'How does that matter? You just do the numbers, we do the rest. You don't need to know or care, men.'

Why not, I thought. It would only be for a short while, just enough to earn my way back to the US, after which I would have the means to walk on the Buddha's eightfold path once again.

'Okay,' I said quickly before I could change my mind.

'Great.' He smiled and gestured with his hand. 'You can stay here.'

'Here?' I asked. 'Won't that disturb you?'

He laughed again. 'The work I do requires no concentration. Besides, I change my address every night to fox the policia and the local goons. I rarely sleep in my bed.'

So he wasn't as cool as he pretended to be. He

must value his life to change his address every night. It made me feel more comfortable.

'There are three rooms here,' he continued. 'One is for my personal use, one is for the business; you can take the third. Stay as long as you like. I will pay you anything you think is fair, men.'

I was suddenly overwhelmed with gratitude. An hour ago, I had no money, no job, no home, and no future; now, I seemed to have a little bit of everything.

'Thank you,' I said, shaking his hand. 'I won't overstay my welcome.'

'It's nothing,' he said. 'You saved my life. You are my guest.'

'Can you show me the account registers, cash slips, receipts, whatever you have?' I asked him. I was determined to be the best accountant Marco had ever seen.

He laughed. 'Everything can wait in Rio, especially work. Why don't you get ready? I will plan a small welcome party in your honour, men.'

I was out of the monastery but the same uneasy feeling of living someone else's life crept over me again. It wasn't supposed to be like this, was it? I was supposed to be a white-collar cubicle-dweller in an engineering firm, with a house in an American suburb and a sweet, pregnant Indian wife. Why was I being welcomed by a drug lord into Rio de Janeiro's most violent slum after spending ten years, first as a Cambodian genocide survivor, then as a Buddhist monk? Just what had happened? And what else was going to happen? More fundamentally, who was I?

'…an idiot.'

'Huh?' I said.

'Where are you lost?' said Marco. 'Go get ready now. You don't want to go dressed like an idiot, men.'

The small party turned out to be at least a few hundred people.

'What is this?' I asked in awe.

Fresh from my first hot shower in years, dressed in Marco's shiny shirt and tight pants and escorted by the gang in a Sedan, I was staring at a large football field with beautiful men and women dressed in slick, skimpy clothes, gyrating to the beats of the buoyant music coming from the thirty-foot-large speakers placed in every corner of the field.

'Favela funk. We organize it every couple of weekends,' said Marco as we got out of the car. 'You got a hell of a lot to learn about rock and roll, boy.'

The DJ, who was scratching and spinning records on the stage where the elaborate music system was set up, saw our entourage and shouted Marco's name on the microphone. A huge cheer went up from the crowd. Much to my discomfiture, Marco dragged me onto the stage.

'Jakeira knows how to party,' he shouted into the mike.

There were whoops of agreement from the crowd, and a few sharp gunshots.

'Today, I want to welcome our friend from nowhere to Jakeira,' Marco said and put his arm around my shoulder. 'Welcome... Buddha, men.'

I cringed at my new name. I had violated almost every tenet of Buddhism within hours of leaving the monastery.

The crowd began chanting. 'Buddha... Buddha... Buddha.'

Marco dragged me off the stage and thrust a large glass into my hand.

'Soak it up,' he said. 'It's a Caipirinha. A few swigs and you can start a new religion, men.'

So be it, I thought, perhaps the tenets of this religion would be easier to follow. I took a sip. It tasted sweet, tangy and harmless, so I took a larger sip. Someone grabbed Marco by the shoulder and he disappeared into the crowd. People came over and introduced themselves to me, slapped me enthusiastically on the back and left.

I stood where I was, gulping down the sweet drink and watching the sensuous movements of the attractive, bronze-bodied couples dancing in front of me. Expertly, they swayed their hips and tapped their feet one in front of the other with the man twirling the woman in his arms.

His arms. I suddenly felt sorry for myself. I would never be able to dance this way.

Someone handed me another drink and I took it happily as I continued to stare, as though hypnotized, at the Samba dancers. Maybe Lara was right, I thought. Love and passion, hope and longing, loss and redemption – these were what kept us alive. How could denial of the most basic human expressions be the greater truth? Lara, elusive and ethereal with her warm eyes, slight smile, long hair – our fleeting acquaintance probably meant nothing to her. The music picked up tempo and the couples grooved harder, hip to hip, fondling, even groping a little.

I was thirty and I had achieved nothing, I thought suddenly. I had never even been in love, unless I counted the puppy love for Lavanya in college and lusting after a model who was unfortunate enough to sit next to me on a flight. I couldn't even claim that I had let go of love to pursue my career; I had nothing to show on that front either. I felt very sorry for myself indeed.

'You dance with me, Buddha?'

A young woman with curly hair and smooth brown skin walked up to me. She was about a foot shorter than my six foot plus and looked stunning in her silky red dress.

Who was I kidding, I thought. Just about everyone looked stunning to me. Either this country had the most gorgeous women in the world or I had lost the ability to discriminate because of my long dry spell.

'Eu falar Portuguese,' I said. 'I speak Portuguese.'

'Very sexy,' she slurred. 'Come dance with me.'

I pointed to my missing arm.

She shrugged and dragged me to the floor.

Alex hooted and handed me another glass of Caipirinha. Balancing the glass in my hand, I drank quickly and followed her lead. She pressed her hips tightly against mine, and I found myself shamefully aroused. Round and round we twirled as I tried to match move for move until I ended up tippling the glass over her in an effort to keep pace.

I watched the alcohol splash on her face and mingle with her sweat. It trickled down her neck and I turned away.

'Lick me clean,' she urged.

I hesitated. 'I can't do that,' I said unconvincingly.

She pushed herself closer. 'You made this mess. You need to clean it up.'

I leaned forward and licked her neck gently. She kissed me softly on my earlobes. I couldn't hold back any longer. Someone, probably Alex, cheered. Another glass was handed to me, the music picked up a notch, and we began to spin.

'Not bad. He has a decent one for such a tall guy.'

'Do tall guys have little ones?'

'Mostly. And I think he is Asian; Asians have the smallest.'

'Does it work as well as it looks, Maria?'

I woke up with a start to find myself lying stark naked in an unfamiliar room, spooning an equally naked woman. I stared at her soft brown body in confusion, shrieks of laughter ringing in my ears. Marco, Alex and Maki were standing in front of us, fully dressed in sleeveless T-shirts and rugged jeans. I moved to cover myself and the woman, who had just stirred awake.

She stretched and swung her legs off the bed unselfconsciously.

'Bastards,' she said to Marco and the others. 'Will you ever grow up?'

She didn't make any attempt to cover herself, and I found myself aroused by her plump, curvaceous figure. Everyone howled, and she smiled.

'You were not bad,' she said. 'You need help with Mr Johnson there any time, you know where to come.'

Only, I didn't. I had no memory at all of last night, except thrusting for an eternity and her writhing, moaning body underneath.

The woman put on her red dress from yesterday.

Much to everyone's amusement, she came and playfully stroked my penis.

'Nice to meet you,' she said. 'My name is Maria.'

She left the room and I stared in embarrassment at Marco and his friends.

'Can you show me the accounts please?' I said in a rush.

They laughed well into the morning.

Chastened, showered, and with a fresh vow of Buddhist detachment, I knocked on the door of the room between mine and Marco's – his office, as he called it. Alex opened the door. He had a big gun in his hand and a bigger frown on his face. He relaxed on seeing me and quickly pulled me inside.

Five or six children, barely ten or twelve years old, were on the floor with their hands in heaps of white powder that had been placed on a rubber mat. They were taking powder from one pile and mixing it in with an identical looking powder in another pile.

'Friends, this is Buddha,' said Marco, who was standing near the window, a rifle slung over each shoulder. The children looked up in acknowledgment and went back to mixing the powder.

'Mixing cocaine with talcum powder,' Marco said matter-of-factly. 'Important for the accountant to know – we get it at five hundred dollars a kilo, we add another kilo of talcum powder and sell it for a thousand dollars a kilo. What is our net profit, men?'

'Three hundred per cent, assuming the talcum powder costs nothing,' I said automatically.

Marco looked at Alex triumphantly. 'Didn't I tell you? You would have taken a year to give me that answer. It took me a month to figure it out myself. We have a genius here, men.'

'You deal in drugs?' I asked quietly.

Why was I surprised? Did I expect a Brazilian slumlord to deal in mutual funds, treasury bonds and credit derivatives? But dealing in drugs and arms was the lowest of sins in Buddhist teaching, was I really going to fall so low? I didn't say anything but my disapproval must have been obvious.

'We use this money to fund everything in the favelas – water, electricity, schools, roads, community projects,' said Alex defensively. 'In Brazil, the government doesn't care about slums. Poverty is a disease here; if you are infected by it, you are shunned like a leper. It's only because of the work we do that people in the community can live like humans.'

Great, I thought, modern-day Robin Hoods. Marco, tattoos shining on his muscular arm, looked about as credible in the role of Mother Teresa helping the poor as I did as a Buddhist monk.

'Don't judge us before you know us, men,' said Marco. 'You don't understand how things work around here.'

I was about to tell him I had seen worse in India when I stopped. He was right. Secluded in my army schools and cantonments, how much of

India's poverty had I really experienced outside the voyeuristic school trips? The context mattered. Hadn't I once almost willed Ishmael dead so I could eat his bowl of rice? From the little I had seen of Rio, the eruption of violence seemed as common as my frequent crises of faith in the monastery. Who was I to judge the impact of growing up in surroundings like these when I had spent eight years in meditation to get over two years of being locked up in a cell?

'You don't need to be involved in the business, men,' said Marco. 'You just look at the numbers. Make sure everything is fair and square.'

What could ever be fair in this business, I wondered. But then, which business was fair?

'This is the account register,' Marco said.

I took it in spite of myself. Numbers were scrawled uncertainly across every page. A few of the pages were torn in half and others blotted with water (or Caipirinha perhaps?) and casual bloodstains.

'It's a mess,' he said, echoing my thoughts.

'How do you keep track of the money?' I asked.

'Money comes, money goes,' said Marco philosophically. 'When it comes, we buy stuff; when it runs out, we don't.'

'What about your investments?' I asked. 'Is there a separate register for that?'

'In our life, there are only two roads,' he said. 'Prison or death. What should we invest for?'

'For the favela you take care of, perhaps? What

happens when you go to prison or die?' I said a little testily.

'Look at these runts,' said Marco, gesturing at the young boys, who had finished mixing the coke and were now packing it into small plastic bags. They looked up dutifully. 'After me, it's them, and so it goes. No one is indispensable in this business, men.'

The realization of the impermanence of life, I thought; the Buddha would have been proud.

'Let me study this,' I said and picked up the register.

For the little time I was here, I would do my best to serve their needs, I decided. I began to walk out of the room.

'Wait,' he said. He opened a cupboard full of guns. 'Choose your weapon.'

No, not this, I thought.

'I don't need to shoot,' I said firmly.

'Self-defence,' he told me. 'You can't step out for a minute unless you have a gun. Remember what happened that day? That sort of thing happens every day.'

'Who were they?' I asked.

'That was Baz, a small-time goon in this favela, who wants to become the Donos. We killed him last night after the funk. But it could have been anyone – the police, a gang from another favela, someone I once shot, even Alex here.'

'Donos, please,' Alex protested.

He raised his hand. 'Don't get me wrong. I trust everyone in the gang, but one day you may think I've become weak and senile; then I will need to be taken out. As I said before, in this life, it's either prison or death.'

'Not for you, though,' he added as an afterthought. 'No one kills the contador.'

I looked at the guns in the cupboard; they all looked the same.

'Choose carefully,' said Marco. 'Everyone has a special relationship with their gun. Soon, using someone else's gun will feel as uncomfortable as wearing someone else's underwear.'

I moved towards the biggest one.

Marco and Alex laughed.

'Not that one, idiot,' said Marco. 'How will you carry that monster? You should stick to the handguns – pistols, revolvers or derringers.'

'But you guys carry them,' I said.

He looked slightly abashed. I had forgotten I was a cripple.

'Use one of these instead,' he said. 'The Anaconda, or the Python, the Beretta, the Glock... all are better for your purpose than the one you chose.'

I picked one up.

'The Glock,' he said approvingly. 'Good choice. Here, just pull back the hammer with your mouth and pull the trigger – like this.'

'Boom,' he said as the bullet escaped, shattering

one in a long row of expensive-looking figurines standing in front of the window.

The runts cheered.

'Now you try,' he said. 'Aim at the head of that statue. It will take some tries to get it right, men.'

'Should we practise somewhere else?' I asked.

He laughed. 'It's just stuff; here today, gone tomorrow.'

To emphasize the point, he shot at a few more figurines, not missing once.

He gave me the gun. It was smouldering hot and I almost dropped it.

'Careful, Buddha.' Marco laughed. 'If it goes off, you may be left with just one leg as well.'

This was the first time anyone had joked about my arm and it felt curiously liberating. I concentrated on the statue he was pointing at. I took aim.

'Easy, cowboy,' said Marco. 'Shooting a revolver isn't half as easy as shooting your load into Maria.'

Alex and the runts burst into peals of laughter.

Suddenly, an image I had tried unsuccessfully to forget for years flashed through my mind – the Khmer soldier stabbing the pregnant woman again and again, her plain white dress gradually stained crimson with her unborn baby's blood.

My hand shuddered as I shot the bastard.

I looked up, as if from a trance, and saw Marco and Alex staring at the headless figurine. My shot had been as clean as Marco's.

I gave the smoking gun back to him. 'Bond. James Bond,' I said with a grin.

'You were meant to be a bandido, not a contador,' said Marco. 'I don't know anyone else who got their first shot right.'

'Thanks, but no thanks,' I said. 'I am better at accounting than at shooting.'

'Go do your accounts then,' said Marco. 'By the way, get ready for tonight. I have kept some shirts and jeans in your room.'

'Where are we going?' I asked.

'A baile.'

'What's a baile?'

'A baile is, well, a baile. Same kind of place we went last night, only bigger,' he said. 'Bigger speakers, bigger field, bigger music, more galinhas.'

'Galinhas?' I said.

'It means hens... like Maria,' he said with a wink.

I hesitated, recalling last night. 'I don't think I should go,' I told him.

He laughed. 'What's left to hide?'

Despite the unpredictable turn life had taken, things soon slipped into a predictable pattern. Mornings were spent in exercising and target practice, afternoons in piecing together the messy accounts. Evenings were spent dancing to baile funk and nights in the company of some girl or the other. I still woke up every morning fighting a strange sense of the surreal, but I no longer lived with the crippling guilt that I had divorced myself from the Buddha's teachings. The longer I stayed with Marco, the more I began to think that morality *was* ambiguous, contradictions made us human and eventually, the only tenets you could live by were the ones that felt right to you.

Casual sex, for instance, was wrong, but what if a culture treated it – as the easygoing Brazilians seemed to – purely as physical ecstasy that came without any emotional baggage? Wasn't joy without accompanying sorrow the broader goal of the spiritual life, after all? Working as an accountant for a drug lord was wrong, but what if you owed him a tribal allegiance for giving you the confidence to thrive in society after your long hiatus from it? Eventually, I thought, I would have to choose the answers that were right for me and chart my own middle path. Or so I thought when I barged into Marco's office one day.

'Marco!' I said excitedly as I entered the room. 'Donos,' I corrected myself hastily. As a mark of respect, I never called him by his name in front of the others.

'One minute,' he said.

He was pulling a plastic bag over the face of someone kneeling in front of him. Alex and Maki stood behind him, egging him on while the children continued to mix coke, unconcerned about the man about to be killed a few feet away.

'We don't shoot in the house because it gets too messy. This way, it is clean,' Marco said in explanation.

The man began to gag as Marco pulled the cord tighter, and his eyes bulged out.

This was the first execution I was being witness to, and it made me feel wretched. Was I any different from the mild-looking guards in that horrendous Phnom Penh school building? Day in and day out, they had seen us die slowly in our cells, but had probably been too afraid, or too indifferent, to say a word.

'What did he do?' I asked as Marco tightened the plastic bag.

'He is a rat,' Marco said in disgust.

'Don't kill him,' I said suddenly.

'Why?'

'Bad karma,' I mumbled.

He laughed his big laugh and loosened his grip on the man. 'It will be worse karma if I let him go.'

I didn't know what to say. In his own way, Marco was right. This was the life he had chosen or that had been chosen for him; his first duty was to save himself.

Sensing a moment of weakness, the man started

blabbering incoherently with the plastic still tied around his face, looking unintentionally comic.

Perhaps it was my weak plea, or perhaps it was the unwitting humour in the situation, but Marco softened. He loosened the plastic bag. The man, his moustache drenched in tears, fell at Marco's feet, begging forgiveness. Marco shot him in both thighs and one arm for good measure, and let him go. He crawled away, leaving behind a trail of blood.

Marco shook his head in disgust.

'That's why I don't like to shoot in the house,' he said to the boys, pointing at the stains on the sparkling marble floor.

One of them had stopped mixing the cocaine and was staring at Marco, wide-eyed in fear.

'You haven't seen anyone shot before, kid?' Marco said calmly.

The boy, eight, maybe ten years old, quivered.

'It doesn't hurt that bad,' Marco said. 'See.'

I watched in horror as Marco shot the boy in his thigh. The child yelped in pain and hobbled out of the room. The other children busied themselves with mixing.

'From time to time you need to remind them about the business they are in,' said Marco to no one in particular.

I couldn't be complicit to this mindless violence any more, I thought. If what I had in mind didn't work, I would get out of here at once.

Marco turned to me. 'You had something to talk to me about, men?'

'Yes,' I said. 'Will you come to the other room?'

He nodded. 'One second,' he said and took a pinch of pinkish-white powder from one of the piles and held it against his nose. 'Fresh stock. Pure pink coke crystals from Peru.'

'Heaven,' he said, snorting it in. 'Try some.'

I shook my head.

'Come on,' he said. 'It's completely harmless in little doses.'

'No,' I said. 'Once I start something, I don't stop.'

We went to my room.

'Do you know how much cash you have in hand?' I asked as I handed him the balance sheets I had prepared.

'Enough to receive the shipment from Colombia this week,' he said.

'How much is the shipment worth?'

'Fifteen, maybe twenty thousand dollars.'

'But your accounts show thirty thousand dollars in cash.'

'Thirty thousand dollars?' he said in surprise. 'That's a lot of money.'

'You're telling me! I am broke as a spoke,' I said. 'Where is the rest?'

'Must be here and there,' he said. 'Some went for the baile you attended last week. I gave some to the gang – they've been working hard these last few weeks. Some went to the favela school for the football field, some to… well, here and there. I can't remember everything.'

'Ten thousand dollars is a lot to give away in one month,' I told him.

'Money comes and goes in this business, men.'

He played with the gun in his hand, his fingers stroking its shiny surface.

'A new Glock from America,' he said admiringly. 'Do you want this one instead?'

'Shouldn't you invest the money instead of blowing it up like this?'

'In our life…' he began.

'Yes, yes, I know about the two roads,' I said. 'But it doesn't have to be that way. You make a three hundred per cent profit in the drug business. I don't know much about Brazil, but I think if you invested this money in a legal business – real estate, the stock market – you would soon have enough capital to get out of the illegal trade.'

He continued playing with the gun, paying scant attention to me. 'Nothing in this country is legal,' he said.

'Just about everything is more legal than what you do.'

He looked at me with narrowed eyes. I wondered if he was going to shoot me. Instead, he talked to me seriously, without scoffing or laughing at me for a change.

'You don't know how things work here,' he said.
'Then tell me.'

'Ten years ago, we had nothing, men, nothing. This favela was just a bunch of super pobre, wretched, miserable folk – no money, no hospitals, no schools. In the eyes of Rio's rich, and the police and the government, we were rabid, unnecessary dogs and treated as such. I was in prison, thrown into a poky cell with forty other men, for no reason other than that I was sitting on Copacabana beach one night, drinking beer. I wouldn't even get a trial for six months. At twenty, I was full of anger at the unfairness of the system that treated us this way from the moment we were born. Most folks in prison had similar stories and we would have gone our own separate ways after a few months of whining about the system had something funny not happened.'

I looked at him expectantly.

'A bunch of college-educated political prisoners quoting Che Guevara, who had been fighting to form a communist party, were thrown into prison at the same time as us. They talked about Lenin and Marx, unity and revolution, and the need to be perpetrators and not victims if we wanted our rights. For the first time, we had an ideology, and that's how the Comando Vermelho or the Red Command was formed. Over the last ten years, the movement has spread across all the favelas in Rio. We stand united, and we play to our strengths. All of us have grown up as thugs on the street, so we control the businesses we know best – drugs, arms, kidnappings – and channel at least a portion of the money into the development of the favelas. Now we have a voice. We count. Politicians come begging for our vote. The police don't dare to enter the favela unless something big happens. Our children have rights. And all this in ten years,' he said proudly. 'I am one of the founders of the Comando Vermelho.'

I paused, trying to take it all in.

'The legal businesses will only help you grow,' I said finally. 'Right now, you earn a hundred thousand dollars a year. If we made the right investments, we could turn that into half a million, maybe a million, maybe even more. Won't that help develop this favela even faster? I don't see the problem.'

'It's a problem because it breaks the… the ritmo,' he said. 'There is a rhythm here. If I break that, others will, too. If I have side businesses, Donos in other favelas will also want side businesses. Then the infighting starts, people will measure each other's wealth, they will want more, they will kill to get more. We won't be united any longer and we'll be back where we started.'

'But…' I began.

He raised his hand to silence me. 'Besides, who will run it? You are here today, gone tomorrow. I'm illiterate. All I know is how to transport drugs from the border, mix them, get them on the streets, and shoot anyone who's in the way. Buy, mix, sell, shoot, kill, die – that's the life of a Donos.'

'I don't know much either, but you're smart. It's not that difficult to learn.'

'I don't have time to learn new things,' he said impatiently. 'Do you think I'm having phone sex when I sit in that room talking to people all day? Every day there is a new problem. Last month, we had to sink our ship from Peru because a coastguard we hadn't paid off materialized from nowhere; three days ago, a truck driver with the Colombian consignment went missing; today, I had problems with a wholesaler. It's not easy running this operation.'

'Legal stuff is easier to run,' I said quietly.

'Maybe in another life,' he said. 'I am okay for this life.'

'Or whatever is left of it.'

He looked at me. I knew I was pushing it, and I almost expected to get shot at. Instead, he burst out laughing.

'You are a cheeky motherfucker, aren't you?' he said.

It was good while it lasted, but a year later, I knew it was time to abandon the life I had built. By paying myself half of what Alex and the others earned, I had managed to save enough money for a one-way ticket to the US by the end of the year. And though I felt a measure of regret for not having accomplished more in my time here, my conscience wouldn't allow me to continue any longer. With my nights spent in illicit sex and days spent accounting for blood money, I could hardly claim to have a conscience, but I was walking a strange path where there was no black or white, just a sea of grey which I navigated based solely on what 'felt' right. Now, it felt right to end this chapter, though I couldn't shake off a feeling of overwhelming sadness when I walked into Marco's room one morning.

'That motherfucker slept with my wife,' a short, dark man was shouting as I entered. 'I need your permission to kill both him and the slut.'

I had walked onto the usual scene of justice being meted out by the coke-snorting Donos, who showed extraordinary acuity in satisfying all the supplicants who came to his kingdom.

Marco laughed. 'When did you last have sex with her?'

'I don't know. Early this week,' the man said, his voice shaking with anger.

'It's not her fault then,' Marco said. 'She has a hot cunt. Shoot her once in the ass so she remembers it every time she is below or on top of anyone.'

'What about Jopa then?' he said. 'He insulted me.'

'I will take care of him,' said Marco and the man walked away, satisfied with the verdict.

Alex brought in a local grocery store owner who had got into an argument with one of the runts for dealing in front of his shop and burst open his face in a fit of anger. Marco shot him in his left arm as a reminder not to hit children again, but spared his right so that his business wouldn't suffer. The man went out, clutching his arm to prevent himself from losing too much blood and thanking Marco for his consideration.

More quick judgment was meted out while I watched silently from the side. I realized with a pang that I would miss Marco despite everything. He had given me a new lease of life, just as David had – and I was deserting him too. Suddenly, I was tired. How many more times would I have to do this, I wondered. Building, destroying, building, destroying, and building again. I had been a nomad for too long. I craved permanence, a community to call my own, someone to love, even children, although I didn't have much to teach them except, perhaps, how not to live.

'I need to leave,' I said when Marco and I were finally alone in the room.

Marco's face fell, or at least I imagined it did. 'Okay, bye,' he said nonchalantly.

'Is that all you have to say?' I asked.

'What else do you want me to say? Anyway,

thanks for saving my life and for handling the accounts and all that.'

I knew he didn't care a rat's arse about either. In his own strange way, he was more of a monk than I had ever been. He didn't care about the physical shell of his body or the inevitability of death, and craved little financial or material gain for himself. Contradictions, I thought, everywhere I went I saw contradictions.

'You can still get out of the drug business,' I said earnestly. 'I have collected all the money-laundering information in the account register. Once the money is white, you can invest in –'

The blast of a gunshot cut me short. He had fired at my feet and the bullet had narrowly missed my toes. I stared at him in surprise, not because he had fired, but because he never missed.

'Get out, paneleiro,' he said. 'You are a fucking ungrateful faggot.'

I went back to my room to pack my belongings before realizing I had nothing to pack. Since I'd come here, I had bought nothing. Everything – the clothes I wore, the books I read, the food I ate, the stuff I used – had been given to me by Marco.

Another unfinished chapter, I thought as I walked out the door, another incomplete journey from nowhere to nowhere.

I was walking down the stairs, lost in thought, when there was a sudden commotion outside.

'He was shot,' Alex shouted, running into the house.

Marco, looking lifeless and dripping blood from his face, was being carried into the house, suspended from the shoulders of Maki and the others.

'Take him upstairs,' Alex told the gang. 'I will call Doctor José.' He sped off.

I watched as the men dragged Marco to his room and stretched him out on the bed. Blood spilled onto the patterned bedsheet. He had been shot in the middle of his head.

'Is he dead?' I croaked out.

The men stared at me, as uncertain as I was. For a moment, I considered running away. I didn't need to be involved. If I walked out now, I could start my life afresh without skipping a beat. I was meant to be a cubicle rat, not a drug dealer.

'What came over him?' said Maki. 'He never leaves the house without a gun. We weren't even around. One moment he is in his room, the next he is smoking a cigarette in broad daylight without a gun in his hand. What the hell was he thinking?'

Probably about my betrayal, I thought with a sinking sensation.

Marco mumbled something and tried to move. The blood flowed from his face in a steady stream.

'He is alive,' said Maki.

'Don't move,' I said. 'Just stay still.'

A foolish comment, if ever there was one. He couldn't move if he tried. His face was shattered, just blood and bone; any move to stem the blood flow would probably make it worse. He won't make it, I thought suddenly. Just as Ishmael didn't.

'It wasn't even a planned attack. I think someone from Jocinha saw him standing alone and took a shot,' said Maki. 'They want to take over Jakeira. Thankfully, a runt spotted them and we got there in time.'

'Isn't Jocinha a part of the Comando Vermelho? Aren't Donos in different favelas forbidden from killing each other?' I asked.

They looked at each other as if they had never considered this question before.

Their surprise made sense. I should have figured it out earlier. The Red Command wasn't set up like a sugared water company with a chief executive in charge; it was a loose confederate of Donos across different favelas, who tried to set boundaries where they could, but ultimately, everyone had to watch out for themselves.

Alex and the doctor, a fair-skinned gentleman who had probably been persuaded to come from a city clinic, rushed into the room. The doctor stared at Marco and went closer to inspect him. He touched the gooey flesh on his forehead and Marco screamed.

'I can try to fix him but I need blood immediately.

Do you know his blood group? Does it match anyone's here?' he said.

The thugs looked at one another. Of course, they hadn't ever found out their blood groups.

'I am O positive,' I said, remembering the results from my US visa application. 'Universal donor, right?'

Another thought had entered my mind which made me volunteer like an idiot. Whether they knew it or not, I was sure most of these thugs had HIV or some other deadly STD. For no other reason than that they all loved to go bareback and alternately called me a pussy and a faggot for insisting on a condom.

'I will need to test both of you first since this is a live transfusion,' said the doctor. 'His blood may show an adverse reaction to the antibodies in your blood, which could kill him – or you.'

'Do we have time?' I asked.

He shook his head.

'Where will you test anyway?' said Alex. 'You know we can't take him to a hospital.'

I paused for a moment. Heck, I thought. I am not a hero, I don't want to be a hero, but here I am in the same no-win position once again. Hadn't I learnt the last time round that there was no karmic justice? What goes around doesn't come around. I had lost an arm the last time I'd tried to be bigger than I was. What would I lose this time?

'Is there a chance I might lose the function of my other arm?' I asked.

I wasn't particularly concerned about death. I had nothing much to live for and not much to look forward to. What I feared was the thought of being fed like a baby and needing someone to wipe my arse. Not that I could even afford it if it came to that.

'There is always a chance,' said the doctor sagely.

Great, I thought. Now what? I looked at the door longingly. I could still get out of here and pursue my dream of becoming a corporate coolie.

'Okay,' I said. 'Let's do it.'

'You are going to die a dog's death,' I said as Marco began to gain consciousness.

The doctor had cleaned his wound and we were now connected with the rickety transfusion equipment. My right wrist, attached to the catheter, hurt like hell, and I rotated it every few minutes to ensure that I hadn't lost control of it. Not this arm, I prayed, anything but.

'Shut up, you fag,' he said through his pain and began to drift away.

'You act cool, like a movie star, but you are as afraid to die as anyone else,' I said, still smarting from being put in this position. 'Why else would you keep moving from house to house every night to avoid getting shot?'

He made as if to reach for a gun and collapsed from the effort.

He made as if to reach for a gun and collapsed from the effort.

Slowly he got better, as did I.

'Are you still going to go?' he said when he had regained consciousness. I was standing by his bed, right arm intact, staring at his heavily bandaged head. He looked like Frankenstein and I felt a sudden wave of affection for him.

'Yes,' I said sadly. 'I've nowhere to go but I can't live this life any more. It is unnecessary and wrong.'

'I chose this life,' he said, sounding less stubborn than usual.

'So did the people who came to kill you,' I said. 'Weren't they from the Red Command as well? Everyone watches out for their own interest here. If you want to have principles, choose bigger ones. You are just a small-time dealer now, but you can become bigger and put an end to this stupid violence – at least in this favela.'

I expected protest but heard none.

'What do you have in mind, men?' he asked.

'That's what I've been trying to tell you. We don't need to do anything dramatic. We will just launder the drug money every month so that it's clean. Once we have enough white money, we can invest in a variety of legal businesses. Money will bring more money.'

'And how do you launder it?'

'It should be pretty simple from what I've read,' I said. 'We need to start a small business with borrowed funds from which we get a regular inflow of clean cash. When we deposit that cash in the bank, we keep slipping in portions of your drug money; once the money is in the financial system, it's clean. Within a few months, we should have enough clean money to start making significant legal investments in stocks and real estate, and soon you can get out of the drug trade entirely – if you want to.'

'What small business do we start?'

'Well, something like… retail, for instance,' I said after a moment's thought. 'Thousands of legal transactions every day, lots of clean cash to be deposited in the banks, no one will notice if we slip in a few thousand dollars of drug money every week. What can we retail in?'

'Guns,' he replied at once.

I stared at him. 'I think I liked you better when the only sound out of your mouth was a groan.'

'Do you know any business yourself, fucker?' he asked.

I paused. What did I know besides silence and loss, and mathematics and cocaine?

'I understand sports pretty well,' I said. 'We could retail in apparel and equipment for basketball, soccer, running, etc. That's a start.'

'Just like that?'

'Just like that.'

'So you are going to stay then, aren't you?'

Unknowingly, we had hit a gold mine. Just as we opened our first sporting goods store in Ipanema in 1990, a wave of international retail chains entered Brazil, and shopping at large stores became the vogue for the growing middle class. One store became two, two became ten, and in three years' time we were operating three hundred stores in Sao Paolo and Rio, generating a few million dollars of profit every year, and growing. What had started as a front for laundering drug money soon became vastly more profitable than the drug business itself, and to further establish its legality, I created shell companies in Hong Kong, Moldova and Seychelles – all laundering havens with no bank-reporting requirements – where we repatriated all our profits. The shell companies, in turn, made profits on local investments that were then re-invested in our retail holdings in Brazil. So intricate was the financial web we spun that it would take years for even the most dedicated investigator to trace the origins of our empire to a coca farm in a small Colombian village. I could now face Marco with some measure of pride – our involvement with the drug business had reduced to a token amount for solidarity with the Comando Vermelho, and we had prospered beyond our highest estimations.

'Can I ask you a personal question, men?' asked Marco during one of our monthly briefings on the state of accounts.

Three years after the shootout, the wound on his forehead had fully healed, but the scars from the stitches had twisted his brows into a perpetual frown. The juxtaposition of his usually smiling face with his scowling brow gave him a comical look, especially when he really was frowning, like now.

I couldn't help smiling at him. 'You sure can,' I replied.

'Why are you smiling, bastard?' he said.

'Because you look like a joker,' I said. 'Anyway, what's bugging you?'

'Look, I'm slow, so it's taken me a while to understand all this stuff but I think I'm getting it now,' said Marco, pointing at the computer. 'What I don't understand is what *you* get from all this, men. You don't have a single bank account to your name, you live in one room in my house, you wear my hand-me-downs, you don't even have a hundred dollars you could call your own. What are you in this for?'

'Just look at what we have accomplished in the favela without relying on the drug trade,' I said, answering his question indirectly. 'Water and electricity are available twenty-four hours, the schools are flush with money, and everyone is more at peace now that gunshots don't ring out every few hours. We could do so much more if we didn't actually have to hide the progress from your Red Command brothers.'

'I know all that but it still doesn't fit. You didn't grow up here, you don't have family here. If you were doing charity, why stop at this? Why not do it in India? Or why not become a nun or a priest or something, men? You were a monk before, you could become one again. Instead, you are one of Rio's rich – one with no money though. How stupid is that?'

'This favela is my family,' I began but stopped. It wasn't true. True to an extent, perhaps, but my primary interest wasn't charity. I had struggled with the same question myself. What drove me? Ambition, perhaps, but ambition for what? I craved nothing, I had no goals. What was I seeking then? I had figured it out for myself, but the explanation required remembering a time I would rather forget. Yet, I owed Marco something close to the truth.

'A long time ago, someone unknowingly taught me the Hindu philosophy of the karma yoga, the path of detached action, of doing your duty without any attachment to the results. His words saved my life and I've tried to follow them since. I am happy and have no goals for myself; neither money nor power nor fame, not even charity. My only purpose is to give myself completely to my work, to unquestioningly perform my duty – even if it is to run a business for a slumlord with a twisted face!'

Marco pretended to shield his eyes from me. 'Ah, ah,' he shouted. 'Your aura is blinding me, o saint!'

'Some saint,' I said. 'You know better than anyone else how much I stumble. And if you don't, just ask Lucia or Regina or Veronica or…'

'They rave about your technique, by the way,' he said. 'They say you are gentle and silent; not like us macho Brazilian men. Are you in love with any of them, men?'

I squirmed. We never talked about that kind of stuff here. Anyone who talked about anything remotely related to love or romance would be called a faggot or a pussy. Women fell for Donos; Donos didn't fall for women.

'No,' I said firmly.

'Have you ever been in love, men?'

'Jesus. What is this?' I asked. 'Can we finish the accounts now? We have a lot to cover today. We should open another shell company in Malta; there has been some change in regulation there.'

'You know I don't understand all that. Do what you want to,' he said dismissively. 'Was she in Cambodia?'

'Love was the last thing on my mind in Cambodia. When I think of the people I met there, you are like a boy scout in comparison.'

I rarely talked about the time before Rio. The

years spent in the monastery had helped me make a grudging peace with the past and I didn't want to open old wounds.

'Where is she then?' he asked.

'Are you sure you didn't mix oestrogen in your cocaine today?'

'What?'

'Nothing,' I said. 'Let's get back to business.'

'My business is to know where she is,' he said stubbornly.

I knew he wouldn't let go.

'It's nothing,' I said. 'Just a schoolboy crush.'

'That couldn't happen to you.'

'Well, it did. We barely met once.'

'Romeo and Juliet dropped dead at their third meeting.'

'To be or not to be taught love by a Shakespeare-quoting mobster! I prefer not to be,' I said. 'Why don't we talk about your love life instead? It's way more happening than mine.'

'Did you sleep with her, men? Did you wow her with your technique?'

'Are you crazy? I told you, we barely exchanged a few words.'

'Where is she now?' he asked. 'Here, in Rio?'

I nodded.

'Tell me her name. I will bring her to you. I run Rio.'

'Really?' I said mockingly. 'Okay, wait a minute.'

I went to my room and came back with a Brazilian fashion magazine I had chanced upon a few days ago. I placed it on the table and it opened to the page I had pored over more than a few times.

'There she is,' I said, pointing to her picture. 'Now tell me, is it an adolescent crush or what?'

'Lara,' he said softly, looking at her glossy picture hawking some French cosmetic. 'I don't know much about this world but she is some kind of model, I think. When did you meet her, men?'

'On the flight to Rio, when I was in my tattered monk's robes, bald, and with my empty sleeve dangling by my side – hardly the Don Juan she was waiting for.'

He looked at me but didn't laugh as I had expected him to. 'You have good taste. From what I've heard, she isn't a slut.'

'That was seven years ago,' I said. 'She probably married a soccer superstar and has three kids by now. Anyway, who cares? I'm not an adolescent in high school. We met, we talked, we said goodbye; no vows exchanged, no hearts broken. I was only reminded of her recently when I saw this magazine.'

'Who cares if she is married? We can get rid of her faggot husband,' he said confidently.

'You are going to do no such thing!' I said in alarm. 'This isn't a Paulo Coelho book. Supermodels don't fall in love with one-armed thugs in real life.'

'Paulo who?'

'Never mind,' I said. 'Just don't do anything foolish. Do you ever see me pining for her or for anyone else? I'm very happy here. Don't screw it up for nothing. If you are looking for things to do, get more involved in the business like I've been telling you to.'

'You should go after her yourself then,' he said. 'If you are smart enough to make so much money from nothing, what is a woman?'

'Go after what?' I said. 'Look, I kind of know what's happening here, though I hate admitting it. Some men fall in love with celebrities or supermodels without knowing anything about them. These are men trying to prove a point to someone – the ex-lover who dumped them, or their mother whom they secretly fantasized about, or the bully in school who stuck it up their arse. Or they are trying to compensate for something, you know, being too short, being gay, stuttering, stammering, a small dick – or a missing arm.'

'You should stop reading so many books,' he said. 'Besides, you know her. It's not like you fell in love with a magazine cover.'

'I've spoken to her once. Of course, that's more than you can say about any of the women you sleep with, so by your standards, yes, I know her very well indeed.'

'Very funny, wise guy,' he said. 'So, will you try or should I do it for you?'

'There is nothing to try.'

'Look, men.' He paused. 'I don't know how to say this, but there is something about you, men. I saw it when you came here, I see it now. You are different, men. You don't belong here; you don't belong anywhere. You are just… bigger than everyone and everything, you know. I don't know how to say it but I think she will see it.'

It didn't seem like she saw anything.

Buoyed by Marco's enthusiasm, I had used our apparel marketing team to set up an appointment with her at our comfortable corporate office in the Ipanema business district. The plan was to launch a branded collection under her name.

I sat at my desk facing her and her lawyer – no doubt an auspicious beginning to the proposed romantic liaison. She looked just as she had in my memory: expressive brown eyes, a cleft below her chin, auburn hair streaked with gold; only the lines on her face had hardened. She would be thirty-six now, to my thirty-seven, and age, though kinder to her than to me, had left its mark.

'What are your contract terms?' she asked.

The greatest pick-up line in history.

'Higher than the industry standard,' I said. 'A signing amount of one million dollars for the use of your name on our new sportswear collection and ten per cent commission on every item sold in that line.'

She consulted briefly with the crusty lawyer before turning back to me.

'The signing amount is fine, but we want higher royalties per item – at least fifteen per cent,' she said coldly.

I was about to agree when I stopped. Business was business, after all.

'I'm afraid that won't work for us,' I said. 'Don't forget we will be undertaking all the marketing costs to promote the line, and it helps your personal brand as much as it helps our product line.'

'12.5 per cent,' she said.

'Agreed, if we have full copyright on your images,' I said. 'We will use them wherever we think appropriate.'

Again, she consulted her lawyer.

'Done, if I get final veto rights on all product designs in the line,' she said.

'Fair enough,' I said. 'You have a deal.'

Her smile did not reach her eyes.

'I will sign the agreement whenever it's ready.'

'If you wait a few minutes, I will get it drafted now,' I said.

She looked at her watch. 'Fine, I guess,' she said haughtily.

For a second, I wondered if I had met her warm, bubbly twin sister on the flight, like that Hema Malini movie from another lifetime.

I told my assistant to draft the agreement and we waited in my office, staring blankly at the walls.

Good, I thought, one more mirage checked off the fantasy list. I'd been right all along. Love was for dummies; soulmates were the creation of pulp-fiction writers; romance was craved by ageing, lonely cat owners. Successful relationships were built on rationality and compromise – and there was nothing rational about a one-armed thug falling in love with a model at first sight.

Eventually, her lawyer filled the silence.

'Why did you decide on Ms Lara?' he asked.

'She is an icon,' I said simply.

'But yours is a young, trendy chain,' she broke in. 'Won't you be better off with a younger face?'

I started spouting the bull I routinely heard from advertising agencies. 'Our target audience associates our brand with certain heritage equities that fit your personality. The brand identity we want to create is…'

I stopped. I was too old, too damaged for this.

'Besides, we've met before,' I said. 'I enjoyed our interaction then.'

She stared at me in surprise. As I had thought, she had no memory of our meeting.

'We have?'

'I have a prosthetic arm now and a head full of hair,' I said. 'Real – the hair, that is, not the arm.'

I sounded pathetic but I bumbled on.

'I wear a suit now, but do you remember a bald guy in monk's robes on your flight from a peace-keeping mission in Thailand?'

She paused, trying to remember.

'Oh, yes,' she said, her face breaking into a smile that reached her eyes this time. 'It's been so many years!'

'Seven,' I said.

She looked at me curiously. 'You've changed quite dramatically.'

'It's been so many years,' I repeated, smiling.

'I know we had a great conversation but I can't remember any of it now,' she said.

So much for Marco's claim that I was special. What had I expected anyway? That she had waited five years to rip my clothes off the moment she set eyes on me? Even Hindi films weren't that fanciful.

My assistant arrived with the papers. I watched her study them in detail and wondered whether we would see each other again. What if we didn't? Nothing. We would carry on, stumbling through our respective journeys, falling in love with someone, falling out of love with another one, breaking up, making up, until our biological clocks went into overdrive and it all got very tiring, and we settled down with whoever was available. Our spouses would become our new soulmates. If life was even 0.24 per cent as romantic as a novel, Sam used to say bitterly at MIT, there is *the one* waiting for me. In reality, as Sam had accurately deduced, jocks had many soulmates and nerds had none. So much for divine providence.

'We should catch up some time,' she said vaguely as she handed over the signed papers.

'How about tomorrow?'

She looked taken aback. 'Okay,' she said hesitantly.

'I could pick you up at seven.'

To hell with self-respect, I thought. I was a one-armed drug dealer.

She looked at me searchingly. 'Seven sounds good.'

I picked her up promptly the next day in my yellow Volkswagen Beetle, ignoring Marco's advice of renting a limousine. ('She should peer into my soul instead of the make of my car, shouldn't she?' I teased him.) However, I did prepare for the date by getting invites to the film premiere of a director she had recently done an advertising film with. He had been compared to Federico Fellini (probably by himself) but I happily sat through the pregnant pauses, stilted dialogues and dark shadows, enjoying her presence next to me. She had taken care to dress for the date, I noted with some optimism, but she didn't turn to look at me even once during the screening. She felt nothing for me except a little curiosity, perhaps, and that was fine since I was no Orpheus or Romeo myself. I was probably attracted to her for reasons much more rational than emotional.

I was surrounded by boundless generosity and a primal intellect in the favela, but I missed the superficial trappings of the privileged background I had grown up in. She represented these for me – someone who travelled the world for leisure, not survival; whose interest in the arts wasn't tinged by the pornography of violence and who had not seen enough hardness to completely blunt her appreciation for all that was good and beautiful in life. No, it wasn't love, but it was good enough to work for someone like me – a dishonest man in a dishonest world; a morally ambiguous observer of a morally ambiguous universe.

'What a charming place!' she said as we entered a small, nondescript café off Copacabana after the film ended.

'It gets better as the evening progresses,' I said. 'Soon it will turn into quite a vibrant Samba haunt.'

'I'm surprised I've never been here,' she said, looking around at the solid wooden tables and soft lighting in the sparse, comfortable room.

'Rio's best kept secret.' I smiled. Known only to well-heeled drug lords who like their anonymity, I almost added.

'Did you like the film?' she asked.

I wished I could tell her that I appreciated the low camera angles and the flickering shadows, but I was too old for pretences.

'Why make a film when you have nothing to say?' I said.

It sounded harsher than I intended. She looked at me evenly with hard, unsmiling eyes and then broke into sudden, kind laughter. She touched my hand.

'I remember thinking you were cute and earnest,' she said. 'That's all I really recall from the flight.'

'I remember a lot more,' I said, holding her hand.

She pulled away. 'So... you didn't like the film?' she asked.

'I liked watching it with you.'

My pulse was racing. Had I moved too fast? I didn't know how to court a woman. I had never courted a woman. In the favela, men and women sized each other up, they didn't romance.

She locked glances with me for a long moment, then looked down.

'I'm not ready for a relationship,' she said.

'I didn't ask for one.'

'I figured,' she said. 'What with Maria, Lucia, Regina, Carolina, how would you have the time?'

It was my turn to be surprised.

'Calm down.' She smiled. 'I haven't been stalking you. My team does a background check on anyone I meet.'

'Impressive,' I said. 'But didn't they tell you that none of them mean anything?'

She nodded, then exhaled. 'Our worlds are too different.'

'We are collaborating on a project,' I said.

'I'm surprised about that. Donos don't like women to work.'

I grimaced. 'I am not a Donos.'

'And they don't like women with a history. I am not pure like you guys want your women to be. My affairs with other men are known to everyone.'

'I'm not a street thug.'

'And they leave their women once they have kids.'

'Stop!' I said. 'I'm not an illiterate goon. All the businesses I run are legitimate. It's a long story, and not one that a background check would easily uncover.'

'Still, we are from different worlds,' she repeated. 'You didn't even grow up here. You come from nowhere, it seems.'

'Aren't you moving too fast?' I said.

'I'm too old to play games.'

'I'm a year older. Don't you remember?'

'No.'

'Well, then, to answer your question, I didn't grow up in Brazil, not even close,' I said. 'But I've lived in a world without boundaries. Everywhere I go, I'm surrounded by kindness. A friend from

Estonia saved my life, an American monk nursed me to health, and now in Brazil, I'm learning how to live. I believe in a world that knows no boundaries. People feel, people care, people love, people hurt; everywhere I've gone, it's been the same.'

She leaned closer and brushed her fingers lightly against my cheek. 'You're different,' she said softly.

I pulled away. 'I don't know about that. I think I'm attracted to you because I'm compensating.' I told her my theory about men who chased models and actresses to make up for their defects.

She threw back her head and laughed.

'By that logic, every pretty woman would be single because all the guys chasing her would be jerks.'

'Isn't that why you are alone?'

'Perhaps,' she said. 'Or maybe I'm the one with issues.'

'You don't have issues.'

'How well do you know me?'

'Perhaps the bigger question is, how well do *you* want to know me?' I asked.

'I'm sorry for being such a bitch.'

I laughed. 'You were very warm when I first met you.'

'I'm different outside Brazil,' she said. 'Here, I'm jaded – too many rich, empty men.'

'I may be empty but I'm not rich,' I said. 'One out of two isn't bad.'

She smiled. 'No, it isn't. You are different,' she said. 'You've known suffering, you have seen pain.'

'I've also known love,' I said.

The music kicked up a notch just then and couples began to descend on the small dance floor.

'Are you going to ask me to dance?' she said.

'Remember how you negotiated the contract terms? You are better at getting your way, you should ask me.'

'May I?' She stood up, barely a couple of inches shorter than my six-foot-three.

She danced expertly and I managed to keep step, though my moves were rough and unsophisticated, an outcome of dancing to the adrenalin fuelled, gunshot pumped favela funk, where the intent of dance was to couple. But she guided me, initially at arm's length, and soon closer, my torso touching hers, her fingers running through my hair, our hips moving in rhythm.

'This is technically our third date. Do you know about the third date rule in Brazil?' she whispered, her lips touching my ear lobes, as the music slowed down.

'I've only been on first dates in Brazil,' I said.

'But they ended like third dates, didn't they?'

'I need to tell you something,' she said as we lay naked on the soft couch in her Ipanema apartment.

We had made intense, unhurried love; fumbling in the beginning as we both tried too hard to please each other, then relaxing enough to enjoy ourselves, until finally there was no pressure to give or get, satisfy or be satisfied, control or be controlled.

'So do I,' I said.

'I don't care about your past.'

'Nor do I.'

'Then what did you want to tell me?' she asked.

'You go first.'

'No, it's your turn this time,' she said. 'I asked you to dance. I made the first move on you.'

Reluctantly, I withdrew from her embrace and got out of bed. Her bedroom overlooked the sea, and I opened the window, feeling the moist breeze against my naked body.

Reflexively, I picked up my shirt from the futon and tried to cover myself. Perhaps she guessed why I did it, because she came up to me and kissed me on my ugly stump, pushing the shirt aside.

'Don't compensate,' she said.

I laughed. And for the first time, I spoke about Cambodia and my despair, Ishmael's death, losing an arm, the years in the monastery and the crushing feeling of loss and failure. I had never told anyone the complete truth – not Marco, not David, nor anyone else at the monastery or the favela. They had probably guessed parts of the story from my sudden silences or my complaints about the unbearable pain in my absent left arm. But I'd never wanted to admit – either to them or to myself – that those two years in Cambodia defined me more than I cared to accept.

Lara listened in shocked silence. 'I'm sorry I had to tell you this,' I said finally. 'But you need to know. I've tried to forget everything but it's complicated, because what happened there is the reason I am here. I'd change everything, and yet I'd change nothing.'

She held me close, her eyes wet with tears.

'Your turn now,' I said.

'I have nothing to say.'

'Say something,' I said. 'Even the contract terms will do.'

'What should I say? You've known such pain, such loss, yet you believe, you laugh, you build.'

'I'm not one of those idiots who thinks that suffering isn't suffering until you lose an arm,' I said. 'Who am I to judge anyone else's struggles? All life is dukha, the Buddha said, everyone feels anguish and no one's pain is any less than another's.'

'My pain is a modelling world cliché,' she said. 'I had an abusive father, who eventually found Jesus, but after taking his beatings for years, my mother couldn't find anything except the bottle. After they died, I vowed my life would be different but I soon realized that consciously or unconsciously, I was seeking the same kind of violence in my relationships. After I was beaten one too many times, I swore off men completely. And then you come along, a monk of all people, a man of god and peace, the sort of man I distrust the most because of my father.'

'I *was* a man of god and peace.' I smiled. 'Now I'm a man of drugs and arms, if that makes you feel any better.'

'Everything about you makes me feel better.' She laughed. Then she became serious again. 'I need to get over my past. I need to get over myself. Look at what you've been through.'

'I didn't exactly set out to win an award for suffering,' I said, suddenly aroused by the soft, vulnerable expression on her usually closed face as she talked to me, her forehead creased in deep concentration. 'But you're right. You need to get over yourself. How about climbing on to me instead?'

We laughed and made love again, surrendering to each other more readily this time.

'I don't think it's a good idea,' said Marco a few months later, when I told him I was moving in with Lara.

'Why?' I said, surprised. 'You're the one who pushed me to meet her.'

'I didn't realize it would lead to this,' he said. 'I thought it would run its natural course after you had had her a few times. Plenty of fish where she comes from.'

'How can you say something as crass as that when you know how I feel about her?' I said, seething.

'Calm down, will you?' he said. 'It's just not right. No good will come of this.'

'I'm not doing it for any good. I love her,' I said. 'What's your problem really, Donos? Be straight with me. Are you feeling lonely because I'm leaving?'

'Don't talk to me like I'm a fucking faggot,' he said, raising his voice. 'After all these years, you think I am going to stop you because of how I feel? I think it's a bad idea because you are drawing attention to yourself. First, you go and start your own business; then, you make us richer than everyone; now, you want to marry a model. Soon your picture will be all over the gossip magazines. Do you think no one is watching? It doesn't pay to be so flashy in this business. Do what you have to, but don't come begging to me for help later.'

'What am I supposed to do then?' I said, calming down a little. 'Should I live in fear all my life just because we own a couple of stores? I have the right to live, don't I? I love her. We want to be together. How is that anyone else's concern?'

'It is my concern,' he said stubbornly.

'Then work with me on this,' I said. 'I'll be careful to keep a low profile. You know I don't want any publicity for myself. No one will even know about us.'

'Just like no one knows you are behind the retail

chains?' he asked. 'You aren't in a monastery any more, men. Nothing is hidden here.' He paused. 'Besides, I don't even think you're in love. You are just trying to make up for lost time.'

His last comment hit home. He was right. I was trying to make up for lost time, aspiring for a semblance of the stability I'd known in my childhood, making a desperate attempt to live the life I was supposed to lead. I didn't know if I was in love. I didn't even know what love meant. But I felt at peace when I was with her. Wasn't that enough?

'Anyway, do what you have to, men,' he said finally, with a sigh. 'We'll cross that bridge when we come to it. Not that you are waiting for my permission.'

I shook my head. 'I am not, but it's nice to have it anyway. You're right. I don't know if I am in love, but I do know that she is a good woman. Don't worry. Everything will be fine. I can feel it in my bones.'

And everything *was* fine. Perhaps it was because Lara and I were two middle-aged, lonely people desperately seeking companionship, perhaps we'd both lost too much to fight over toilet seats and dirty dishes, or maybe we really were soulmates, but we settled into a comfortable, easy companionship. The wedding came and went. It meant nothing; at best, an affirmation of societal rules in lives that had never known rules before; at worst, a desperate attempt to inure one to the vagaries of the other's nature. We fought as often and as hard as two strong-willed people who had spent too much time alone would, but we never held on to our resentment for long as we deeply valued what we had built. Soon, even that surreal feeling of living someone else's life which I had woken up with for years, came to pass. All I felt was a quiet bliss. *This* was my life. My choices had led me here; nothing else mattered. I was in Brazil now, married to a beautiful woman I loved and who loved me back unconditionally; I was running a thriving business as an insignificant but not entirely unproductive cog of the human wheel, staking his own small claim to happiness. And I wanted nothing more; not now, not ever.

For all my joy though, I don't think I fell completely, selflessly in love until Lara became pregnant after two years. If any doubts held me back until then – residual guilt at thumbing my nose at the Buddha's teachings or thoughts of overcompensating for my arm – I lost them completely at the sight of her tender, tired face aglow with the anticipation of our baby. We were about to become parents, we would have a child who would never know pain, and though at thirty-nine I wouldn't exactly be a young father, we had as much life ahead of us as we had left behind.

And this chapter would be less interesting, I vowed to myself as I entered our bedroom, which had been converted into a quasi-operating room a few hours before her Caesarean.

'…you just connect it like this and, maneiro, you can monitor every sound, every image within five hundred yards.' Marco was sitting at Lara's bedside, explaining the uses of a bulky contraption made up of a monitor and a tangle of wires.

I felt a deep sense of contentment. Despite his disapproval of our relationship, Marco had never mentioned his doubts to Lara. Instead, he had accepted her, welcomed her, and cared for her without a grudge.

Lara, heavily sedated, was trying to pay attention, but kept drifting off to sleep between his enthusiastic words.

'An electronic baby monitor smuggled directly from California,' he said, looking up as I entered. 'It's not even in the US market yet.'

'What better way to induct the baby into our world than with a newly smuggled device to monitor its first movements?' I said sarcastically.

'It's very useful,' said Lara loyally.

'Ignore him,' said Marco to her. 'He goes through a Buddhist phase whenever he is under stress. He will snap out of it as soon as the baby is born.'

He turned to me. 'Good you are here. I was about to head out.'

'Stay,' I said. 'In a few hours, you will be a real godfather.'

'Pele is playing an exhibition match in Maracana today. I can't miss that,' he said.

'You would choose football over me?' I said mockingly.

'You've already scored, and a model, no less.' He smiled as he got up from his chair. 'Now it's time to watch Pele score.'

He gave me a quick, embarrassed hug.

'Good luck,' he said quietly. 'I will be by my phone.'

I nodded.

'He loves you more than I do, I think,' Lara said after he left.

I shrugged.

'He has been hovering around me all these months as though it were his own child. No, much more. He grew up in a favela where children are born every minute and no one even cares.'

'He is a good man,' I said. 'The best kind there is.'

'This is more than that.'

'We've been through a lot together.'

She looked at me as her eyelids started to close. 'What kind of man can inspire such loyalty?' she said. 'How did you come into my life when…'

'Ssshh…' I placed my finger to her lips. 'Rest now.'

She closed her eyes.

The doctors and nurses came into the room. 'We

should be ready to start in a few minutes. Do you want to stay inside?'

I nodded. 'If it's not a distraction,' I said and sat by the bed.

Lara drifted into sleep and the doctors got busy when suddenly, the unmistakable sound of a gunshot being fired at a distance made me sit up.

My heart sank. Not now, I thought, not when everything seemed to have settled down for once.

The doctors continued, oblivious. Our penthouse faced a busy street and it required ears attuned to such sounds to recognize them.

I tensed as I held Lara's sweaty hand, praying it was a stray shot and unconnected to me.

A volley of shots ripped through the air in quick succession. The doctors looked at each other, then at me, demanding an explanation. They probably knew my background. Lara awoke with a start.

'Sleep,' I said, brushing my hand across her forehead. 'It must be the gang celebrating early.'

Her face relaxed.

'I will go and stop them,' I said softly as she drifted off again.

I gave a reassuring glance to the doctors and rushed out of the room. I had lived on the edge since Lara and I had been together, knowing something like this would happen.

But not now, please.

Glock in hand, I dashed through the apartment

into the stately lobby of the luxury condominium. We shared it with respectable lawyers, bankers and actors, and it was unlikely that any of them could be the target of the Comando Vermelho. Marco stood alone in the large lobby, gun in hand, ears cocked, intently watching the glass doors. The concierge was cowering in fear as he stood flattened against the wall on the far side. I saw nothing unusual in front of the building, nor did I hear any more shots.

'Get out by the fire exit and take a taxi to Ary Franco,' he said without turning around. 'I will look after her.'

Wordlessly, I rushed down the back stairs and hailed a taxi to the Ary Franco prison on the outskirts of Rio.

A quiet calm descended over me on my way to the jail as I tried to piece together what had transpired. The Comando Vermelho had come for me. They had chosen this time deliberately, knowing I would be at home because of Lara's delivery. I wasn't surprised. Marco had warned me again and again that they would attack, and I had chosen to ignore him. But this wasn't the time for regrets. There would be plenty of time for that later because life, as I knew it, was ending today. Marco was sending me to prison because it was a safe haven, at least for the time being, and he probably knew the guards there. I knew the drill. False charges would be concocted so I could spend

time there while he negotiated desperately with
the Comando Vermelho for my life. But it wasn't
money they were after. There was enough money
flowing in the system to keep everyone happy.
What would they want in return? Would I ever
see Lara again? Would she be safe? The last time
I had felt this surging sense of hopelessness was
in Phnom Penh. But I had been alone then, and
falling had been simpler.

The prison security guard was expecting me. He
came out as soon as he saw the taxi pull up in front
of the imposing iron gates.

'Donos,' he said as I got out of the car. 'It's an
honour.'

'I'm not a Donos,' I told him.

He stared at me disbelievingly.

Similar greetings were exchanged when I went
inside.

'You will be safe here, Donos,' said the jail warden
as he escorted me to my cell. 'We will arrange for
you to stay as long as you like.'

I walked with him through the long, dark
corridors. The prison was six floors high, filled with
tiny six-by-six cells, each one packed with half-
naked prisoners. Angry screams disturbed the air,
chewed food and rotten pieces of fruit were flung
through the bars, and mould grew on the stained
walls. I felt a creeping sense of unease, like I hadn't

felt in years, only now it was tinged with panic. What was I doing in a prison thousands of miles from where I grew up as the son of a law-enforcing officer? I just wanted a simple life with my wife and child – what was I doing here?

'You can pick any cell you like, Donos,' said the warden.

There wasn't much to choose from. There were convicts stretched out on hammocks strung from the walls of every cell because the floors were filled to capacity.

'I'll take this one,' I said, pointing at the first cell to my right. It was filled to the brim like every other cell but had enough space to give me a little standing room to think – which was all I wanted.

The warden entered the cell, with me trailing behind him.

Immediately, five people jumped down from the hammocks and joined fifteen others on the floor.

I wondered if they would attack me. My years of training, first in Thailand, then in Rio, convinced me that I could take three, maybe four of them, but not twenty. I crouched to defend myself.

Instead, the warden asked them to get out of the cell.

Without a whimper of protest, they walked out, staring resentfully at me. I lowered my eyes, hoping I wouldn't have to pay for the privilege later.

Alone in my cell, I waited for word to come. I willed myself not to allow my regrets to overwhelm me, concentrating instead on thoughts of Lara and the baby. The Buddha had taught me about the aatma, the universal soul, the life-force that runs through every being, concentrating on which connects you to a supreme energy. After years of ignoring his wisdom, I focused on the energy, imploring it for Lara's health and safety.

'Donos Marco is here,' said a voice.

I broke out of my trance and looked up at the jailer.

Quietly, I followed him outside the cell, a sinking feeling in the pit of my stomach. We walked through the corridors once again. A bloody brawl was in progress in one of the cells. Arms, legs and fists – two men slugging it out in a no-holds-barred encounter, fifteen people around them, watching and clapping.

The jailer ignored them.

'It's an everyday affair here,' he said, following my glance. 'I'll come back to stop them once I have escorted you to the Donos.'

By which time one or both of them would be dead, I thought. Life came cheap in Rio, especially in a prison cell. I averted my eyes, feeling no anger, no pity, no sorrow at their fate. I had turned into an animal.

'How is she?' I asked him as soon as the jailer had left us alone.

'*They* are fine,' said Marco, red with exhaustion. 'It's a boy covered in blood and goo, uglier than you are, but as healthy as any newborn baby ever born in Brazil.'

A colossal weight lifted off my shoulders. Despite the mess I was in, I had never felt happier.

'Will she be safe?' I asked.

He nodded. 'The enforcer has word not to harm the wife and child unless they are witness to...' He stopped.

'...my execution,' I completed the sentence for him. I sighed. 'Give it to me,' I said. 'Spare me nothing.'

'It's not the Comando Vermelho, at least not directly. Griselda Blanco, La Madrina, the Godmother – you know who I am talking about. She's called the Black Widow because she killed all three of her husbands. It's she who has taken out a hit on you. She runs a big Colombian cartel which controls most of the cocaine supply in South America.'

'But why me?' I asked. 'I'm not even in the business any more.'

I didn't need to ask the question and Marco didn't insult me with an 'I told you so'. He had warned me about this two years ago. I was an outsider who had overstepped his limits, first by running a business, and then by marrying Lara. I had taunted them, scoffed at their disorganization, laughed at their powerlessness. This had to happen sooner or later. If not Griselda Blanco, it would have been Pablo Escobar, or Jorge Vazquez, or Carolos Lehder. I had known I was a marked man, yet I had chosen to ignore the threat, endangering not only myself, but also Marco and Lara – and now my son.

'Will they come after you too?' I asked.

'Unlikely,' he said. 'That would start a full-fledged gang war in which no one wins. You, on the other hand, are an outsider, so no one cares.'

I sighed with relief, glad I hadn't sucked him into it.

'That was the bad news,' he said. 'Now, I have some good news. I spoke to Pablo, one of her front men. He says that the Black Widow *may* agree to a jail sentence of ten years instead of killing you. She's got nothing personal against you. All the cartel wants to do is send out the message that an outsider can't enter the system.'

So, this was the best I could hope for. Stay in jail for ten years and watch Lara lose the best years of our son's life, waiting and pining, begging and pleading, building hope only to see it crash. Ten years was a long time to be suspended without an anchor. And then? Suppose the Godmother changed her mind once I was out? My family would be destroyed. No, this wasn't even an option.

'Can't we pay them off?' I asked. 'As much as they want – twenty, maybe thirty million dollars.'

Marco shook his head. 'I tried. They don't even want to talk money. I think you should agree to jail, at least for now. Meanwhile, I will keep working on them and try to get you out sooner.'

'What are my chances?'

'Slim,' he replied honestly. 'I can't even hit back at her because she is lodged comfortably in a prison in Chicago. We have no connections there and it's going to take a while to build some. Besides, her people will come back with a vengeance… and you can't afford that now.'

He was big enough not to remind me that I had been forewarned about the dangers of having a family. I had wanted to recreate the stability of my childhood so badly that I had forgotten to consider the impact of all the wrong choices I had made in between. How could I have been so selfish?

'You have to decide quickly if you want to spend ten years here,' he said evenly. 'She will start filling this jail with her men soon and make the decision for us if we don't give her our answer.'

We sat quietly for a while.

'I have another option in mind,' I said finally.

I told him what I wanted. 'Just do this one last thing for me,' I said.

'Are you sure?' He sighed.

I nodded.

I called Lara from the jailer's office after Marco had left to make the arrangements.

'I'm sorry,' I said, ruing the inability of words to express what I felt.

'It's not your fault.'

'How does he look?'

'He doesn't look like much yet. But your worry was unfounded: both his arms are intact.'

'I've ruined everything.'

'You made my life better than I ever thought it could be,' she said.

'I could be in jail for ten years, maybe fifteen,' I said, willing her to say that she couldn't wait, that she would have to move on.

'I was alone for thirty-six years before I met you. What's another ten?'

'Listen, please…' I began and stopped.

Nothing I said would make a difference; we were past the stage of rationality. If I wanted her to go on with her life, I had to get out of it. She was beautiful, she was accomplished, we had taught each other to love; she would live without me, be happier perhaps.

'I need to go now,' I said, blinking away the tears.

I returned to my cell as night descended. The lone light bulb outside was switched off and the corridor was plunged in darkness. Occasional sobs and whimpers swept through the prison compound, the policeman on duty clanked his heels against the concrete floor, rats scurried past. I stared at the wall and waited.

I'd known that it was a house of cards, yet I had tempted fate, scorned it, tried to live a life I wasn't meant to live. There were so many alternate turns I could have taken. We could have left for the US after marriage; between us, we had enough money to never have to work another day in our lives. We could have chosen to go back to the monastery and worked for a cause greater than ourselves. We could have returned to India, or even done volunteer work in Cambodia. Instead, I had tried rashly to make up for lost time and destroyed more than one life in the process. I claimed that money and fame meant nothing to me, but wasn't that the real reason I had stuck on in Rio despite the risks? Could I deny that I felt a tiny stab of pleasure when we were written about in the newspapers or when we evaded the flashbulbs of media cameras while returning from a late night movie? Hadn't I started to take these incidents as proof that my life finally mattered, that it had some significance? Hubris follows pride. I had tried to be bigger than myself and the gods had struck a blow once again. Only, this time, I hadn't fallen alone.

How could things have unravelled so quickly?

At midnight, the door to my cell opened.

'Marco?' I whispered.

'It's me, Donos,' said the jailer. 'Donos Marco has sent me to fetch you.'

Could I trust him, I wondered, then laughed silently in the darkness. What were my options?

I followed him quietly as we walked through the corridors, barely glancing at the whimpering prisoners in the overcrowded cells. When we reached his office, he went to his desk and took out a revolver from the topmost drawer.

Instinctively, I reached for mine, forgetting it had been checked in.

But he made no move to shoot me. Slowly, deliberately, he fitted a silencer on top of the gun and handed it to me.

'Shoot me, Donos.'

I had a sudden flash of clarity and silently applauded Marco for his meticulous planning, despite the short notice.

'Where?' I asked quietly.

'One above the calf in my left leg, and graze the other through my right arm. Let me turn the other way so it seems like I was caught unawares. Donos Marco tells me you are the best shot he has ever seen.'

I nodded and walked a few steps back.

My hands were steady as I shot him twice. He crumpled to the floor and I was relieved to see just a light trickle of blood by his side. I had fired accurately.

I went up to him. 'Are you okay?' I asked.

He gave me a thumbs up. 'I will press the alarm two hours from now. Remember to shoot the padlock on your way out.'

Marco and Alex were waiting for me outside in an unmarked car.

'He was good,' I said as Alex began to speed away.

'A million reals, plus he gets to keep his job and become some kind of a hero – that kind of money brings out a lot of good in people,' said Marco. He paused. 'Are you sure about this? We can still turn back.'

I nodded. 'I'd rather have stayed in jail but I know Lara. She won't let go and ten years is too long to waste on someone. And who can guarantee their safety when I'm out after ten years?'

'Just lie low for a while. I will find a way out of this,' he said.

'What does she know?' I asked.

'Lara will know what the papers report tomorrow – that you made a violent escape from prison and deserted her like a coward.'

I grimaced.

'This is your passport,' he said.

I flipped through the American passport with my smiling face on the first page.

'I found a guy with the name Nick. Thought you'd appreciate the touch.'

Nick Bolton. A registered plumber from Minnesota. I practised saying the name a few times, trying to get the American twang right.

'Is he dead?' I asked.

Marco nodded. 'Not dead in the US, though. He had come to fuck in the carnival, but got fucked instead. A sad story you don't want to hear.'

'How did you put in my photograph?'

'A simple lamination job. Five-year-olds at the favela could do it. Getting the passport was the tricky part. I couldn't get you an Indian one, no matter how much I tried. Indians seem to be careful people who don't travel much, at least not to this part of the world. How did you turn out like this?' He smiled. 'Anyway, I thought America would do since you've lived there before.'

'Will they recognize me at the airport?' I asked, still examining the passport.

He laughed. 'Not unless you do something foolish. You have an inflated sense of your fame. Every day, there is a new celebrity in Rio – no one remembers anyone.'

'I don't know how to thank you. I don't even know how to *begin* to thank you,' I said.

He waved his hand. 'I've done nothing, men,' he said. 'All of us partied for the last five years while you worked. Yet, you took the fall alone. But we will get back at them, you wait and see.'

'Don't do anything foolish,' I said.

'I won't,' he said. 'I've learnt from you. Silence and business will be my weapons now.'

I grimaced. 'Get out of this business. No good comes of it.'

'Cocaine is my life, my karma yoga, you might say.' He smiled at me. 'You know me. I have no concept of right or wrong, good or bad; there are some things I do and some things I don't, that's all.'

The car drew up at the airport.

'Here is your bag,' said Marco. 'It contains five hundred dollars, toiletries, a few clothes and shoes. This is the maximum cash you are allowed to carry, and I didn't want to take a chance.'

'That's more than enough,' I said. 'I've lived on less.'

'Now here's the tough part. No matter what happens, don't call me and don't call Lara; not for a couple of years at least, until I have sorted out this mess. The Godmother won't forget and the police will be under a lot of pressure from the media to do something. You will have both on your back. Every phone call, every message, every movement that Lara and I make could be traced.' He paused.

'You are on your own from now on,' he said. 'I have no contacts there. Just keep this one number, but don't call him unless it's a matter of life and death. I mean it. Don't call him unless you have to. He is an important man and will know how to help you – but he'll extract a price you will find hard to pay. Just trust me on this.'

'I trust you,' I said quietly as we stood outside the terminal.

He looked me in the eye and hugged me with all his strength.

'Stop being a faggot now, will you?' I said, tearing up as I walked off.

The Entrepreneur

Make mistakes of ambition and not mistakes of sloth.

Niccolo Machiavelli

25 January 1995, Shelter for the homeless, Minnesota, USA

'Where are you from?'

I looked up from my bowl of watery soup to see a middle-aged African-American man with long, knotted hair and needle marks all over his eyelids. His hand trembled as he tried to guide a spoonful of soup into his mouth. Despite his best efforts, he kept spilling it over his tattered overcoat which looked like it hadn't been washed in years. There were scars all over his wrist and white foam dribbled out of his mouth. A far gone crack addict, I noted, someone who had to stick needles into his eyeballs to get the drug to flow into his bloodstream faster: the veins in the arms and wrists took too much time. The seed money for the business I ran in Rio came from feeding junkies like him, I thought shamefully. I had no right to complain. I deserved to be where I was.

'Where are you from, brother?' he asked again.

'Very far,' I said.

A gust of Arctic wind blew in through the broken windows of the large dining hall and I shivered. Three months in Minnesota and I still wasn't used to the weather. The first thing I would do once I got a job was buy an overcoat. Just after I bought a shaving razor. Just after I bought a toothbrush. Just after I bought a second pair of underwear. Just after…

'Why are you here, brother?' he asked, his hands still shaking violently. His teeth chattered – or what was left of them anyway. Half were broken, the rest chipped at the edges. His lips were sore and chapped and his gums showed remnants of dried blood. I had an eerie feeling that I would end up like him soon. Another week in this cold and I would probably need to shoot up something to give myself an illusion of warmth – crack was cheaper than overcoats after all.

Everyone around me had already capitulated. Unshaven faces, unkempt hair, rotting, decaying flesh, men and women freezing in the cold, every item of clothing except the bare essentials sold for crack. They appeared stunned into stoned silence, like zombies silently awaiting a passage into the afterworld.

'Why are you here?' the man demanded again, his rough voice breaking the silence in the icy dining room.

No one paid any attention except the two kind-hearted volunteers who had brought food for the homeless today. They looked at him warningly, but I don't think he noticed – or cared.

Why indeed, I wondered. Because Nick Bolton, the wayward plumber whose identity I had now taken, had made Minneapolis, Minnesota his home. Because five hundred dollars ran out in three months in this city even if you stayed in cheap motels and scrounged for leftovers outside budget diners. Because I had no means to get more money since I'd already bartered my only asset, my prosthetic arm, for a sweater at the midnight black market on Hennepin Avenue.

'I'm here to look for a job,' I said.

He thrust some soup into his mouth excitedly.

'There are no jobs here,' he said, shivering. 'No chances for the poor. No chances for the yellow, brown or black.'

I nodded. Despite his piteous state, he made sense. I was no longer an MIT graduate. I was a plumber who had dropped out of high school, and in the twenty years I had been out of the country, it seemed that even plumbers needed a high school education to fix leaking toilets.

'The only jobs are in drugs. Do you deal?' he said.

Did I deal? Just a few months ago, I was a drug lord of sorts with a fifty million dollar empire, I wanted to tell him.

'No,' I said.

He sensed my hesitation. Suddenly, his authoritative voice turned squeaky and pleading.

'Just one hit, please, brother. One hit only, please.'

'No, no,' I said, shaking my head violently.

'One hit please.' He was getting hysterical now. 'I'll do anything for you, brother. Just one rock. I'll blow you, brother. I'll give you the best blow job you ever got, by Jesus.' He opened his mouth and ran his tongue over his bloody gums. 'See. No teeth. I put you in nice and soft. Please, please, one hit, brother.'

'I don't deal drugs,' I said, nearly shouting now. 'I didn't deal drugs. Not now, not ever.' I slammed my soup bowl on the table, held my head in my hands and began to sob silently. Why had I entered her life just to ruin it? Would she ever be able to move on? Had I given up too quickly? Should I have taken my ten year imprisonment instead of running away like a rat?

The man calmed down a little at my outburst.

'Jesus always creates a pattern,' he said unexpectedly. 'When you are close, you only see unravelled threads, but with time and distance, it will reveal itself as a mosaic. Just wait and watch. Everything was meant to be exactly the way it is.'

'What?' I said, raising my head, surprised at his sudden lucidity.

'Jesus creates a pattern. Jesus creates a mosaic,' he said animatedly.

'It's a pattern; you just don't know it now.' His hands were shaking even more.

'A pattern,' he said, banging his fist on the table. He upset his bowl of soup all over himself as the volunteers came rushing to our table to hold him down.

'It's a mosaic; you wait and watch,' he shouted as they led him out of the room. 'Just one hit, please. One hit, brother. One rock. Best blow job ever.'

I shuffled away from the dining hall to the sleeping area, more than a little shaken at his outburst. There were thirty bunk beds here – no mattresses, bedsheets or pillows, just bare iron frames from volunteer donations. No one could lay claim to a particular bed. Every day, the occupants changed; some died from the cold or one of a hundred diseases, some slipped back into the streets because of the rigid drug-free rule enforced by the volunteers and some just disappeared, never to be heard of again. I'd been in the shelter for a few weeks and in a strange way, it had begun to provide a measure of comfort that I once used to associate with home. Today, once again, I felt a quiet sense of pleasure when I saw that my favourite bed – the one farthest away from the broken window – was as yet unoccupied. I curled up in it, trying desperately to keep warm. I closed my eyes, watched her cry silently and prepared for another sleepless night.

An advertisement for an accountant's position in the *Minnesota Star Tribune* Classifieds caught my eye the next day. This time I decided to get rejected in person, instead of over the phone. I scraped my week long beard with a blade in the mirror in the common bathroom, careful not to nick myself like I had the first time. Other people came in and out of the bathroom. No one asked to use the basin. Grooming, shaving, washing – these were unnecessary for the living dead. Sometimes I envied them. It was so much easier to drift away, speed up what destiny had designed for one, and not fight the battle any longer. I was touching forty, had fewer years ahead of me than behind, and I no longer had the will to build my life again.

I winced as I nicked myself, and a small bewildered droplet of blood appeared on my dry skin. I wondered what it would be like to slash my face until it turned into a bloodied mass of flesh and bone.

I stared at my reflection a while longer before wiping off the drop with the back of my hand, and forced myself to finish shaving without incident.

Dressed in a suit I had rented from the local dry-cleaning shop, I looked almost presentable. There was a scar on my forehead, my mouth was still a little swollen from a scuffle in the shelter a few weeks ago, and my left arm was missing, but on the whole, I didn't look like the homeless bum I was.

Outside, the freshly fallen snow which had looked so beautiful twenty years ago now seemed dangerous and threatening. I couldn't afford to slip on the ice and fall, not today, when a small voice in my head told me things would work out – the same voice that had accurately forecasted doom when Lara was in the throes of childbirth and the gunshot had sounded. I decided to splurge one dollar of my seven on a bus to the St Louis Park office in the Twin Cities.

'You don't look like a Nick Bolton if I may say so,' guffawed the tall, bald man who was interviewing me.

I smiled noncommittally, although my heart skipped a beat. This was my chance, I thought. I was finally inside an office. Not plush or luxurious, by any means. It was a small, uncarpeted two-room suite on the first floor of a strip mall in a forgotten part of town. But it was warm. That was all that mattered. There was a receptionist in the other room, doing her nails, and inside was this military looking guy who looked like an ageing Mr Clean, the genial giant who cleaned bathroom tiles in the billboard advertisements opposite the shelter.

'Pardon me,' said the military guy. 'I'm a private investigator, so I am suspicious of everything.'

I stiffened. What if he managed to sniff out my past?

'But I know a good man when I see one, and I like you. You are homeless, right?' he said, his eyes boring into me. He wasn't offensive at all, just a man used to calling a bum a bum.

I nodded cautiously.

'That's not a problem with me,' he continued. 'I am no one to judge you. I spent years climbing the ranks of Homeland Security, but look where I am now. We all make choices, son. I made the wrong ones. But that's the past, let's not go there.'

I had no desire to go anywhere. I just wanted to stay in that warm office.

'Have you handled accounts before? Real cash?' he asked.

I nodded.

'My clients are all respectable citizens, but for obvious reasons, sometimes they have to pay in unrespectable ways. I've had trouble with the law, so I want to ensure everything is legal – or can be made legal. I need someone who understands enough to know what's right and what can be made right.'

I told him briefly what I knew about both legal and illegal accounting – escrow, onshore, offshore, laundering, Moldova, Malta, Seychelles, etc.

'Wow,' he said. 'Aren't you a little overqualified to be here?'

I let that one pass.

'Your salary won't be much, just five hundred dollars a month. I've just started so that's the most I can afford right now. It will grow as the business grows, and believe me, I know what I'm doing. God knows I am not a saint, but you can trust me on this,' he said. 'Is that good enough?'

Twenty years ago, I had earned exactly that amount as my graduate scholarship. But it didn't matter. Money had never meant anything; now it meant even less. If I could have a warm roof above my head, I wanted nothing more.

'At times, very few times, I may need your help in some private investigation activities. Very basic things, like following someone, and you will have a licensed gun in case something goes wrong. Can you handle a revolver?'

I could probably handle every revolver made by man.

'I think so,' I said.

He nodded approvingly. 'I thought as much.' He paused. 'I have nothing more to ask you. Do you have any questions for me?'

I shook my head.

'Well then, it's all settled,' he said. 'Congratulations, you are hired!'

A wave of relief swept through me. Warmth, I thought. Now I would have nothing to bother me, except my memories. I thanked him profusely.

'I just have to run a quick background check on you and we're good to go,' he said.

I froze. The moment he ran the check, he would know. I couldn't con a CIA man. My fake ID notwithstanding, he'd know I wasn't a plumber who grew up as a ranch hand on a Minnesota farm. I couldn't predict what he would do then. Would he dig up my real story or would he let it go? What happened to me was inconsequential, but I couldn't in any way endanger those I'd left behind.

'Could you spell your name for me?' he asked. 'And your birth date, please.'

I thought of the icy evenings and bitter nights in the shelter and felt a crushing sense of despair. But once again, I had no choice.

'I don't want the job,' I said with sudden resolve. 'On second thoughts, the pay is too low.'

He looked at me, astonished. Our eyes locked for a moment, then he relaxed.

'I understand,' he said slowly. 'If I venture into the dark side again, I'll track you down. And I won't do any background checks then.'

I left the office.

Down the stairs of the crumbling staircase I went, dreading the bitter winds that awaited me outside. I'd be asked about my past, no matter what I was being interviewed for. Where could I go now? What could I do? The only option, I thought, was to start where Nick Bolton had left off, and enroll in high school again. Then I could slowly rebuild my life, perhaps even get into MIT again. If I didn't mess up – and given my track record, that was unlikely – in five years I would be where I was twenty-five years ago. Not that it mattered. Time had lost all meaning, achievements meant nothing, I had already lost more than I could gain in several lifetimes, and I wasn't looking to reach anywhere – except perhaps a warm place.

I was so engrossed in planning my future that I didn't realize I had walked all the way down to the basement instead of the ground floor.

A white middle-aged man with long, Santa Claus hair stood outside what looked like a storage room, smoking a cigarette.

'I'm sorry,' I said and began to walk back up the stairs.

'Will you help me?' he asked.

'Sure,' I said, thinking of the few extra minutes I would spend in the warmth of the building. He probably wanted my help to move some stuff. Maybe he would tip me. I cheered up at the prospect of a double-digit bank balance.

'Come in,' he said.

I followed him into the storage room, which was actually set up as a rumble-down office. A lone wooden desk with a computer and a telephone stood in the centre with two cheap plastic chairs placed on either side. But it was warm, warmer even than upstairs, perhaps because the room had never seen air or sun.

The phone began to ring as soon as we entered.

'Could you tell them that Philip is busy with a team meeting?' he said. 'No, can you say that he is leading a team meeting? Or... no, say he is with clients, but...'

I picked up the phone.

'May I speak to Philip North?' said a woman's voice.

'Mr North is leading a client meeting,' I said.

'Are you his assistant?'

'Yes,' I replied without thinking.

'Could you give him a message to call Mr John Brochkardt at Cerberus Capital? I am Shauna, Mr Brockhardt's assistant.'

'Sure,' I said. 'He will be in meetings all afternoon, but I'll request him to spare some time.'

I put down the phone.

Philip looked at me in awe, a large smile spread across his cheery face. He was about my age, though his white unkempt hair and thick, dark spectacles gave him a weary look. There was a vague, distracted air about him as if his mind was elsewhere, in higher planes than the small, dark room he currently inhabited.

'That was unbelievable, man. Just incredible,' he said. 'I'm Philip North.'

'Nick Bolton.'

He expressed no surprise at hearing an American name from an Indian mouth.

'You caught on really fast, man. I need to give the

impression that I'm busy and have a big, thriving office. Venture capitalists dig that kind of stuff.'

I was suddenly transported twenty years back in time to MIT.

'What are you seeking VC funding for?' I asked.

He warmed up to someone speaking the same language as him, and didn't seem to notice – or care – that I was an armless hobo.

'Oh, I have tons of ideas,' he said. 'You name it, I've got it. Things are really starting to look up. I am developing a live internet gaming device for mobile phones, the biggest online fashion marketplace ever built, and a comprehensive virtual pet shop. The VCs love the ideas; they just want to see the user interface and the business model and then, Eureka! I'm done, retired a billionaire at forty.'

I gave him a suitably appreciative look. There were lots of questions I wanted to ask to make sense of what he had said – online, internet, gaming, etc – but they could wait. I had a more fundamental question to ask first.

'Er… do you need an assistant or an office manager? Someone to handle your phones and stuff?'

'Sure,' he said.

Just like that.

'I mean, can I get a job?' I said, taken aback.

'Of course.'

I stared at him stupidly.

'The only problem is, I can't pay you anything more than minimum wages – twenty dollars a day. But I can pay you in stock. How about ten per cent of the company?'

I stared at him open-mouthed.

'Okay, twenty per cent then. Don't ask for more. Soon your stake will be worth millions, maybe billions of dollars, and you won't know what to do with it,' he said, eyes shining with excitement.

'That's fine,' I said, unable to believe my luck.

'Any other questions?'

'Well… I hate to ask, but can I sleep here at night?'

'Of course,' he said. 'We are partners now.'

A deep silence descended on me in the days that followed. I strove for nothing, I wanted nothing, I felt nothing. I just sat in silence, suspended, it seemed, in a state of un-being. I was used to remaining alone for extended periods of time and this job demanded nothing more. In the beginning, I attended a few phone calls and manufactured stories about Philip's unavailability. Later, I scheduled meetings, but Philip's software code wouldn't be ready so I would re-schedule the meetings. And so it went, taking calls, arranging meetings, scheduling and re-scheduling appointments – work that required neither physical nor mental ability, which suited me perfectly. In the long, lonely nights, I would sit – sometimes on the plastic chair, sometimes on the wooden floor – and think. I would think of the past: losing Mom and Dad; gaining a friend in Sam; losing my arm and my sanity in Cambodia; grudgingly learning to accept my situation in the monastery; finding love and a family in Rio; and losing everything in a moment. I tried to coax a pattern from these events but all I saw were unravelled threads. Where was the tapestry the homeless guy had mentioned? I'd been running in circles for forty years and I was now behind the starting point. Perhaps this was why I saw a kindred soul in Philip.

'Where did you go to school?' he asked one day as I was sitting on the floor, smiling at Lara's earnest expression as she challenged my life-denying Buddhist philosophy.

'MIT,' I replied without thinking.

'Really?' he said, looking up from the computer on which he was always tapping away. 'Which class?'

'I mean, I wanted to go to MIT,' I said hastily. 'But I haven't even completed high school.'

As usual, he was too distracted to notice my slip.

'Oh,' he said. 'I was in the class of 1973.'

Just a couple of years senior to me. Sam and I were in the class of 1975. He would have been in the campus at the same time as I was. But it had been a large campus – almost five thousand students across four classes – and a lot had happened since then, rendering those years almost meaningless.

'That's great,' I said, not knowing what else to say. We rarely talked to each other, comfortable in our individual cocoons. I, in my thoughts and regrets; he, in his programming books and computer.

'It's great if you do something with it,' he said unexpectedly. 'But I have done nothing. My classmates from twenty years ago, and even those many years junior to me, are all millionaires many times over. MIT has produced partners in consulting firms, heads of investment banks, CEOs of Fortune 100 organizations and entrepreneurs of the hottest startups. All of them have big houses, one or maybe more wives, and at least two kids. Everyone has achieved something of consequence.'

There was at least one exception that I knew of, I thought ironically, and I knew him very well indeed.

'I live in a rented apartment with three cats.' He said it so matter-of-factly that we both burst into laughter.

'But you are on the verge of something big,' I said when we had stopped laughing.

'I've been on the verge of something big for twenty years now,' he said. 'I've been moving from job to job, running in circles, searching for the next big thing which always seems to be around the corner – but isn't.'

If the last three months were any indication of how he had lived twenty years, I knew exactly what he meant. He'd been 'about to crack it' every few days, and I had scheduled and re-scheduled venture capitalist meetings until they had stopped calling altogether.

I kept quiet. He looked expectantly at me. Perhaps a word of comfort from one failure to another, his expression said.

'This time it's different, isn't it? You have venture capitalists lining up to fund you,' I said.

'Didn't I tell you about the internet? VCs are breaking down the door of everyone who has a computer. Every twenty-two-year-old kid with a finger has a million dollars in funding from a VC right now. But I've been through this cycle with the telecom boom. I'm not going to make the same mistake again. I will accept VC funding only if I have a plan, else they will sue my ass off later, forcing me to file for another bankruptcy.'

'What about the one-stop pet shop?' I said. 'That's a really cool idea. Who wouldn't want to buy supplies online instead of trudging to the grocery store in this bitter cold?'

He called me over to his desk. 'Look,' he said and opened a slew of websites, all with assorted pictures of dogs, cats, mice, goldfish, horses, guinea pigs, turtles, iguanas, even tigers and snakes. Each website claimed to provide pet food, pet supplies and luxuries, including coupons for spa treatments. 'Nowadays, before you even have an idea, somebody has already executed it.'

'What about the others – the fashion store and the mobile game?'

'All taken.'

He didn't appear sad, just resigned, as if the same thing had happened many different times in many different situations.

'What are you going to do then?' I asked.

'What can I do? I'll keep working, trying new ideas, blowing up my meagre savings, and file for bankruptcy again.' He smiled.

'I'm sure something will work out,' I said soothingly.

He shrugged. 'I can only control the work, not the result. I just need to give the best to what I do.'

I stared at him in surprise. An image I had long tried to forget flashed through my mind. Ishmael gritting his teeth and passing on the secret before he died; a karma yogi, the highest of all beings, performs his karma without attachment to the results thereof.

That night, instead of shutting my eyes and surrendering to thoughts of Lara, or trying to imagine what my son looked like, I began to glance through some of Philip's computer programming books. I had no idea what I wanted to accomplish, only that it was my karma, my duty, to learn – and contribute – to the business I was a partner in and shamelessly pawing daily wages from. A host of unfamiliar terms leapt out of the pages and I tried to shake off the weariness I felt at having to apply my mind to something new again. C, C++, Unix, Linux, Java, Microsoft, Office Suite, http – everything I read about seemed strange and incomprehensible. Computers had changed a lot since I had studied engineering at MIT, I thought; all I remembered studying then was BASIC, which was now referred to only sparsely in the books. I had a lot of catching up to do.

The bleak winter gave way to a bright summer. Every time I ventured out, I was assaulted by happy, smiling faces and athletic bodies jogging without a care around the turquoise Minneapolis lakes, kissing, hugging, laughing, talking, holding hands. I would retreat to the basement office quickly, seeking refuge in the darkness and the computing books. Night after night I read them, slowly piecing together the puzzle of modern computing. Philip, to his credit, turned out to be a more effective teacher than an inventor.

'Read this one first,' he would say, delighted at my newfound interest. 'You need to learn an operating system before you understand programming languages.'

He would mark particular chapters for special attention and quiz me when I finished a book. My mind, which had regressed to its most primal state in the last twenty years – run, fight, survive, eat, shoot, defend, run – relished the inherently mathematical challenges of programming and I began to make a little progress.

'Java is the language of choice for programming now,' Philip told me when I finished learning operating systems. 'But you should start with C; it lays a good foundation. Anyway, what's the hurry?'

There was no hurry. Time had frozen and I was content being in the state I was in, learning without thought, working without ambition, living without desire.

'More than anything else though, you should know all about the internet. It's going to fundamentally change the face of the world. Nothing, I repeat, nothing could possibly be more revolutionary for civilization.'

I began to understand his enthusiasm for the internet in due course and was amazed at its possibilities. No wonder Philip was always bursting with new business ideas and, like Mr Micawber of David Copperfield, believed that the one that would change his life was just round the corner. The ongoing dotcom boom fuelled his fancy and he picked, discarded and re-picked ideas at such frightening speed that I began to tire just hearing about them. Soon, I began doing more and more of my study at night when he was at home feeding his cats.

On one such night, I was trying to create a graphic interface using Java applets and the mobile gaming software that Philip had downloaded on his computer when a message popped up on the screen.

'Wanna chat MITstud? I am 24/F/Istanbul.'

Philip had probably forgotten to log off from the chatroom he had started frequenting recently. He had insisted I use it too, to ward off loneliness, but I desired no companionship. The thought of sharing my life – or even a chatroom – with anyone but Lara repulsed me; my guilt was too deep and solitude was my only balm.

Another message popped up. 'Please, I am lonely.'

I paused. Why was a twenty-four-year-old girl in the capital of vibrant, colourful Turkey lonely? I felt unexpectedly irritated. What did she know about loneliness? Had she ever abandoned a family and run a thousand miles away? I don't know what came over me, but I replied to lonelygirl24.

'You can do a lot more about your loneliness by meeting real people instead of chatting with perverts.'

I thought she'd sign out. Surely she wasn't seeking emotional counsel from 'MITstud'.

But she replied immediately. 'No one likes me in real life.'

My heart thawed just a little bit.

'You are young,' I wrote back. 'Things can be confusing when you are young.'

I was something of an expert at that, after all. I spent my twenty-fourth birthday tied to a wall with a bleeding, dying man at my feet. Things can be *very* confusing when you are young.

'I'm not young,' she said.

I nearly laughed out loud. If she was old, what did that make middle-aged losers like Philip and me? But then, age was relative; the older you got, the more your definition of 'young' kept changing. I was about to pass on this nugget of wisdom to her when a thought struck me. What if she wasn't twenty-four? Lonelygirl24 could be a fifty-five-year-old balding, potbellied, foul-mouthed forklift operator from Ukraine for all I knew. Or she could be a man or a transsexual, how would I know any better?

'Who are you really?' I was about to write, when I stopped.

Did it even matter? Clearly, here was someone who wasn't satisfied with the hand life had dealt her, or him, and had decided to take control and change that in the best way she knew. If she couldn't be young and attractive in the real world, she would be so in the virtual.

I looked for the statistics of the chatroom. Sixty-five thousand members, it said, and most of them were under thirty.

How many were really who they said they were? Were most of them cranky old men with shrivelled dicks parading as young, virile Rambos or lonely old women with ten cats posing as eighteen-year-old virgins? For that matter, even Philip, usually honest to a fault, called himself an 'MITstud', and though he didn't lie about his age, he didn't make it a point to reveal it either. It had been twenty years since I'd thought about what a stud was, but something told me that a broke, middle-aged nerd with three cats wouldn't qualify as one despite his golden heart.

There was another message. 'Talk to me MITstud. No one has talked to me like this before. I am wet and waiting.'

It was a liberating idea. You could be anyone you chose to be. Everything was controlled by *you*. In the real world, fate and destiny teased you, tormented you and tossed you about mercilessly; in the virtual world, you could regain control in a moment. Wouldn't I do so myself, given a chance?

I could go back to being Nikhil Arya and be with a Lara I met in the chatroom; I could even find a little son in the chatroom if I put my mind to it. I would find my family and be happy once again. Would it feel any less real if it happened only in the virtual world? Who said happiness was an emotion confined to the physical world? For that matter, what was real and what was virtual?

'Are you there MIT Stud? I am real.'

'Yes, I know you are real. It's just a matter of perspective after all,' I typed as an idea struck me.

'What?'

I left the chatroom and worked on the idea for the rest of the night.

'You look tired,' said Philip the next day.

I was surprised he even noticed. But I didn't want to tell him my idea just yet. I would develop a prototype before he quit working on everything else, as he was prone to do every time he heard a new idea.

'I was wondering if you could teach me three-dimensional user interfaces,' I said.

As usual, he had time to spare. We spent the rest of the day working on graphical interfaces.

'You are really good,' he said when we finished.

'I'm good?' I laughed. 'You are the one teaching me!'

'I've never seen anyone pick up things this quick,' he said.

'How many people have you even *seen*?' I smiled at him.

'You are way quicker than me, for one,' he said. His eyes narrowed. 'You said you've never been to school? That's funny.'

'It's not funny when you don't get the chance,' I said with as much self-righteousness as I could muster.

'When I think about it, you are quicker than almost all my MIT classmates – even the ones who are hotshot technology entrepreneurs now. I can't believe you didn't go to school,' he repeated with a shake of his head.

I kept quiet lest I say something damaging.

'I used to teach my classmates at MIT when they fell behind,' he continued when I didn't answer. 'Now, of course, I'm the one who has fallen behind.'

'I'm sure you will catch up soon,' I said, glad that he had changed the subject. But it wasn't for long.

'Tell me, how did you lose your arm? You know, it suddenly struck me that we've been together for so long – more than a year now, right? Yet, we don't know a thing about each other.'

The less you know about me, the safer we both will be, I thought. I am bad news: a mobster, a fugitive, a deserter. Every time there is a fork in the road, I take the wrong turn.

'Did you grow up in India?' he asked. 'You look Indian, but you are tall and don't sound like one. You don't even sound American actually. You have this curious mix of so many accents like a… you know…'

'A mongrel,' I said with a forced laugh.

This conversation had to stop, I thought, nothing good could ever come of it.

'No, no, no,' he said. 'I didn't mean that at all. I mean you… you must have travelled a lot.'

'A little,' I said guardedly.

'Were you in the Peace Corps?'

I almost laughed. First in Cambodia, then in Brazil, I had seen more blood, guns and violence than anyone should see in one lifetime – and done just about nothing to stop it. I would hardly be on the Peace Corps recruit lists.

'No,' I said. 'But I had a friend who worked for the Peace Corps.' I thought of David. He was in a monastery, not the Peace Corps, but it was close. I was filled with unexpected emotion. 'He was a good man, a very good man indeed. Were you in the Peace Corps at any time?'

'Not me,' he said. 'But I sometimes wish I had decided to pursue a career in non-profit. Not that I am generating a lot of profit here.' He smiled. 'I'm just not cut out for this – business models, VCs, cash flows, pre-empting competition, etc.'

I clucked sympathetically.

'Have you worked in a non-profit before?' he asked.

I couldn't handle this any more. 'Philip, it's getting late. Don't you have to take care of the cats?'

He looked at his watch.

'Oh, it's nine already! Tell you what, why don't we grab a beer tomorrow and talk? We rarely get out of office. It will be a nice break, won't it?'

Just the break I was looking for, I thought. One thing could lead to another, and this entire pack of cards would collapse – like it had so often before. My life was shot anyway. I would end up wrecking Lara's life too – if I hadn't already done so.

'Sure,' I said.

I wouldn't let it happen. I would have to discuss my idea with him tomorrow as I began to work on the prototype. I had to get him off his newfound obsession with my background. I forced myself to concentrate on the code I was writing.

'Are you ready?'

I looked up from the computer to see Philip in a Hawaiian T-shirt and yellow flip-flops.

'Yo boy! Today is our team offsite. Have you forgotten?' he said cheerily. 'Why are you working so early? And what are you working on anyway?'

I blinked and looked at the time on the computer screen. Ten a.m. I hadn't moved from my seat in fifteen hours.

'Anyway, forget all this,' he said. 'I thought we'd catch an early lunch and take the rest of the day off. It's a beautiful morning. We could grab some beer and kayak on Lake Calhoun. What say?'

I flicked a tongue over my gums to remove the bitter taste of the sleepless night. 'I've been working on an idea I wanted to share with you,' I said groggily.

'Can't it wait?' he said, looking a bit hurt. 'I thought we could have some fun today for a change, get to know each better and stuff. I was thinking about your accent last night. You know, I had a friend from Brazil in MIT, and you have the same twang. Were you – '

'Sorry to cut you off, Phil,' I said, my heart skipping a beat. 'Why don't we talk about my travels in the kayak? I don't want to be late for our fun time! I thought I'd quickly show you the idea before we left.'

He didn't look very happy but he bent over the desk.

'So, it's a kind of computer game, but not entirely. It's really a whole world in itself…' I began taking him through the prototype, feeling the same knot in my stomach that I'd felt when I told Marco about the business plan for expanding beyond the drug trade.

'You did all of this in one night?' he said when I'd finished.

'I've been thinking about it for a while.'

'This is impressive,' he said. 'Un-fucking-believably impressive. And you've checked that there is nothing like it out there?'

I nodded. 'Not that I could find.'

'Are you sure you never went to school? I mean, MIT PhDs couldn't do this stuff in years. And you did it in a day? You are a bloody genius, like I always knew.'

Please don't get started on that, I pleaded silently.

'What do you think about the technicalities?' I said. 'Can we make it work?'

'*You* can make it work,' he replied. 'Yes, I am sure you can. This is already almost there. Don't give me credit for anything.'

'We are partners, remember?' I said. 'Eighty per cent of this is yours. Besides, I couldn't care less. I just want to build this for, err, personal reasons.'

'What personal reasons?'

'It doesn't matter.'

Thankfully, he let that pass.

'I can help you take it to the VCs,' he said. 'At this pace, we could go as early as a week from now.'

'You think so?'

'You have to agree to my terms, though. This is *your* idea. We reverse the agreement. You get eighty, I get twenty.'

'That's unacceptable, Philip,' I said. 'You taught me everything. I used your office, your computer, your books, your knowledge. It has to be…'

He cut me short. 'Don't insist,' he said quietly. 'The only thing I have left, twenty years after graduating from MIT, is some kind of honour. Don't take that away from me. Besides, I think this will be so successful that I could retire on just one per cent.'

I nodded reluctantly.

He began to get more excited and to my delight, the kayaking trip was soon forgotten.

'I can do the soft stuff – the pitch, presentation, marketing, bells and whistles; you concentrate on the real stuff. We don't need anything fancy, just enough to host the website live and get a few subscribers. Can you do that in a week?'

I nodded.

'Then all we need are good answers to the objections that the venture capitalists raise,' he said.

'What objections?'

'Nothing you should worry about. They just like to ask tough questions to check whether you've thought everything through. It'll be a breeze for you.'

'What kinds of questions?' I asked, worried that there would be questions about my background again.

'Believe me, that's the least of your worries. They are just normal questions about you and the project.'

About *me*, I thought, now seriously concerned. If it came to that, I would rather abandon the project.

'What questions?' I persisted.

He gave me a surprised look. 'What's the matter with you? If you are so worried, let me just do a dry run with you, okay?'

A dry run wasn't what I had in mind at all, but he started before I could come up with a good excuse.

'How is your website different from a computer game?' he began.

'Oh, those kind of questions!' I said in relief.

'Yes, what did you think? Go on, answer me now.'

'Well, nothing about our website is like a game...' I began.

'No, don't be condescending,' he said. 'They are the ones with the money, after all.'

'Okay, try this,' I said. 'Another Life, or anotherlife. com, is much more than a computer game. It's an alternate life, a complete world in itself, a virtual world where a player can be anyone he wants to be, live anywhere he likes, be with anyone he chooses to be with, do anything he pleases. There is no victory or defeat, no points to gain or lose; just being in this virtual world is winning.'

'That sounds corny,' said Philip, playing the role of a VC. 'If there is no game, what would people do in Another Life?'

'Well, they would live in the virtual world – exactly as they live in the physical world they inhabit every day,' I said. 'They would take on a name and an onscreen image that represents them in the virtual world. They would work for a living in the virtual world, earn virtual money, own virtual property, drive virtual cars, go for virtual vacations, buy virtual things, meet other virtual people like themselves; talk, love, mate, marry – or choose to do none of these things and just be a name and an image. It's just like living life... another life beyond the real world, hence the name. All they have to do is sit at their computers and manipulate their virtual selves with a click of the mouse.'

'But what's the point then? Why would you go to a website in your free time to live exactly the same way you live in the physical world? People come online to take a break from their mundane real-world existence and become warriors who slay dragons and explorers who conquer the solar system. Why log in to live the dull lives they sought to escape in the first place?'

'Because there is one big difference,' I said. 'You have choices here. You are in control of your destiny, your situation; you aren't a mere pawn in a larger, incomprehensible game. The website allows you to choose your own identity, complete with an onscreen image that you can create from the huge menu of virtual body and skin elements, and attire from multiple catalogues of virtual clothes. For instance, if you are someone who wants to be young forever, you can be a ripped hunk in Another Life. With a click of your mouse, you can manipulate your image on screen and there is your icon – young forever, partying all night, meeting attractive young women, becoming a DJ at a nightclub – whatever you want. Can you imagine how liberating that is? Here is a defeated, fifty-year-old, balding, divorced accountant who made a series of wrong choices that left him broke and full of regret. Now, he can take control again. For twenty-four hours a day, he can be young, healthy and rich, an object of envy – in contrast to the real world, where everyone looks at him with pity and derision. Is his happiness at this change in situation any less because it is only in a virtual universe? He sits on the chair in front of his computer and, without any change in his physical self, with one click of the mouse, he is in Another Life; young and happy, a master of his fate and immune to the cruel twists of destiny. He interacts with everyone on the website with his alter ego; nobody he meets in Another Life cares about who he is in the physical world.'

'Your eloquence is impressive, but how is this different from lying about yourself in a chat room?' Philip asked. 'The internet is full of places where old men are posing as young men to lure nubile girls. How is this any different?'

'You said it yourself. They are *lying*. The people they are chatting with don't know that they are posing as someone other than themselves, but they do care if they find out. In Another Life, no one will care because it doesn't matter. You choose to live an alternate life. You choose who you are going to be and people choose to talk to you – or not – based on who you are in *this* environment. All other dimensions of space and time cease to exist. You are living in a parallel world as real as the physical world.'

'What is your business model?' he asked.

'The same business model that exists in the physical world! I told you, Another Life is an alternate, more pleasing reality; everything else is the same. We charge money for people to enter the website just as they pay taxes to live in the physical world. People earn money when they work in offices in Another Life; they spend it on the goods and services we offer in Another Life. The manufacturers of the goods and services, in turn, employ people whom they pay a salary. In a simplistic scenario, our young hunk would earn his wages in a virtual BMW manufacturing factory and spend it on a virtual BMW, while we make money on sales tax. It's self-sustaining. Money comes in, money goes out; and we get a margin on the operation.'

'It's an interesting idea, but it isn't tangible; it's all make-believe. How can you live an alternate life in a virtual world, when you know it isn't real?'

'But what is real, sir? How do you define real? Isn't everything around us fundamentally incomprehensible? Where do you and I, the mountains and rivers, the stars and planets which you consider "real" come from? You will say it is evolution, but what was point zero? What was the origin? Hindus think of the world as a maya jaal, an illusion. If that real world is an illusion, then so is this; and if that is real, so is this – only better. In Another Life, you can be a lawyer if you want to be a lawyer, instead of becoming a paralegal bulled by a lawyer just because of destiny or your own limited abilities.'

'Bravo,' he said. 'Your software is robust, your business model is strong, but it's your passion for the project that is most inspiring. It seems that you feel a compelling need to own your destiny?'

'I've lost so much that I am tired of losing,' I said mechanically. 'Every time I build something, it crashes. Then I build again and it crashes, and so it goes. Here, I will preserve what I build forever. If this were Brazil…'

I suddenly noticed Philip listening intently to me, and snapped out of it.

'Did I do okay?' I asked.

'You will be a legend,' he said warmly. 'I haven't heard anything quite like this before. They'll whip out their passbooks faster than Jenna Jameson reaches an orgasm.'

'Jenna who?'

'Never mind,' he said. 'Why did you stop? What happened in Brazil?'

'Not relevant,' I said shortly.

He eyed me curiously.

'Should I line up venture capitalist meetings then?' I asked.

'I'm your assistant now. I will do that.'

I began to protest.

'Please,' he said. 'Don't embarrass me further. For

twenty years, I've been chasing mirages and blaming my failure on fate. Today, you made me realize that it was my ability that was at fault, not my destiny – and I find it oddly liberating.'

'But…' I began.

He cut me off. 'You don't understand, but this helps me. I'm no longer a victim. I'm no longer envious of the success of others. I am a second-hander who is meant to follow, not lead.' He paused. 'One week from now should be okay, right?'

I nodded. 'I can build enough of an online community on a beta site to get initial feedback.'

'I still can't believe you haven't even been to school,' he said wondrously.

'Err… Philip, another thing, and please take this the right way,' I said. 'Would you mind if I worked outside the office for the next couple of weeks? I will be able to concentrate better, I think.'

Certainly I would be more efficient if I wasn't constantly worrying about my past being uncovered.

'I totally understand,' he said.

I hope not, I thought.

'I can set you up in a hotel close by,' he continued. 'I have a little money in my retirement account from when I was a research assistant at MIT.'

'Oh, no need for that,' I replied. 'I have a place in mind.'

He looked confused. How could I possibly

know the city when I had never ventured out of the office?

'Don't worry,' I said. 'I will call you once a day to give you an update.'

I meant to call him – and probably would have, had it not been for the events that transpired the first night in the shelter.

'Welcome to Another Life,' I typed, awaiting my first set of unsuspecting visitors while I fiddled around with the graphics of the virtual environment. A greener tree, a bluer tinge to the sky, a deeper sea, a brighter star, shinier cars, more elaborate buildings – a replica of the real world, only richer. In direct contrast to the plush surroundings of the Another Life environment, I sat in a chair without a backrest in a small, infrequently visited storage room in the homeless shelter. The room was dark, save the flicker of light from my computer screen, but darkness was an old friend now and I was most at peace when I was in it. No one probed into my chequered past here, though from time to time, someone would come in, smelling of sweat and vomit, quietly take a hit from a crack pipe, and leave without saying a word.

Soon, the first few online visitors dropped in.

They asked questions, they raised objections, they fought the rule of purging your physical identity when you entered, they got angry at the make-believe nature of the game – but they stayed.

As the night progressed, Another Life acquired a hunky firefighter, a female astronaut, a few actors and models, a policeman, an engineer and a doctor. Almost all of them chose to create lean, tanned and fit avatars, though some adorned theirs with glasses and briefcases. Most identified themselves as single but some came with spouses who were as colourfully employed as they were. They interacted with each other as folks in the physical world would, only, they typed instead of speaking. No one seemed to feel the absence of speech, though. Words typed in the text boxes that I designed to look like speech bubbles were enough for the models to hit on the firefighter, the doctor to dispense advice on a myriad ailments, the astronaut to describe how the moon looked from close, and the engineers to discuss the insides of the virtual black Jaguar parked outside the virtual building. Maybe they were models and astronauts in real life, maybe they weren't, but this was what they were in Another Life, and they were treated as such. In a matter of hours, the community had grown to thirty people and no one seemed to be in a hurry to leave. A universe had begun to form.

In the darkness of the room, I didn't even realize when it was morning. Soon, people began to sign out with passionate promises to return in the evening. When I probed them for feedback, they wrote that they had enjoyed the break from their mundane jobs, nagging spouses and ordinary, indifferent lives; it felt as though they had reclaimed their entire lives in the few hours they had spent on the site. Well worth another sleepless night, I thought, as I rubbed my weary eyes. I began to get out of my chair to inform Philip about our initial success when something caught my eye.

'Lara,' I typed, stunned.

A spitting image of Lara, wearing the black cocktail dress that she had worn when we met for our first date, stared at me from my computer screen. She was walking on blades of grass (as she often liked to do), and had stopped in front of an office building. She turned her head to look at the building and my heart skipped a beat.

Had she noticed the sign?

A lifetime ago, when Lara and I had made love for the first time, I had told her about the statue of the smiling Buddha in the monastery, which had haunted me for years. Initially, the half-knowing, half-condescending smile had angered me; later, it had become a symbol of the transience and impermanence of life. Nothing mattered, the Buddha seemed to say, everything you craved was ultimately an illusion. Now that I was rebuilding my life, I had embedded the icon in every structure

I created in Another Life, blending it into the background so no one would notice. Everything could crash once again, it reminded me. It had happened before, it could happen again, but ultimately, even loss was transient.

She continued to look at the sign. Could it really be her? But that would be too easy, and the one thing my life could never be was easy. But how else would she know about the sign? Why had her icon stopped in front of it? Why was she wearing the same cocktail dress that haunted my mind every time I shut my eyes? My heart skipped a beat – maybe *this* was the mosaic, the reason why I came to Minnesota and ended up in Philip's office. Maybe she had been online warding off loneliness – just like me – and chanced upon the website, and realized immediately that I was the creator. But no, it couldn't be, that was just too fanciful.

'Lara,' my fingers typed of their own volition. 'It's me.'

I navigated the mouse to move my icon closer to hers. If it was her, she would recognize me in an instant. I had no desire to be younger, taller or better looking, and my icon mirrored my person, including a missing arm.

She looked away from the building and stared at me.

'And who is me?' she typed.

My heart fell. I had wished so fervently for it

to be her that I'd almost believed it. Of course it couldn't be her. Such a coincidence wasn't logical. Maybe there was still a chance though, I thought desperately. Marco might have told her why I left Brazil. Maybe she was worried that the Godmother was following her actions in this universe as well; maybe she wanted to be certain before she revealed herself.

'It really is me. Nikhil. I created this – for us.'

She didn't respond. Anyone could pose as me and say those words, I thought. That she didn't respond was itself a sign of her typical calm and repose. I would have to be more specific to convince her that it really was me. My icon was almost touching hers now, as I manipulated it closer using the keyboard. I pointed to the building and the car and the trees.

'Don't you see the signs, Lara? Who else could have made this? Everything is in the past now – La Madrina, prison, the drug trade, Rio – nothing can touch us here. You and me, here and now, that's all that matters.'

Again she didn't speak, but she didn't walk away.

'I missed you, Lara. I can't even begin to tell you how much I missed you. I am sorry for everything. I am so…'

She cut off my message as I was typing.

'I missed you too, Nikhil,' she typed back.

I felt a crushing wave of joy envelop me. Was this really her? How had this happened? Why had she come here? Was this just a coincidence or had she known? But how would she have known? No one knew that I had created this website, except Philip. But why was the icon wearing the same black dress that Lara knew I loved? I bombarded her with messages. Her response was stoically simple.

'Remember what you said? You and me, here and now; that's all there is. I don't want to talk about the past.'

I was puzzled. We had shared the most beautiful moments of our lives together. Did she really want to forget them? But I had also hurt her deeply. I could understand why she wanted to start afresh.

'Did you name our baby?' I asked. 'Our baby,' I repeated, liking the way the words appeared on screen.

She kept quiet.

'What happened?' I asked, terrified.

'Let's not go there,' she said.

What had happened to our son? I was petrified, but what right did I have to ask? I had deserted them in their greatest need. Something must have transpired in my absence, perhaps she didn't want me to be crippled by guilt.

'I'm sorry, honey,' I said. 'I am so terribly sorry for everything.'

She replied, 'Love means never having to say you are sorry.'

I was surprised. Wasn't that a cheesy line from a

pulp novel she didn't care for? Almost two years, I reminded myself, two long, miserable years. She had gone through so much in that time; she must have sought solace in familiarity.

After that, I spent every moment I could glued to my chair; only my fingers on the mouse moved, edging my icon closer to Lara's so we could always be together – although it gnawed at me that we didn't share the same chemistry any more. Her silences were longer, our conversations seemed stilted, and she studiously avoided all mention of our past, our son, and the future. I blamed it on the conditions in which we parted and the trauma of our separation. With time, I was sure we would rekindle what we had shared, for I felt a joy that I could feel only in Lara's presence. If it felt right, it was right, I thought. It had to be right.

Day and night lost all meaning for me in that small dark storeroom. When she signed out in the evening (to take care of our son, I thought hopefully) I would start working on the virtual environment, adding tools and options that I thought would please her. I knew she loved going to local hole-in-the-wall bars, so I built a slew of virtual bars that played the quaint thirties music she loved. Only, her tastes seemed to have changed and she now preferred raucous nightclubs – perhaps a reflection of the turmoil I had caused in her life – so I scattered the streets with discotheques and pubs instead. She used to love running on the beach, so I created a turquoise blue ocean with gleaming, animated sand alongside. But it seemed that she now preferred hiking in the mountains, so I created several virtual snow-capped mountains. Once, she had read books voraciously, now she preferred movies, so I created both libraries and movie theatres. I created schools for children to hint at our future plans and she did take the bait – but not in the shy, touchingly beautiful way I remembered.

'Why are you being so nice to me?' she asked.

'Do I need to tell you that I love you?' I said.

'But where is this going? Where will it go?'

'I want us to plan our future now that things have settled down.'

I guided my image closer to hers. Finally, it seemed like we were getting back to the way things had been.

Purposefully, we walked to a small cove in the virtual ocean where no one seemed to be present. I moved my virtual icon next to hers and kissed her. She didn't resist and kissed me back. I silently made a note to add more hidden enclosures in Another Life. As a result of all the changes I had made to please Lara, our virtual community was now ten thousand people strong; everywhere you went, you ran into happy, laughing figures.

Lara seemed to have lost her earlier inhibitions about public displays of affection. Her image undressed itself and her warm, supple body, looking every bit like it did in the physical world, came into view.

'What are you waiting for?' she said.

A rush of desire overcame me. I had missed her touch, her feel, her soft, suggestive voice. I couldn't hold myself back any longer. Our figures moved rhythmically on the screen.

'Harder, harder,' she cried. 'Make me come, you bastard. Fuck me hard. There, yes, faster, faster.'

This didn't sound like Lara. Unlike some of the other girls I had been with before I had met her, Lara never talked dirty when we made love. She would sigh deeply and bite me hard when she was reaching an orgasm, but she never shrieked in ecstasy.

'Now take me from behind. Do it *now*.'

Lara had never liked it from behind. She had probably been with another man, since – which was fine with me. I was the one who had wanted her to move on.

'Take me like a bitch. Make me scream, you bastard. Faster, faster, move your package.'

Her body writhed under mine, and though it was hard to reconcile her newfound passion for rough sex with the gentle, loving memory of our past, her obvious pleasure excited me into an...

'Computer porn, eh?'

The beam from a flashlight blinded me.

'Turn that off,' I said.

The words rolled out of my mouth with great difficulty. I tried to stand up, feeling light-headed and disoriented. I fell back but missed the chair and crashed to the floor instead. Where was I?

'You look like hell. Are you high?'

I shook my head. A thin young man with acne on his face stood before me holding the flashlight. With his crew cut hair, he looked like alfred62, one of the first members of the Another Life community.

'Alfred,' I said.

Every time I opened my mouth to speak, my head began to pound.

'Is your name Alfred?' he asked.

I shook my head. It hurt.

'I am Jason, one of the volunteers at the shelter,' he said. 'You look very weak. Have you eaten anything?'

Hunger was an old friend, I thought vaguely. I didn't need food. I had no time for food. I slowly dragged myself up and managed to sit on the chair. Lara seemed to have vanished from the screen. I moved the cursor frantically but I couldn't see her anywhere. Where was she? I couldn't lose her again. Every minute spent without her was futile.

'Lara, Lara,' I whispered and began to search desperately for her once again.

It felt as if a hand was touching my forehead. But I couldn't see anybody on the screen.

'You have high fever. It looks like you haven't slept in a while.'

Who was speaking? I looked around wildly. I couldn't see anybody on the screen.

Someone shook me. 'Are you there?'

I still couldn't see anyone.

Someone shook me violently. I turned around. It was Alfred but I couldn't see him on the screen. My mind was playing tricks on me, I thought. I needed a break, but there was still one thing I needed to do before tomorrow when Lara came back again.

'Listen, brother…'

'Get out,' I snarled.

'You should eat something, brother. You look like you are about to die.'

'Please leave me alone,' I shouted. 'Please, please,' I begged as I typed.

'Okay, man. Relax, will you?'

My head hurt and my eyes began to water as I returned to the computer. I still couldn't see Lara anywhere despite searching frantically through the entire span of Another Life. She would be angry at the interruption, I thought, and I cursed alfred82 for being so insensitive. How could he say I looked unwell? Just look at me standing tall, well-built and healthy, not an ounce of excess fat on my body.

I would make it up to Lara when she came back tomorrow. I spent the next few hours working on a surprise for her.

*

'It wasn't my fault. I'm sorry,' I pleaded as soon as I spotted her on the screen the next day.

'When is it ever your fault?' said Lara.

'A guy nearly tore my only arm apart,' I tried to joke.

'Which guy? There was no one around.'

'Let's not talk about it, please.'

The numbness seemed to spread from the tips of my fingers to my right shoulder. The phantom pain in my left arm had returned, strong and crippling, as it had been when it was first amputated. I felt dizzy and faint – hardly in the best condition to take this significant step. But it couldn't wait. Over the last few hours, I had felt as though Lara was slowly drifting away. She was colder and more reserved than usual, she remained tight-lipped about our past and showed even less interest in talking about the future. All she seemed to enjoy was sex. I didn't want to lose her again. I wanted to see our son – hold him, touch him, feel him, play with him; I wanted to know how Marco was; I wanted my old life back. Given time, I knew I would thaw her. All I needed was time – and commitment.

'I have a surprise for you,' I said.

'I hate surprises.'

I took it out.

'What is this? A cock ring?' she asked.

'No, silly,' I said affectionately. 'It's a ring alright, but a more special kind. Can't you guess what it is?'

'What special kind? Come on, I told you I hate surprises.'

Although I looked sturdy, I felt a sudden wave of nausea. It wasn't hard to go down on my knees.

'Lara, will you marry me – again? This time I won't let you down.'

There was so much more I had to say. I wanted to tell her how much I loved her, how I hadn't known or believed in love until she entered my life, and how empty every moment was that I spent apart from her. I wanted her to know that I would be a better father to our son than I had been a husband to her.

She didn't respond for what seemed like an eternity.

'Everything will be just like it used to be,' I managed to say.

I moved closer to her, feeling fainter and dizzier.

'Get away from me, you freak,' she said. 'Oh heck, it's my fault. What am I doing playing this silly game anyway?'

It didn't sound like Lara at all.

'Lara, please…'

'Enough already with this Lara nonsense, psycho,' she said. 'Who is she anyway?'

What was happening? I began to shiver uncontrollably. The nausea came to the fore and I vomited all over the floor, clutching my stomach in pain. Strangely though, I didn't move and remained standing right next to her, looking fit and healthy as ever.

'I am not feeling well, Lara,' I said. 'I don't know what's happening.'

'I am *not* Lara,' she said.

'But you are. Why are you saying that? You…'

'Jesus, why am I even typing this nonsense? Listen, creep. I put together my image from the menu of skin tones, elements and clothes available on this website because the combination resembled a supermodel in a fancy Brazilian clothes catalogue I had recently seen. If I looked like her in real life, do you think I'd be wasting my time on this stupid online game?'

'But…' I suddenly felt exhausted and my eyes began to close of their own will.

'I thought you were like a cute puppy dog initially. But I should have known you would turn all psycho on me,' she said.

Had it all been a lie then? But I had felt her presence. Could I have imagined it?

'Did you really create this? Some job you've done here,' she said. 'It's the greatest collection of nuts in the world.'

The image on the screen wasn't me, I thought suddenly. *I* was me, here in this... where was I?

'It's twisted in a cool way, though. But tell me, why would a brilliant guy like you behave like such a jerk?'

Why indeed, I thought, as I regained consciousness and stared at the white ceiling of the bare, neat hospital room that I shared with four others. A plethora of tubes were connected to my body, and I felt heavy. But my head felt clear – or about as clear as could be expected after coming out of a major psychotic episode. I could recall every detail of the madness that had seized me over the past few weeks – but I had no idea why it had happened.

'The nurse told me you are awake now.' Someone had entered the room. I recognized him at once as the kind, acne-scarred volunteer who had interrupted me once during my psychosis.

'How long...' I began, and started coughing incessantly. I felt my torso under the covers – skin and bones, but nowhere as bad as it had been in Cambodia. The one benefit of screwing up so many times, I thought detachedly, was that no matter what you did, you'd probably done worse before.

'Take it easy, man,' said the volunteer who I had mistaken for alfred82. 'You are suffering from severe starvation, fatigue and pneumonia. I checked your in date. You hadn't left that room in four weeks.'

An entire month, I thought with a sinking sensation; all the VC meetings must be long over. I hadn't contacted Philip since the day I left. He had trusted me to the point of giving me his only computer and I had let him down. What would he be thinking? That I had run away and partnered with someone else so that I didn't have to share the profits with him?

'Jesus Christ! I don't think I've seen a stranger thing,' the volunteer said, shaking his head. 'What was happening in that room? Were you working on that damn computer all the time? I've seen a crack addict saw off his little finger and a meth junkie give a blow job to sixteen men in a row for just one hit of a crack pipe, but I have never seen anything quite like this. What were you thinking?'

I drew a blank myself. What had made me lose my sanity until I could no longer tell the difference between the virtual and the physical world? Everything had blurred together – real, virtual; fact, fiction; day, night – yet it had made sense. I had wanted it to make sense so badly that I had abandoned all rationality. Unconsciously, I had recreated Lara in minute detail from her skin tone to her wardrobe, and someone had combined these to create an image that I mistook for her. But I had wanted to make that mistake. I had become a pathetic addict of a game I had created myself. And what was worse, I had made Philip suffer – he must be shattered at the sabotage of his dream project. He would never trust anyone again.

'The doctor says you are suffering from some kind of extreme post traumatic stress disorder because of severe psychological trauma in your past,' said the volunteer. 'But I don't know all that fancy stuff. All I know is that you are lucky to be alive.'

It would be so easy, I thought. Marco had once told me that it was easiest to kill someone in a hospital – all it required was an air bubble to enter the veins. I looked up at the catheter. Just a little pressure at the valve, and a bubble would enter my blood stream and choke me. But I knew I was too yellow to get even that right.

'Are you okay, man?' the volunteer asked. 'Do you need something?'

For what it was worth, Philip needed to know that despite my insanity, our idea had attracted hundreds of people. Maybe he could still do something with it.

'Could you send this computer to an address, please?' I managed to say between bouts of coughing that made me double up in agony.

'Gladly.'

I wrote a brief note to Philip, explaining the

additions I had made to the website since he had last seen it. I didn't write an apology, nor mention my psychosis. Words weren't sufficient to express how I felt, and I didn't try.

'I have no money to pay for the hospital,' I said.

'Don't worry about that,' the volunteer said kindly. 'It's covered by the Goodwill Army and other charity donations to the shelter. As you can imagine, coming here is a regular occurrence for us – if not exactly in these circumstances.'

What had I reduced myself to, I wondered. At forty, I was broke and homeless, addicted to a computer game like a five-year-old might be, feeding on the charity of good people born in far less privileged circumstances than I was. Would there be any end to my debasement? This time I couldn't blame destiny, nor could I blame La Madrina or the Khmer Rouge. I had run out of people and situations to attribute my failures to.

'Do you need anything else?' he asked gently. 'Otherwise I must hustle along. These days, I have to look out for guys with computers as much as guys with needles!'

I looked at his smiling face. A life spent helping others, I thought. All I'd done was think of myself, and what a thorough job I had done of that! I looked at the catheter valve longingly. Just one turn, I thought. But no, I would try to die with courage – if not with dignity.

'Would you please get me a phone?' I managed to say.

'At your service, Mr President.' He laughed.

He left the room while I stared blankly at the ceiling, and returned moments later with a phone.

'Thank you,' I said. 'I hope I get a chance to repay you in a different life.'

He touched my hand. 'Take care, brother,' he said gently. He paused. 'Shit happens. What looks like a series of unravelled threads from close is actually a pattern from a distance. Just give it time.'

I had heard those words before but I was too distracted to remember where. All I could think about was the phone number Marco had forced me to commit to memory as a last resort. It was finally time to call him. I was left with nothing, and this time I had no desire to try and build anything. For everyone's sake, I was better off dead than alive. I would gladly pay any price he demanded.

'Yes,' barked a thick, unrecognizable accent from the other end.

'Marco told me...' I began.

'Call me from a pay phone,' he said and disconnected.

I called him from a pay phone after a few hours. I had been discharged and was wearing the same clothes I had worn when I'd first come to Minnesota a couple of years ago.

'I called a few hours back...' I began.

'Yes,' he said in his thick accent. 'I've been thinking about it. Do you want to die more than you want to live?'

However surprising the question, I didn't need to think about it for too long.

'Yes,' I said without hesitation.

'Can you go to Asia in a couple of days? To India or Thailand or Vietnam?' he asked.

I thought for a moment.

'Only India,' I said. A poetic end to an unpoetic life; from ashes to ashes, from dust to dust; back to the place where this whole miserable journey had begun.

'I can do just one assignment,' I added. 'I have no will for more.'

'I don't deal in small stuff,' he said. 'It's all or nothing.'

Click.

The sharp sound of the blank was followed by a sudden silence. Then there was clapping, hesitant at first, but soon it rose to a crescendo like the roll of funeral drums. Someone thumped my back, another shook my hand which still held the smoking gun, someone else banged on the table.

'You did well. You won half a million rupees,' said the handler. 'Now hand him the gun.'

I passed the gun to Dayaram. He took it with trembling hands. I looked into his eyes. He seemed to have lost his fear and held the gun to his temple with an air of inevitability.

The crowd cheered wildly.

Finally, an end to a saga that couldn't have been better scripted in a Hindi film: five bullets blank, the last bullet would draw blood. I watched dispassionately as Dayaram released the barrel and placed his finger on the trigger. He began to pull the trigger…

In one swift movement, I reached across the table and pulled the revolver from his hand.

Dayaram looked at me blankly, his empty hand still pointing towards his temple. The applauding crowd fell silent.

'What the fuck?' The tight muscles in the handler's neck twitched as he reached for the gun.

I jumped up from my seat and pointed the gun between his eyes.

'Don't move,' I said. 'There is a bullet here and you know I won't miss.'

A hush fell upon the crowd.

I looked around at the surprised faces. Bastards, I thought with sudden anger, they lived lives that people like us could only wish for; if drama was what they craved, I'd gladly exchange my life for theirs.

Now that the gun was pointed at them, however, their quest for a thrill seemed to have ended.

'Come with me,' I shouted at Dayaram.

He was still rooted to his spot with his hand on his temple.

'Daya,' I said sharply. He seemed to wake from a trance. 'Follow me.'

I began to inch backwards towards the door with my gun still pointed at the handler. I didn't care about the others. They could easily jump me if they wanted to, but I knew they wouldn't. If they were so insulated from death that they paid money to seek it out, they wouldn't have the guts to face it themselves. Violence was entertaining only as long as others were spilling blood.

'You know we will find you,' said the handler flatly.

I had no doubt that they would and I didn't care. I had come here to die. Instead, I had almost killed another man. No, I couldn't die with more blood on my hands.

'I don't want the money. You take it back,' I said, gun still level. I pointed at Daya. 'I just want him alive.'

'You can't do this for me...' began Daya.

'Shut up,' I said, pointing the gun at him as we reached the door.

He followed me quietly.

We left the basement room and I locked the door

carefully behind me. Almost immediately, the men inside began pounding on the door.

'We have five minutes before someone comes,' I said. 'He would have called already. Just follow me. Don't ask questions.'

We ran up the stairs and rushed past the closed furniture showroom and onto the busy street.

There was still too much light for us to merge into the crowd. It would be dark soon, a long familiar ally; until then, we had to drop out of sight. I saw a lifeline and ran towards the main road.

'My friend has an auto-rickshaw here, sahib,' Daya panted behind me. For an old man with a cancer ridden body, he ran surprisingly well.

'They will track him down,' I said. 'We need to take a bus.'

I looked down the street and saw a public bus rumble in our direction. 'This one,' I shouted. I managed to hold on to the railing with my arm and hopped on, closely followed by Dayaram.

I stood still in the middle of the crowded bus, sweat pouring down my face as the bus rolled forward, weaving through the crowded intersection in Mayapuri where Sam and I had once knocked down a cyclist while learning to ride a Lambretta, past the Rachna theatre in Patel Nagar where we often went after bunking school, the Moti Mahal in Karol Bagh, my mother's favourite restaurant – Delhi was full of happy, uncomplicated memories from the days before I began this Faustian journey of self-destruction. We passed my old school on Pusa Road. I'd been the head boy once, the captain of the basketball and football teams, everyone's unanimous pick for the one who would be the most successful in life. Would my old teachers be alive? What would they say if I walked in right now in my torn clothes, sans an arm, broke and homeless, a man who had deserted his family and was wanted by drug barons and the police in multiple countries?

'Where are we going, sahib?' Daya asked timidly as we stood next to each other in the bus.

'Haan?' I said, shaking out of my reverie. 'Where does this bus go?'

'CP,' he said.

Another blast from the past. 'Connaught Place?' I said. 'I will go there.' I paused. 'You will be safe. You did nothing wrong, so they won't come after you. You don't need to run with me. Go back and die with grace.'

'Why did you save me, sahib? Why didn't you just take the money and go?'

'Money doesn't stick to my hands,' I replied. 'Why do you need it so much?'

'I told you I'm dying of cancer, sahib. My life means nothing,' he said. 'My daughter is getting married tomorrow and the groom's family will call it off if we don't give them money.'

The same old story, I thought uncharitably. After

so many years, nothing seemed to have changed. Only I had changed. Twenty-five years ago, this story would have roused some pity in me, maybe even anger at society's injustice. Now, I felt no sympathy, no anger, no sadness. Life is tough, get over it.

'If he wants money to get married, he will want money to stay married. It won't end. Your daughter is better off without him,' I told Daya.

'Easy to say, sahib. You won't understand until you have your own children.'

His words pierced me, a misdirected barb that hit an unintentional bulls-eye.

'What's this sahib business? Don't call people that. You are oppressed because you want to be oppressed,' I said.

A strange sense of the surreal gripped me. What was I doing here, mouthing Marxist bullshit to a guy who I had just played Russian roulette with? It wasn't meant to be like this, was it? I shook my head and tried to snap out of it.

'Would she be happy getting married if she knew you had killed yourself for her?' I said.

'I'm going to die anyway.'

'Says who?' I asked as the familiar white pillars of Connaught Place came into view. 'You don't die until you die.'

A memory of my mother writhing in pain on her bed as the cancer spread from her urethra to her bladder to her bloodstream struck me as the bus stopped at CP. More images of people lost and places forgotten flashed through my mind. I had to get out of Delhi, I thought, as I stepped off the bus. Everything I saw unlocked dark closets of memories; some joyful, some miserable, but all tinged with regret. I couldn't take the agony of these multiple worlds any more.

'The New Delhi railway station is nearby, right?' I asked Dayaram.

He nodded. 'But you can't get a train today,' he said. 'There is a railway strike for the next two days.'

Nothing had changed, I thought again.

'You can get a bus from ISBT, though.'

'That's okay, I will just find a hotel here,' I said. ISBT would open another box of memories: trips to Shimla, Jodhpur and Dharamsala; more people, more images. Besides, I was tired and wanted this to end. If I were in Delhi, they would find me soon enough. If I was somewhere else, I would keep waiting for them to show up – and I had nothing to accomplish in that extra time.

'Arre sahib, how can you even think of staying at a hotel? Please come to my house,' he said. 'We would be honoured to have you as our guest.'

'That's okay. I'm used to being alone.'

'No, sahib,' he insisted. 'You saved my life. How can I let you stay in a hotel?'

'No need to be so dramatic,' I said.

'No…'

'Shut up. Don't you understand it's dangerous, you idiot? They will come for me,' I snapped. 'Just leave me alone.'

And I walked away.

Every block I crossed evoked memories. Tired, I stopped at the first run down hotel I saw.

'How much?' I asked.

'Where are you from?' asked the inconspicuous looking clerk standing behind the crumbling reception desk, a desire for conversation and confrontation shining in his eyes.

'I don't have time for this,' I said.

He appraised me from top to bottom.

'Will you get any girls?' He smirked.

'I don't do girls,' I said. 'Only men. I have a special weakness for hotel clerks.'

I took the Glock out of my pocket and placed it on the table. He shrank back.

'How much?' I repeated.

'How long?' he asked in a small, scared voice.

'One night,' I said. I was certain they would find me within twenty-four hours.

'Four hundred rupees,' he said.

I took out all the money I had from my shirt pocket. Four dollars.

'That's all I have,' I said.

He stared at me for a moment. 'Okay,' he said and handed me the room key.

'Do I get you free or do I pay extra?' I asked.

He recoiled in disgust as I climbed the creaky stairs to my room.

⚬

What do you do on the last night of your life, I wondered as I lay spreadeagled on the dirty pink bedsheet. The small unreliable bulb in the room flickered on and off, casting eerie shadows on the wall. Soft strains of Hindi music wafted through from an adjoining room. The ceiling fan whirred slowly and I closed my eyes, trying to remember all the good moments – of which there were plenty. In Lara I had found love that knew no boundaries. I hadn't seen my son, but I had experienced the joy of bringing a new life into the world. Sam, Ishmael, David, Marco, Philip – everywhere I went, I met strangers who loved me more than I deserved. A good life, I thought, all in all. And I bore no ill-will; not to the Khmer Rouge, not to La Madrina, not to the girl who had pretended to be Lara in Another Life, not to the local mafia, who would surely get me tonight. They all had their reasons and I was never a hapless victim. I had dived headfirst into the deep end; I couldn't blame anyone if I sank.

I woke up with a start. Someone was knocking frantically. The sun beat steadily against the dusty windows and I was covered in sweat. I looked at my watch. It was one p.m. I had slept for fourteen hours straight and I was still alive.

The pounding on the door continued.

They had come for me, I thought, and felt oddly excited. My dying wish, I announced to an absent audience, was not to be tortured before death; just a simple shot in the temple or the back of the head would do just fine. Maybe it was the good night's sleep or the abundant happy reflections, but I felt weirdly optimistic as I opened the door.

'You!' I exclaimed.

My heart sank. I had expected the handler and his henchmen with sleek revolvers loaded with silencers.

'Yes, sahib,' said a smiling Dayaram. 'I went from hotel to hotel asking for you. I've come to take you for the wedding.'

'Didn't I explain yesterday? Please get out of...' I began, but he interrupted me.

'Everything is fine, everything has been taken care of.' He smiled. 'Yesterday you gave me a new life and everything fell into place. The groom's family has agreed to the marriage if I promise to pay the money later. I will figure something out by then.'

'Don't give your daughter to a man who asks for money to get married,' I said. 'He will keep asking for more.'

'That is our destiny, sahib.'

'I told you not to demean yourself by calling people that.'

'Sahib, please bless us on this auspicious occasion. You saved me. The marriage can't take place without you.'

'Don't watch so many films,' I told him.

'Please come with me. I beg you,' he said with folded hands.

'I told you it's not safe.'

'It's okay, sahib,' he said. 'It will give me a chance to die with dignity. Please come with me.'

'Look...' I began to argue but felt too exhausted to resist. 'I don't even have a set of clean clothes,' I said lamely.

Immediately, I regretted the statement. 'Arre, that's no problem, sahib. I am a big man's servant, and he won't notice even if ten suits are missing from his cupboard.'

☞

I found myself inside a small gaudy shamiana, surrounded by happy faces and boisterous voices. I felt distinctly uncomfortable, not just because the big man's small suit stolen especially for me for the occasion was tight, but because I was being treated like a guest of honour.

'No,' I said for what seemed like the hundredth time as Dayaram came up with a plate of oily samosas.

'Please, I insist,' he said. 'You saved my life, you are the reason...'

'Okay, okay, don't start with the dialogues,' I said and stuffed another samosa into my mouth.

He disappeared to search for more things to load me with, while I nursed an orange drink in my hand, trying hard to think of it as an orange drink and not Gold Spot. Gold Spot would bury me in an avalanche of memories, just as thinking of this as a wedding would. Memories I wanted to purge my mind of – wanton childhood days spent stuffing myself at marriage buffets, oblivious to who was getting married and unconcerned about what marriage meant, except for a vague fantasy of marrying Waheeda Rahman's daughter one day.

Stop, I told myself as my mood began to darken, you are doing it again. Think of this as a loud, gaudy affair; unknown faces streaked with garish face-paint exchanging false pleasantries to the accompaniment of coarse music.

'Arre, sahib!' I heard Daya's voice behind me. 'I've been looking all over for you.'

I turned around, determined to improve my mood and at least pretend to share in his happiness – and saw a ghost.

Curiously, the first thing I noticed was the make of the security guards' rifles – a Marlin, a Browning, another Browning – perhaps because I didn't want to admit to myself that I had recognized the face of the man who was flanked by the guards.

I recognized him immediately, not by his eyes or

his face, but by his sloppy, clumsy gait – unchanged, it seemed, even after twenty-five years.

Dayaram went up to him. 'Sahib, this is the man who saved my life,' he said. 'He is like a bhagwan, an angel in human form.'

Dayaram turned to me. 'This is our big sahib,' he said proudly. 'He runs India's largest film studio and cable television network, yet he was kind enough to attend a minor servant's daughter's wedding. What a great man!'

The big sahib stretched out his hand.

'Sameer Srivastava,' he said. 'Call me Sam.'

I must have turned white because I felt my blood stop for a second. Suddenly, I didn't want him to know it was me. I couldn't see my failure reflected in his eyes. I didn't want to share my past with anyone. I shook his hand mechanically without meeting his eyes, but couldn't think of a name to make up.

'I must go,' I whispered and turned away.

I began to walk away quickly. Why me, I wondered. Why this cruel twist when all I wanted was to die in peace?

'Hey, wait.' I heard his voice behind me.

I didn't stop.

'Nikhil. Nick. Nikhil Arya,' he shouted. 'Stop, for god's sake!'

I stopped and turned as Sam came up to me. He had lost his puppy fat and looked tanned and fit. The boyish impulsiveness had given way to a measured, almost arrogant swagger, though his face looked like he had seen a ghost as well. He looked at my face searchingly.

'Nick?' he said. 'Oh my God.'

Tears began to stream down his face, softly at first, and then torrentially – just like in high school, when he was legendary for frequently bursting into tears.

A small crowd had gathered around us, though thankfully the cacophonous band music kept the others distracted.

'Should we get out of here?' I asked.

He nodded, recovering a little.

☞

'You've done well for yourself,' I said awkwardly as I looked around the swanky furnishing inside the limousine.

'Why?'

'Why? Well, you are being driven in a limo…'

'After all these years, why did you turn away when you saw me?' he said. 'Why haven't you contacted me all this while? Once the Khmer Rouge was thrown out by the Vietnamese in 1979, I spent months in Cambodia and Thailand, but they didn't have a single record of you – not of you coming in, going out, living, dying – nothing. Remember that crazy guy we met at the airport?'

I nodded. I remembered Ishmael well. Too well, perhaps.

'Even his picture was there as one of the victims of the regime's misguided attempts to find traitors,' he said. 'But you seemed to have disappeared from the face of the earth. What the hell happened?'

It made sense that they would purge my name from the records. There were so many bodies all around that one less made no difference; to obliterate an existence was far easier than explaining an escape.

'I didn't join GE, you know. I couldn't have faced myself if I had. I became a journalist for the *New York Times* in Asia instead, hoping, always hoping that somewhere I would discover some clue that led me to you. But after years of finding nothing, I gave you up for dead like everyone else had. No foreigner survived the Khmer Rouge years, not even one. You were either very lucky or very smart.'

I was neither, I thought, I was the idiot who kept chasing away his luck.

'Tell me what happened,' he said. He looked at me and began to cry softly again. 'Did you lose your arm in Cambodia? You look so weak and unwell. When did you get out of there? Why didn't I find you when I searched the length and breadth of the country?'

'I don't want to talk about the past,' I said stiffly.

'But I want to, Nick,' he cried. 'I'm living the life you were supposed to live. I'm crippled by guilt every time I remember the moment you thrust the passport in my hand. Why did you do that if you want to run away on seeing me now?'

'Bloody Hindi films,' I said. 'Everyone in this country is over the top.'

The car stopped in front of a palatial white marble house in a part of town I remembered as Lutyens Delhi, the playground of diplomats, ambassadors and the uber-rich.

A guard opened the imposing gates and we entered a long cemented driveway. Sam rolled down the car windows and the air filled with the familiar fragrances of my childhood.

A familiar sense of loss and regret began to creep over me as we stepped out of the car and walked through the manicured garden onto the front porch – when an angelic, curly-haired boy, about five or six years old, came running out of the house.

'Nikhil, meet Nikhil,' said Sam as he hugged his son. 'This is the uncle after whom you were named.'

I shook his son's hand awkwardly, feeling uncomfortable and protective at the same time. At least he would never be under pressure to live up to his name, I thought.

'You're back early. I just tucked Nikita into bed,' said a woman, presumably Sam's wife, as she stepped onto the porch.

'Nikhil. Nikhil Arya,' she gasped.

She looked like a model, but not in a glamorous, sexy way; more in an intelligent, news anchorish way.

Dusky, with sharp features and long black hair, she wasn't the kind of person one could forget – which was why I was surprised that I didn't remember her from school or anywhere else.

'Yes,' I said. 'Err…'

'Alisa,' she said slowly. 'You don't know me, but I know you well. I don't know what to say. We have pictures of you all over the house.'

'He knows, Liz,' said Sam. 'He knows we think he is dead. Come, let's go in.'

We walked into an elaborately designed hall with a fountain in the centre.

'You were blind to beauty,' I said. 'When did you develop such taste?'

He pointed to Alisa. 'I never did. Pearls before a swine.'

'In more ways than one.' I smiled at her.

'You are alive,' she said, still looking stunned. 'I'm sorry, I mean…'

'Don't worry, I have to keep reminding myself as well,' I told her. 'Most days, I don't even feel alive.'

'I'm sure you guys have a lot to catch up on,' she said, looking meaningfully at Sam and me. 'I don't want to bother you tonight. I'll go tuck Nikhil in bed – the other Nikhil, I mean.'

'The boy, not the ghost, you mean,' I said.

'We are all ghosts,' said Sam sagely. 'Ephemeral and transitory; here today, gone tomorrow.'

'Bravo!' I said. 'The years haven't taken a toll

on your gift for spewing meaningful sounding bullshit.'

I watched as Alisa walked up the stairs.

'You overachieved,' I said to Sam and we laughed like old times.

'What!'... 'No way.'... 'Really?'... 'But why?'... 'Are you serious?'

'We'd move faster if you stopped peppering everything with buts and whys,' I said. 'I don't know why I did what I did. It just felt right at that point, though it all turned out wrong later.'

I held nothing back. I wanted to share it all with Sam, but I also wanted to hear myself talk. I wanted to explain my decisions to myself and understand why I had made all the wrong choices I made.

The hours ticked by. Midnight turned to dawn as Sam's expression changed from bewilderment to pity to occasional laughter to grief. We sat on a couch with a bottle of whiskey untouched in front of us as I talked feverishly, arranging the pieces together in my head, trying to find a pattern in the events.

'The funny thing is that I don't know what I would do differently. I would change everything, yet I would change nothing. What if I hadn't lost my arm in Cambodia, for instance? Would I have joined the monastery then – and would I have met

Lara on the flight? You don't know her, but trust me when I say that any man would gladly give both his arms to be with her. See, that's what confounds me. My happiest moments are linked inextricably to the saddest, and my worst choices are connected to my best. I know that forty-year-old MIT graduates aren't usually broke, crippled, homeless, separated from their family, and on the run from police and mafia dons, but I don't know what I would do differently. Except that whole Another Life fiasco of course – but then I wouldn't have met you.'

When I finished, Sam had tears streaming down his face.

'As my friend Marco would say, don't be a faggot,' I told him.

He didn't smile. Instead, he came and shook my hand.

'What the hell are you doing?'

'You have suffered, but you are a hero,' he said. 'I always knew you were meant for greatness. You were different, you were special, but this is beyond incredible.'

'Some hero,' I said bitterly. 'The only clothes I have, except my underwear, were stolen from you. Forty years, and I have built nothing, achieved nothing.'

'You are a hero,' Sam repeated.

'Can you stop calling me that?' I said. 'Or should I curse you alternately in Hindi, Khmer, Thai,

Spanish, Portuguese, English, and even Java to get the message across?'

'Everywhere you went, you touched people's lives.'

'Everyone touches someone's life.'

'You didn't just touch them, you fundamentally changed them. Marco and I will never find a better friend than you, the monk a better student, Philip a better employee, and Daya a better opponent. And if you were so good to us, I can't even imagine what kind of husband you were to Lara,' he said. 'If I was even half the person you are, I would die a happy man.'

'If you were half the person I am, you would be without either arm and wouldn't even have your own underwear.'

'Don't keep talking about being poor, for heaven's sake,' he said. 'My blood boils, as Dharam paaji would say. Everything I have is because of you. Take everything. I need nothing now that I have found you.'

'Is it a requirement for the CEO of a media corporation to be so filmy?' I asked. 'Anyway, money is the least of my concerns. I can make it again if I want to, I know that.'

I also knew that it wouldn't stick. In my life, loss was as inevitable as breathing. That was why money, beyond what was required for the basics, had never meant much.

The doorbell rang just then. I stiffened. Had they tracked me down already?

'Oops, my squash partner!' said Sam.

I relaxed.

'You are into sports now?' I shook my head in disbelief. 'Remember how I used to nag you to get yourself into shape – but you never listened. Why now?'

'Even this is because of you,' he said simply. 'You let me get out of Cambodia because you thought I wasn't fit, didn't you?'

'I didn't think, I knew,' I said with a smile.

'I didn't miss a day of exercise after that. In fact, everything that happened afterwards was because of you. I went into journalism instead of GE, that's how I got to know of cable television before the others; one thing led to another and the film studio happened. In between, I met Alisa, who was a news anchor on one of my TV channels,' he said. 'I should be based in Bombay for my work but I run things from Delhi because of all the memories from the past.'

The doorbell rang again.

'Well, don't miss today's exercise then,' I said, touched by Sam's generosity.

'Are you sure you are going to be all right?' he asked.

'Yes, big sahibji. If I could survive Phnom Penh and Rio, I can get by quite well in your palace, don't you think?'

Sam got up to open the door. 'By the way, don't tell this guy your real name. Unless you want to spend the rest of the morning explaining how a ghost came back to life. Everyone has heard of you here.'

The door opened and a short, lean guy with a busy air entered the house. He walked with quick, short steps and with his angular face and slightly curved posture, he looked like, well, a lizard. I chided myself for the thought. Who was I to judge him? For all I knew, my missing arm made me look like a kangaroo.

'What's happening? You aren't even ready yet,' he told Sam.

Then he noticed me and stared curiously.

'This is Nick, a friend from MIT,' said Sam. 'And Nick, this is Ram.'

'Ram Lal,' said the man, shaking my hand. 'Partner and Managing Director at MSG Consulting.'

Sam laughed.

'I'm going to change into my gear. You two keep each other company.' He winked at me. 'You have a lot in common.'

'What do you do?' Ram asked as soon as Sam left, his tongue darting in and out of his mouth.

I was silent for a second.

'I am between jobs,' I said finally.

He looked at me with the expected disdain. In his eyes – and mine as well – I was a loser in a poorly fitting suit who had just spent the night on his friend's couch.

'You should have hired better lawyers,' he said.

I looked at him quizzically.

'You've just been through a divorce, haven't you?' he said.

'Not exactly,' I replied. 'I just kind of ran into Sam last night.'

'Oh,' he said. 'Did you lose your job?'

I thought about this for a moment and nodded.

He looked at me triumphantly.

'Solving problems is what I do for a living,' he said. 'What work did you do?'

Waiting, running, scrounging, meditating, drug-trafficking, sharp shooting, money laundering, computer porn – you name it, I've done it.

'Last, I was in software,' I said.

'Ah, technology,' he said, as if it explained everything that had gone wrong in my life. A Cambodian rebel army and a Brazilian drug cartel be damned, the root of all my problems was technology. 'It's a bummer, but I always knew the bubble would burst. What do you plan to do next?'

'I don't know,' I said.

Never was a truer word spoken. I didn't even know what I would be doing a minute from now.

'Have you thought of management consulting?'

'Not really.'

'I work for MSG Consulting,' he said proudly. 'I run the India office, as a matter of fact.'

'Okay,' I said.

'You know MSG, right?'

'Vaguely,' I said – which was true. The name did sound familiar, but his eyes popped out at my response.

'I've been out of the business world for a while,' I said, more to console him than to cover my ignorance.

His eyes continued to bulge.

I felt so bad for him that I almost told him that I hadn't done a decent day's work in twenty-five years, when Sam entered the living room.

'Has he told you yet that he pulled ten million last year in M-fucking-SG?' said Sam.

'We didn't get to that point,' said Ram haughtily.

'I told you. You have a lot in common.' Sam laughed again.

An army of people descended on me as soon as Sam left. A motherly housekeeper gave me sweet, milky tea; another made piping hot paranthas; a third poured me a bath; Alisa fawned on me; the kids spoke shyly to me, probably at their mother's insistence; a male servant escorted me to another palatial room while another turned down the bed for me. I was comfortably tucked in when Sam walked into the room, hot, sweaty and in remarkably good humour.

'You live like a feudal lord,' I said. 'I counted at least ten housekeepers, and Alisa said the day is just starting.'

'Generating employment, my friend.' He laughed. 'It's my moral duty, just like your moral duty is to give up your life for your friends. By the way, you made quite an impression on Ram. He thought you had a great sense of humour.'

'Bastard, you knew what would happen,' I said. 'How the hell was I supposed to know what MSG is?'

He doubled up with laughter. 'There are many things you don't know, my friend. I have another special guest for you to meet tonight.'

'Fuck off. I am not meeting any more of your corporate types,' I said. 'I crashed off that path a long time back.'

'No, no, he isn't a corporate type at all. I'll ask Alisa to prime you. Why don't you get some sleep now?'

I was running as fast as I could but the black clad soldiers were catching up, their red bandanas flying in the air. Lara and my son were playing on the street outside the favela amidst groups of children mixing cocaine.

'Run,' I shouted, but they didn't listen. I tried to bundle my son in my right arm, but I couldn't touch him.

He isn't real, he is a computer image.

Wake up, this is a dream, I urged myself. Someone caught me by the shoulder. I resisted, but he pulled harder.

I opened my eyes and saw my son in front of me. I gasped in horror – and then I saw Alisa.

'Wake up, uncle, wake up, Amar uncle is here,' said Sam's son, shaking me as I lay on the bed.

I lay back in bed, exhausted. Another nightmare. Why couldn't I get used to them? Why did I always wake up covered in sweat and thrashing in bed?

'Who?' I asked, feeling disoriented in the dark. It was probably evening. I had slept through the morning. I couldn't sleep this long, I told myself, it wasn't safe.

'Amar uncle, Amar uncle,' shouted Sam's son as he rushed out of the room.

'Would you like some coffee, Nikhil?' Alisa asked.

I nodded, and invisible hands came in with a plate of biscuits and a mug of steaming coffee within seconds.

'Are you feeling okay? You twitched a lot when you were sleeping,' said Alisa.

'I have bad dreams.'

'Sam told me everything,' she said softly. 'You are the bravest man I've ever known. I will be proud if our son turns out to be even half the person you are.'

I let that one pass.

'Amar Kumar is here to meet you,' she said.

'Who is he?'

'A bad actor but a big movie star.'

'Why is he here?'

'He always comes by when he is shooting in Delhi, not because we're great friends but because Sam's company bankrolls all his movies. We thought we would cancel since you were here, but Sam thought it would be fun for you to meet him,' said Alisa.

'A lot of fun,' I said cynically.

'Sam has told him all about you.'

I choked on my coffee. 'Can't he keep his mouth shut? I didn't intend my life to become fodder for Tulsi Ramsay and Dada Kondke movies.'

She laughed. 'Your life is more like a Guru Dutt film,' she said. 'Would you like to meet Amar?'

I didn't really want to, but I didn't seem to have an option since Sam walked into the room just then, accompanied by a diminutive young man. He was almost half a foot shorter than my six foot plus, and he had a pleasant, if not altogether handsome face.

'Nick, boss, meet the Indian superstar, Amar Kumar. I'm assuming Alisa has told you that he is bigger than Dilip Kumar, Dev Anand and Rajesh Khanna were in our time.'

'Kya Sameer bhai, aap bhi na,' said Amar Kumar in a soft voice that seemed to suit his frame. 'I am nobody.'

'We are starting shooting for a new film in which Amar plays a superhero. I thought he could meet you before that – to gain some inspiration, you see,' said Sam. 'I thought you both would have a lot in common. Just like Ram and you.' He winked at me.

I shot Sam a dirty look as I got up from the bed to shake hands with Amar.

'A pleasure to meet you,' I said.

'The pleasure is entirely mine, sir,' said Amar. 'I'm just a hero in movies; you are the hero in real life.'

If this was what being a hero did to you, I thought, I would rather be a movie star – or just about anyone else for that matter.

'I'm a method actor, sir,' Amar continued. 'I like to get under the skin of my character to do justice to my role. You've had some very emotional experiences and I would love to understand them better for the film. Would it be possible for me to ask you a few questions?'

'Sure,' I said. 'What would you like to know?'

From the corner of my eye, I saw Sam grinning like a cat. Fuck you for making a mockery of my life, I mouthed silently.

'How did you feel when you were in that small cell in Phnom Penh?' Amar began.

My face fell as I recalled the blackness and blood, Ishmael's body decomposing next to me, and the unending hours spent waiting for the rice soup. What did I feel during that time?

'I don't know,' I said. 'I just felt... nothing, actually. Just a funny kind of acceptance.'

Amar looked disappointed. 'You didn't feel any anger against the system that had chained you there?' he said dramatically.

I shook my head. 'I was too hungry to feel anything, I guess.'

He seemed to like that and made a note in the small diary he had with him.

That was probably the only note he made during the course of our conversation. I disappointed him the rest of the time with a series of 'I don't know… I didn't feel anything… it's hard to explain,' while Sam shook with silent laughter on the couch.

'You didn't feel anything when you lost your entire business in Brazil?' Amar said, sounding exasperated. 'You went from a hundred million dollars to zero in one minute for no fault of your own. Surely you were angry.'

'At whom?' I said. 'I was the outsider. I fully understand their motives for doing what they did.' I paused. 'Look, I know I'm being of no help, but you have to understand. Things happened so fast that I thought nothing; I felt nothing; I just did what I could to keep afloat at that time. The anger only came later, and it was directed wholly at myself.'

He looked at me blankly.

'Thank you for your time, sir,' he said finally. 'You are an inspiration.'

For a star he was quite a decent guy, I thought.

He got up to leave and paused for a minute. 'Sir,

I have one suggestion for you and please take it the right way.'

'Sure,' I said.

'I think you should change your name.'

'My name?' I repeated in surprise.

He nodded. 'As soon as I added an extra R and an extra K to my name, all my films became superhits. The audience doesn't even notice that my name is Amarr Kkumar now, but the gods have noticed.'

'Why an extra R and K and not something else?' I asked.

'My numerologist suggested it after consulting all my charts,' he said.

I must have looked sceptical because he added, 'I know it sounds silly, sir, but who knows how God works? Who really knows the mysterious secrets of the universe? After all, everything around us is fundamentally incomprehensible, isn't it?'

I recalled hearing or saying those words sometime in my past, but I couldn't remember when.

'If an extra Y can change fate, then Y not?' He grinned at his own joke.

So be it, I thought. But with my kind of luck, extra Rs, Ks and Ys wouldn't do the trick. I needed to change my whole name, and I wouldn't even need to consult a numerologist. Any name would bring better luck. I tried thinking of a new name as Alisa escorted Amar Kumar out of the room.

'Nick, you idiot, you aren't seriously thinking of

adding Ns, Ks, or As to your name, are you?' said
Sam. 'You are an MIT graduate for heaven's sake!'

The screen credits of a Dev Anand movie began
to roll on the television in front of me.

'Who's Nick?' I said. 'I am Johnny. From today,
Johnny mera naam. So, you were saying?'

☞

'I need to head out,' I said.

Sam and I were sitting in the living room as usual,
after the children had gone to bed. He was scanning
the business dailies, peppering it with the occasional
'bastards' and 'cocksuckers'. I was staring into space,
my mind empty of thought, yet too preoccupied to
concentrate on anything.

'Sure, Johnny boy,' he said without looking up
from the newspaper. 'Sutta-chai?'

He picked up the intercom on the table to call
the driver.

'No, I mean, I need to get out of your house and
start my own life,' I said.

He put down the newspaper.

'Why are you running away again?' he said.

'I'm not running away,' I said. 'It's been a couple
of weeks already. How long can a forty-year-old
man live in someone's guest bedroom?'

'Is space an issue? I could easily add another
floor to the house. Let me get started on the plans
tomorrow before...'

'No, no,' I interrupted. 'This is like the Taj Mahal compared to where I've been before. Seriously, I have really enjoyed being here and being so carefree and silly once again, but I need to move on now.'

'What's the hurry?' he said. 'Take some more time to recover and figure out what you want to do next.'

'It's been a few weeks already, Sam,' I said, shaking my head. 'I've recovered as much as I can.'

'Are you ready to date again?' he asked. 'That's the real measure of recovery.'

'Then I won't recover in this lifetime.'

'I know several actresses. You name one and…'

I held up my hand. 'It's demeaning to have this discussion. I don't want to love again. I can't love again. And I've spent so much time alone that I won't have any problem spending time by myself.'

'Why do you want to go then, Johnny boy? Just be alone by yourself in your room.'

'Feeling very funny today, aren't you?' I said.

'I can't lose you again,' he said, suddenly serious. 'Despite Liz, despite the kids, I lived with this vacuum all my life until you showed up.'

'That sounds really gay.'

'If something happens again, I won't be able to forgive myself.'

'That's my point,' I said. 'Something *will* happen again. Disaster doesn't leave my side for long. You have to understand that this isn't like the movies,

Sam. Those people whose Russian roulette thing I screwed up are the South American mafia. I know what they are capable of. The cartel will strike like a viper as soon as things get cold. And I'm not an Amar Kumar who can beat ten baddies with a flick of my little finger. I can't put your family in danger.'

'You forget that I have the best security team in Delhi,' he said. 'All of them are ex-police and goons.'

'Trust me, you don't know these guys. I've seen them in action,' I said. 'I've been awake every night with the Glock in my hand, waiting for them to come.'

'Are you out of your mind, Johnny boy? Nothing can happen here.'

'You haven't seen what I have,' I said. 'They strike when it's cold, and it's starting to get cold now.'

'And you'd rather be alone than with this security cover?'

I nodded. 'I've been trained by the best.'

I didn't mention that no matter what I did or which security cover protected me, I'd be eliminated. Sooner or later, everybody with a hit on their name was executed. You could run from yourself but you couldn't run from the cartel – especially if you'd screwed them twice. My only wish was to protect Sam's family. The assassins were honourable people, but eliminating all witnesses was the first rule in the book.

'I need to think about this,' he said. 'Let's talk tomorrow.'

'Listen, Mr Studio Boss, I am not Amar Kumar asking you for permission to re-shoot a song sequence in Switzerland,' I said. 'I'm informing you that I am leaving tomorrow.'

'*Please* give me time to think about this, Mr Johnny,' he said. '*Please* can we talk tomorrow, Sir Johnny?'

I nodded reluctantly.

It was midnight when I went back to my room and prepared myself for another sleepless night. The Glock, always a companion, went from the back pocket of my jeans to a small fold I had cut out in the mattress. I positioned light rubber-soled shoes next to the bed and lay down with my eyes wide open, alert for the sudden, silent thud of a security guard falling outside or the soft, quiet scratch on the tall patio windows facing the garden. If I told Sam about my nightly drill, he would laugh it away as being obsessive – and perhaps it was, but then the *New York Times* Manhattan headquarters paled in comparison to Rio de Janeiro's Jakeira favela as a training ground in contract killings.

Twelve a.m. One a.m. Two a.m. Another uneventful night, I thought, with a slight tinge of regret. I was no stranger to waiting in the darkness for nothing, but sometimes I wished it would happen quickly. If only they knew I had no desire to harm them, they probably wouldn't waste so much time in preparation. All I wanted was to face them before they ran into anyone else in the house, pretend to fight, and get mowed into blood and dust – alone. I had accumulated enough bad karma in one lifetime to be born an insect for the next ten; shooting a few more people wouldn't really help my karmic cause.

Three a.m. Time to drift off. A lease of life for another day, I thought, stretching out on the bed. And then I heard it. A soft movement of the sofa, a body bumping into another. They were here. I put my well-orchestrated drill into action with tense excitement. In a few seconds, I was downstairs, waiting behind the mahogany staircase, the gun pressing against my palm. A few silent seconds passed. I listened, every nerve end alert, and tightened my grip around the Glock. It would probably go unused tonight unless they decided to go after Sam's family, in which case I would empty it out on them.

Suddenly, I heard the click of a lamp being switched on and a portion of the living room lit up with soft yellow light.

This wasn't like them, I thought urgently, they worked in darkness. What the hell was happening?

Revolver in hand, I rushed out into the open.

'Jesus Christ, keep that damn thing down, will you?' Sam shrieked. He was sitting on the sofa with a laptop. He stared open-mouthed at me, his eyes wide with terror. 'What the fuck, man, can't you ever relax?'

I took a few deep breaths and put the revolver in my back pocket.

'Sorry,' I said evenly. 'Why are you up so early? I thought they were here.'

'I almost died from a heart attack,' he said, his face still flushed with fear. 'Why are you up this early?'

'I told you, I can't sleep,' I said.

'Oh yeah, Johnny boy, well, you can sleep now. You can buy all the peace in the world and then some more.'

I looked at him, puzzled.

'You are a psycho, Johnny boy. Another Life is the coolest thing ever, especially for middle-aged men with diminishing libidos. I just banged a couple of chicks this morning. I haven't felt more alive in years.'

'How the hell…' I muttered.

'The website is live now!' he said. 'Check it out. You made a cool hundred million dollars or so on it. That guy Philip has been saying in all the interviews that he is desperately searching for you. They are talking about you as some kind of urban legend; a mad scientist who stalks homeless shelters stealthily – like Bigfoot or the Yeti or something.'

'How do you know all this?' I asked, still confused.

'I had put my media team on the job of tracking mentions of Another Life and checking websites which came up with that or variations of that name. The launch press conference just happened around midnight India time and the website went live immediately after that. I would have called you if I knew you were playing night-watchman. Check it out, will you?'

I let the news sink in.

'Here, let me open the website for you,' said Sam.

I didn't know how to react. I was happy for Philip, but I didn't want any part of that madness again. Not just Another Life; everything – MIT, Brazil, Cambodia, Minnesota. I wanted to move on, cut off all ties with my past, pretend that it had all happened to someone who no longer existed.

'Why are you standing there with your hands on your hips like Shilpa Shetty?' said Sam. 'Come on, check out the website.'

I didn't budge.

'What the hell is wrong with you?' said Sam. 'You should be jumping with excitement.'

'It's over, it's the past. I don't want to think about it.'

'Don't be a dick. Stop running away from yourself. All of this is you, you can't not think about it.'

'Thanks for the free psychiatric consultation, but no thanks.'

'At least call Philip. I've read his interviews and he seems very emotional about you. Don't do to him what you did to me.'

'I want to protect him,' I said.

'Balls! The only one you are protecting is yourself,' said Sam. 'Face the past, else you'll always be a victim. Plus, you did nothing wrong. You are a hero.'

'Don't get started on that.'

'Just pick up the damn phone, will you?' Sam exclaimed. 'You need to come to terms with things.'

I called Philip despite the knot in my stomach. In his own way, Sam was right. I could never be at peace until I accepted my failures, apologized to everyone I had hurt, and grovelled for some kind of forgiveness.

'Hi, Philip, it's Nick,' I said in a rush as soon as he picked up the phone.

'Nick! Is that really you? Tell me it's you.'

'It is me. I can't even begin to tell you how sorry –'

'Nick, boy, why the hell did you disappear?' Philip cut me off. He sounded more concerned than angry. 'You didn't mention anything about your whereabouts in the letter, and there wasn't even a return address on the box that computer came in.'

'Philip, I am really, really sorry,' I said. 'I don't know what came over me. After everything you did for me, I deserted…'

'Stop, for god's sake,' said Philip. 'I'm the one

who is sorry. I know I pressured you too much with the one-week deadline, so you bolted. I searched and searched for you, kept waiting for your call, but there was nothing. Eventually, I contacted the VCs myself, and of course, they bought it immediately. We have more money now than we ever dreamt of, even though I think I undersold it because I didn't fully understand the technology. I need to apologize to you for that.'

'You don't need to apologize for anything,' I said. 'I'm the one who screwed…'

'By the way,' he interrupted. 'There is someone else who is looking for you desperately.'

Had they traced me already? Eventually, their path would lead here. As if one wasn't enough, now I would have two mafia groups duking it out to get me.

'Who?' I asked.

'I've forgotten his name. He scared me because he kept calling me a faggot and said he would shoot me through the phone if I didn't quickly find out where you were. He spoke in a funny accent. I would peg him as a Spaniard.'

'Marco!' I said.

'Yes, yes, yes,' said Philip excitedly. 'That's his name. Please get him off my back if you can. He scares me.'

My heart sank. Why was Marco trying to contact me when we had agreed not to speak for five years?

Something had happened to Lara. He would never contact me otherwise.

'We need to talk about the money transfer,' said Philip. 'It's a lot, so you will need to create multiple accounts in multiple banks…'

'Later, Philip. I need to rush now,' I said. 'Thanks for everything.'

I put down the phone.

'That wasn't too bad, was it?' said Sam, smiling at me. His look quickly changed to one of astonishment. 'You look like you've seen a ghost. Now what has happened?'

'Something has happened to Lara.'

'What? How? When?'

'I'm going to find out,' I said and dialled Marco's number.

He picked it up at the first ring.

'Marco!' I said. 'Are you okay? Is Lara safe? Why did you try to contact me?'

'Buddha, finally,' he said softly, a voice ashamed to show emotion. 'I've been worried. You shouldn't have fucked with him.'

'I know,' I said, unexpected tears welling up in my eyes. 'It's a long story.'

Marco laughed and my spirits lifted. It couldn't be all that bad if he was laughing, could it?

'I know the story, men. Why do you think you are still alive? He would have found you in a day. All of us from Brazil to Peru to Chile to Ecuador to Venezuela to Colombia are working for him in a way,' said Marco. 'But it worked out well, actually.'

'What worked out well?' I asked, my voice barely a whisper.

'I struck a deal to give him ten years of free distribution in Brazil without taking a commission, besides expanding from coke to crack, speed, meth and acid. He agreed to get the Godmother off your back as well if I deliver.'

This wasn't what I wanted. I wanted peace, but not at Marco's expense.

'Don't do it, Marco,' I said. 'You will get into big trouble.'

'I *am* trouble, men,' he said, the usual cowboy bravado returning to his voice. 'This is a blessing in disguise. I've expanded the business significantly since you left, and this will take me to the next level. Just like the retail stores, right? It will take a while to break even, but then the profits will pour in.'

I knew this was no business decision. What had I done to deserve such friendship? I was a fundamentally flawed person who wrecked lives wherever he went. I didn't deserve such unconditional love.

'Pay him off, Marco. I have all the money in the world and then some more,' I said, thinking of Another Life. But I knew it wouldn't work even as I said it.

'Rather than interfere with my future plans,

do you want to plan your future with your wife instead?'

Suddenly, I didn't want to speak to her. I didn't trust that the Colombian mafia would let me go. I didn't believe that the handler, whom I had humiliated in front of his customers, would forgive and forget. I didn't want to re-enter her life and destroy it again.

'Are you there, men?' he said. 'We've both been trying to track you down since I agreed to his terms a couple of weeks ago. You move fast, don't you? Every time we reached somewhere, you were already off. Here, speak to her. She is pissed off.'

She deserves better than me, I thought. We had taught each other love; she would love again. I wanted to put down the phone but couldn't bring myself to do it.

'Nikhil,' she whispered at the other end.

I began to cry, my mind a confused jumble of emotions.

'Lara,' I said softly.

'You silly man, you silly, silly man,' she said. 'Couldn't you have told me once? Did you really think I could just move on after all these years?'

'Lara,' I repeated.

'I love you, Nikhil.'

I waited for the joy to envelop me, but I felt nothing except a growing unease. It had taken just a couple of hours, and everything had resolved itself.

It was too easy, too perfect, too neat – and I didn't trust it. It couldn't be over. I had been deceived in the past before. There was a shadow lurking somewhere in the corner.

'Are you still there?' she asked, her tone alarmed.

'Yes,' I said silently. 'I missed you. I am sorry. I am sorry for everything. I love you.'

'You are coming tonight, Johnny boy, aren't you?'

I looked at my son, who was knocking himself out silly with his inflatable green monster and Lara, who sat on our futon, smiling as she read a book. How could anyone leave these two and go anywhere, especially me, still paranoid about losing everything in a flash once again? There had been way too many coincidences that had got us together – and I didn't trust coincidences. We were safe here in Delhi, thousands of miles from trigger happy South American cartels and from the bleak loneliness of the US, yet I knew things could unravel any moment.

'Of course not,' I said.

'You need to get a life, Johnny boy. It's been six months since they got here and you haven't ventured anywhere without them,' Sam said on the phone. 'They need a break, even if you don't.'

Lara looked up from her book. 'Go,' she said.

'It's not about them,' I said to Sam. 'I have

nothing to say to anyone in this MIT reunion. You guys will be on a dick measuring trip. I am a managing director, you are only a CTO, oh no, I am a CFO. I've nothing to contribute. I am no better than a college dropout.'

He laughed. 'Yours will be the biggest dick in the room tonight! I'll pick you up at seven,' he said and put down the phone.

I looked at my watch. Six p.m. My son squealed with pleasure as he finally knocked out the monster doll. There was no way I was going, I thought.

'You need to go,' said Lara, pushing strands of her hair back into her ponytail as she looked up from the book. I felt the same tenderness towards her that I'd felt when she was pregnant.

'I don't think so,' I said. I looked longingly at my son. 'I would rather play with him.'

'Did I ever tell you about the misguided botanist this writer wrote about?' she said.

'Look, let's not get...'

'The gentle botanist saw the butterfly struggling in her cocoon and felt so bad that he pulled her out so she wouldn't have to suffer,' said Lara. 'Of course, she shrivelled up and died instead. The botanist didn't realize that struggling in the cocoon, fighting and stretching the larvae, is what makes the ugly, fat moth a butterfly.'

'Profound,' I said. 'But what has that got to do with anything? I just want to play with my son.'

'Like the botanist, you want to make sure he doesn't suffer, but you'll end up smothering him instead. You don't realize that your struggles were essential to make you what you are. You can't deny him his own.'

'So he can become like me?' I said, pointing at my prosthetic arm.

'Yes, exactly, so that he can become like you,' Lara said. 'So that he touches lives everywhere he goes, so that he has friends who won't think twice about giving up their life for him; so that he meets someone who loves him more than he loves himself.'

'You don't love me,' I said bitterly.

'Are you going to get ready or not?'

Reluctantly, I went to our room to get dressed for the non-occasion. We had been fighting about my supposed over-protectiveness ever since we had been reunited six months ago. Why didn't she understand that I couldn't shake off this vague feeling of impending doom when we made silent, unhurried love in our sprawling bungalow in Lutyens Delhi, or when large sums of money kept flowing in from Another Life so that my days passed just watching my son play, or when we sat together in our garden, lazy and quiet, basking in the warmth of the winter sun.

Despite having everything I ever wanted, I wasn't happy. It was too perfect – a picture waiting to be sullied; calm waters about to turn tempestuous; the lull before the crashing storm – it had happened before, and it would happen again. Only, this time, I didn't have the will to fight it. I was forty, Lara was thirty-nine; we weren't getting any younger and we had a three-year-old son to think about. I knew I was protective, but I didn't want my son to become like me – jumping at unknown sounds, recoiling at strange faces, and sweating in his nightmares. I wanted him to experience life, but not at the price I paid for it.

'You look good,' she said when I emerged from the room in my suit. 'You will have to fight away the women.'

'I might just take one as a mistress. Perhaps she will want to spend time with me.'

'That's a really good idea,' she said, returning to her book. 'You won't be in my hair so much then.'

I went to play with my son, but he seemed so annoyed at being distracted from the monster that I thought he'd punch me instead.

I called Marco. 'Now is not a good time,' he said and put down the phone. I thought I heard a gunshot in the background.

I called Philip. 'Oh yes, now that this is steady, I have another big idea I wanted to talk to you about…'

Sam's arrival, announced via our sophisticated security system, was almost a relief.

'I'm going,' I said stiffly.

No one cared. I double-checked the alarm systems and ensured that the three security guards on duty were fully awake before I joined Sam in the waiting car.

'You go in, Johnny boy. I have a phone call to make,' said Sam as soon as we reached the sprawling farmhouse on the outskirts of Delhi where the MIT Indian alumni reunion was on.

'What's this now? Busy CEO Sameer Srivastava arrives after everyone else? Anyway, I'll wait. What will I talk to them about?'

'Arre… all our old friends will be there,' he said. 'You have so much in common with them. Tell them all about your new name, Johnny. Go on now! Unlike you, I work for a living and need to keep my business running.'

I cursed him as I got out of the car.

I saw about two or three hundred identically dressed men and women ranging from their twenties to their sixties, scattered in small groups around the farmhouse. In their tailored suits and expensive sarees, their flushed, confident faces and easy, textured smiles, they conveyed an effortless air of importance. They ruled the world after all, these CEOs, CFOs, consulting partners, hedge fund owners, managing directors, studio heads, billionaire entrepreneurs – all that we'd been trained to become.

I didn't belong here, I thought, as I made my way towards the bar in the corner. I chatted with the middle-aged bartender, a kindred soul who seemed to have graduated from the same hard knocks school as I had, before others assailed him with cocktail orders. I fetched myself a stiff whiskey and stood comfortably in a corner, nursing my drink. I had no desire to talk to anyone. MIT was a distant memory from another lifetime, and I felt neither nostalgia for the past nor aspirations for the future. There was no one I wanted to swap memories with or network for the future with. I wasn't going places; I didn't *want* to go any place.

'Hey, you are Sam's friend, aren't you?'

I turned around and saw the man who had come to play squash with Sam that first day in Delhi. A lot had happened since then and I no longer remembered his name.

I nodded. 'Jahangir Khan, right?' I smiled.

He laughed. 'Yep. Ram Lal,' he said. 'And you are Nick, right?'

'No, I'm Johnny,' I said.

He looked puzzled. 'Surprising! I don't usually forget names. We can't afford to forget in our line of work.'

Ah, the consulting partner, I recalled.

'Have you found a job yet?' he asked.

I considered this for a moment and shook my head. 'Unless you consider fighting a green monster with my son,' I said. 'But I'm not looking for one.'

'Oh, you can't give up hope so soon,' he said. 'You

should network at events like these. Everyone here is very well connected.'

'Actually, Sam and I…' I began.

'Shall I tell you something?' he said, cutting me off. He came closer to me, his eyes bulging. 'You can't trust Sam. He won't do anything for you unless you do something for him in return.'

'Really?' I said, amused. I would never let Sam live this down, I thought, laughing to myself.

Ram nodded his head vigorously. 'You come with me. I will introduce you to the others.'

I looked towards the entrance to see if Sam had arrived yet, but couldn't see any sign of him.

'Sure,' I said and followed him.

We headed over to a group of four men – all of medium height, clean-shaven, balding, with gold-rimmed glasses – and a few women, also looking identical with their permed hair and wide foreheads. They were engaged in an animated discussion when we joined them. To my relief, Ram seemed to have forgotten his altruistic mission of helping me find a job, and proceeded to regale them with stories of his latest accomplishments while I quietly introduced myself to the others.

'What is your take on the recession? Will it end this year?' Ram was asked by one of the suits.

He stepped back to give himself room. 'The fundamentals are still weak, but if I were to make an educated guess…'

I tuned out the rest of the discussion as the others listened in rapt attention.

I could have been them, I thought suddenly. Successful, confident, stable, secure – none of them would know any serious crises other than a delayed promotion at work or a failed marriage. I *would* have been them, I thought, just a few different turns and I would be mouthing grand theories about complex credit derivatives, mortgage crises and the ongoing recession. Instead, I thought regretfully, all I knew of were genocides and amputations, Buddhism and Vipassana, guns and drug cartels, and homelessness and insanity.

'Where are you lost?' said Ram, looking at me kindly. 'When do you think the economy will get better?'

The others looked at me expectantly.

'I don't know,' I said. 'I haven't been following it closely. To be honest, I haven't paid any attention at all.'

Everyone looked at me with incredulous expressions. 'But this is everything,' their expressions said.

But it isn't, I thought, suddenly, inexplicably irritated. There is so much more out there, I said silently as Ram continued to drone on and his circle of listeners became bigger and bigger. There is an entire world that is completely oblivious to Mckinsey and Goldman and vacations in French

Polynesia and company retreats in Swiss villas and MIT and the latest econometric theory. Do you believe that knowing the latest Federal Reserve interest rate trumps knowing that a Glock can shred your temple from two hundred yards away? Why don't you try telling the crippled Cambodian survivors who lay in their blood for years on end that the chairman of XYZ bank is a more influential figure than Pol Pot, the CEO of the greatest genocide in Asian history?

'Hey Ram bhai, stop this intellectual discussion, please yaar,' said someone and the others laughed in chorus.

'That reminds me of Sodhi, Sukhdeep Singh Sodhi, who started the anti-intellectual movement at MIT,' said Ram. 'You guys remember him? 1979 batch? Must be your batch, Jassi, wasn't he?'

More names were thrown around. Do you remember him? Do you remember her? None of them meant anything to me. Either I'd never known them or they had been replaced in my limited memory by far more significant events.

'Arre yaar, don't talk about those days. I get all nostalgic,' said someone. 'Those were the best days of my life. It's so good to catch up with everyone. I've never made such friends again.'

Everyone agreed whole-heartedly, again in sync.

Such friends, I thought dryly, that you don't even remember their names. I thought of Sam, Ishmael and Marco. I didn't even know what 'catching up' with them meant because I couldn't think of them as separate from me. Could it even be called friendship? It was beyond that, beyond any 'we are close as brothers' clichés. Hell, I was alive because of them. What do you call such people? 'Friends' seemed too limiting a word.

'Now, my only friend is this,' announced Ram, proudly pointing to his Blackberry, 'and the boss in New York.' Again, he looked at me a little condescendingly. 'You are lucky, man. You don't have to answer to anyone.'

I thought of David, the monk who had nursed me to life and taught me what was worthwhile in it, and Philip, who selflessly taught me everything he knew and willingly allowed me to take over. Were they bosses? Or mentors? Again, I struggled with words. They meant so much more. Like Ishmael and Marco, they had both given me another lease of life just when everything seemed to have ended.

'Our real bosses are at home,' said someone. 'Cheers to the "no spouses and kids" MIT reunion tradition.'

Everyone cheered in unison.

I thought of Lara, and felt the same heady emotion I had felt the first time we went on a date. Now we had a son together. She had waited without an end in sight, despite everything I had put her through. Did I really deserve such a blessing? Would I ever be able to take our marriage for granted as spouses reportedly did after years of living together?

'Cheers also to the MIT India chapter!' said someone who looked like he had had a drink too many. 'Desi rocks! Aren't you glad we guys came back home? Anywhere else in the world you would be a second-class citizen.'

But you aren't, I thought. I had lived in a world that knew no boundaries. Everywhere I went, people had overwhelmed me with their generosity. Was Marco, a Brazilian, less of a friend than Sam, an Indian? Or David, the wandering Buddhist monk, less effective as a teacher than Philip, an American who had never ventured out of America? What about Ishmael from Estonia – a country I would still be hard-pressed to locate on the map? There were no borders, there was no distance; people felt, people cared, people loved, people hurt. Everyone was the same.

'Desi rocks!'

Everyone clinked glasses in agreement.

Another middle-aged, balding man with gold-rimmed glasses and a bushy moustache joined the group just then.

'There you are!' said Ram excitedly. 'You all know him, right? Sharad Raj, CEO of Lever Oil.'

People made space for him. He was important, he had a title after his name.

A startling realization hit me with a sudden

force. I didn't want to be them. I now understood the strange feeling that had haunted me since the time I had arrived at the reunion. They were all clones. They all looked the same, they thought the same thoughts, they even talked the same way – and none of it was my way.

It was, well, small, for lack of a better word.

All my life I had thought I wanted to be *them*, but I realized now that I wasn't supposed to be them. I had thought I was unlucky. But no, quite the opposite. I was lucky to have been chosen to live this patchwork quilt of a life. How could I wish any different? Damn, I thought as I drained my glass, so this is what Lara meant. I was turning my son into them by denying him the very things that made life worth living – friendship and loyalty, openness and vulnerability, love and loss, complexities and contradictions, falling, picking up the pieces, rising and falling again, a world that has no boundaries, a life that knows no limits.

I would relieve the security guards as soon as I got home.

Sam came rushing in just as I moved away from the group.

'Johnny boy! There you are,' he said in a rush.

'Who is Johnny? I'm Nikhil,' I said. 'Johnny's gone down.'

'What?' he said, looking confused.

'Johnny's gone down,' I repeated. 'I'm me again.'

'Screw you and your name games. You won't believe what just happened. Wait till you hear,' he said, his face red.

And here we go again, I thought.

'Don't sweat it,' I said. 'He was right, the homeless man in the shelter. I kept seeing unravelled threads because I wasn't looking at it right. But I can see the pattern now.'

'Are you high?' asked Sam.

'Soaring.'

Acknowledgements

First, a note of gratitude to the many readers who took the time to share their thoughts with me via e-mail and letters after reading *Keep Off the Grass* and also the critics who reviewed the novel, including a venerable scribe who termed me and some of the more illustrious authors of my generation as the 'Rakhi Sawants of Indian literature' (I'm still trying to figure out who the remark was intended to offend, Rakhi Sawant or us). I'm being honest when I say that I have valued each and every critique that came my way, both positive and negative, and though I can't claim to be the Shabana Azmi of Indian literature just yet, I hope I've improved significantly with my second novel. And as always, I greatly welcome your comments on *Johnny Gone Down* to guide me along my journey to be a better writer – and a better person.

To my parents, both heroes among a thousand faces, my father for his character and dignity, my mother for her strength and resilience; noble traits that have influenced Johnny, my protagonist.

To Anshuman Acharya, Renuka Chatterjee, VK Karthika, Neelini Sarkar, Ashwin Bhave, Jason

Chrenka and Regina Brooks, the very best set of early readers that an author could wish for. Your respectful, considered comments made the book stronger than it was ever capable of being in my rookie hands. I've learnt tremendously about writing from each of you and for that I will forever be in your debt.

To Sonali and Avneesh Arya for giving Johnny a name without reading his story!

To the uniquely Indian familial networks that never cease to fill my life with warmth, comfort and interesting stories, from grandmother down to maasis, chacha, bua and cousins.

To Vinod Raghuwanshi, Saurabh Nanda, Kent Wolf, Ajay Srivastava, Trupti Rustagi, Sundip Gorai, Keith Melker, Jana Malinska, Ben Rekhi and Samrat Chowdhury, old friends who constantly surprise me with new ideas – as you did this time.

To Hinoti Joshi and Bhaskar Shankaran, and their team, Nrusingha Choudhury and Bhautik Siddhapura, the most creative folks I know. I'm proud to work with you as colleagues, prouder to know you as friends.

To the marketing and editing team at Harper Collins, Text 100 and Mr Pradeep Guha; humble, hardworking, competent folks who often have to bear the brunt of my marketing MBA!

To all the terrific institutions I've been extraordinarily fortunate to be a part of – BIT

Mesra, IIM Bangalore, Procter & Gamble, Boston Consulting Group and now, Kraft Foods. Any novel is ultimately some version of one's experiences and I wouldn't have lived half a life is not for these establishments. Also to JP Kuehlwein, Shailesh Jejurikar, Maile Carnegie, Stephen Ripple, Steve Robinson and Gopal Pathak, just some of my mentors in these institutions who fundamentally changed the trajectory of my life.

A note of gratitude for Jackie Kennedy's immortal quote used at the beginning of the book. Finally, I'm greatly obliged to all the films and novels which inspired *Johnny Gone Down*, both in terms of research and ideas. There are way too many to mention all of them here, but a special word of appreciation for *Forrest Gump, Cocaine Cowboys, Oldboy, Travelers and Magicians, The Deer Hunter, The Killing Fields, City of God, Elite Squad, Bus 174, Crime School: Money Laundering, The Novice, Lucia, Basic Teachings of the Buddha, Voices from S-21, Children of the Killing Fields, Amores Perros, Second Life for Dummies, English August, Delhi is Not Far, Bangkok 8, Bangkok Tattoo* and many, many others. I've travelled extensively in most of the countries these books and films originate from, and have been amazed at how well they capture the ethos of the environment they are set in, something I aspire to emulate in my writing.

Q&A with Karan

Excerpts from an editorial interview with Karan Bajaj

Q: **First things first, congratulations on publishing your second novel. From India to Cambodia to Thailand to Brazil to the Silicon Valley back to India, you've covered quite a bit of ground in a pretty slim novel!**

KB: Thank you. Yes, the story does run through several countries, but since the intent was to follow the protagonist rather than to make any comment on the historical or political context of his environment, the size of the novel didn't increase with its span. In Thailand, for instance, the story remains within the four walls of the monastery where the protagonist becomes a Buddhist monk.

Q: *Johnny Gone Down* **is very different from your first novel,** *Keep Off the Grass*. **I know writers hate this question but I feel compelled to ask – do you like one more than the other?**

KB: I guess the correct answer would be to say that I like both equally as a mother loves both her children or something. But I will be honest and say that I have a stronger affection for *Johnny Gone Down*. I was young when I wrote *Keep Off The Grass*, both in terms of age and experiences. I think I've grown up since and this is a deeper, darker, more heart-felt novel with a much stronger story.

Q: **Yet *Keep Off the Grass* was a significant commercial success and reasonably well-reviewed. This leads me to my next question. Literary critics have come down heavily on the new generation of Indian writers. Does criticism bother you?**

KB: On the contrary, I think criticism is tremendously helpful. When your novel is reviewed by seasoned critics, who've read everything from Salman Rushdie's epics to Salman Khan's biography, you get a free education of sorts. I deeply valued the feedback I received from critics as well as the hundreds of readers who wrote to me after reading *KOTG* – and consciously acted upon it. Given the mixed reviews on plotting, I focused heavily on *JGD's* plotting while trying to retain the pace and freshness that made *KOTG* a success.

Q: **How long did it take you to write *JGD*?**

KB: I usually start with a big theme in mind and allow the story to work itself in my head for a while before I put pen to paper. The theme I was playing around with for *JGD* was around success and whether living a stable, even-keeled life is better than a rich, interesting life with towering ups and abysmal lows. During this time,

I was also backpacking for a year in between jobs and travelled to some pretty interesting places and ended up meeting quite an odd assortment of people on the road and in youth hostels. Somewhere in the middle of the trip, I began to realize that no matter where I went, whether Cambodia or Brazil or Mongolia or India, there seemed to be more similarities than dissimilarities in people, feelings and ideas. Hence this intercontinental journey of the protagonist began to fuse with the original theme. So I guess the story was playing around in my head for almost a year, but the actually act of writing took four or five months which began when I joined my new job.

Q: **So you wrote while pursuing a full-time job? Do you find it difficult to balance your corporate career with writing?**

KB: No, I don't think my corporate career is coming between me and the Nobel Prize for Literature! The lack of skill and ideas limits me more than a lack of time. I'm lucky that I'm in a very fulfilling line of work which actually infuses my life with energy rather than sap it out of me. I work in Brand Management, which requires a lot of leadership, teamwork and creativity and you work with a lot of diverse, interesting folks – advertising agencies, design agencies and such – which always keeps things interesting.

I also feel that having a steady career makes me a better writer. I can choose to write what I want to and compose from the heart because I don't have to cater to the latest publishing trends or specialize in the genre I've written in before or lobby for author awards or worry about networking for film deals. I don't really need the money from writing, nor is writing my only source of self-worth.

Q: **From a film deal perspective, your first novel was optioned by a Hollywood studio and received a lot of Bollywood interest as well. Do you envision a similar response to _JGD_?**

KB: I don't know. It occurred by happenstance the first time around as well. The book was picked up casually in airport and hotel bookshops by the directors who contacted me. I hope something similar happens this time, but ultimately writing has to be its own reward. Rather than a great film deal, I'd probably feel a greater sense of accomplishment in writing an honest, engaging book which touches some hearts.

Q: **_'Write about what you know'_ is said to be the mantra for good writing. Have you lived through any of the varied events that happened to the protagonist in _JGD_?**

KB: No, I've never been a drug lord, a Buddhist monk, a genocide survivor, a homeless accountant, a deadly game fighter or even a software mogul! I'm more of a believer of 'Write about what you can feel'. I deeply relate to Nikhil, Monk Namche, Coke Buddha, Nick,

Johnny and the other avatars of the protagonist. In various stages of my life, I've experienced the same sense of displacement and failure as also the unconditional love and friendship that the protagonist experiences. Of course, my life has never been this dramatic but then these leaps of fancy are what make fiction so compelling.

Q: Who are your writing inspirations?

KB: I'm inspired by both films and literature. *Johnny Gone Down*, for instance, was inspired by the dark, futile mood of films like *Oldboy*, *The Deer Hunter* and *Amores Perros* as it was by the incredible journey of *Forrest Gump* (which is one of my favorite novels and a mighty decent film as well) and the surreal adventures of Sonchai Jitpleecheep, the Buddhist detective-protagonist of John Burdett's Bangkok novels, *Bangkok 8, Bangkok Tattoo* and *Bangkok Haunts*. Closer home, Ruskin Bond, Upamanyu Chatterjee and Mohsin Hamid are among my favorite contemporary writers.

Q: Indian writing in English has gone through a great transformation. What do you think about Indian publishing today and where it's going?

KB: I'm too small a person to attempt a knowledgeable answer to this big a question. All I can say is that like any other era in Indian publishing or anywhere else, I think there are a few good novels and many more bad novels.

Q: What is your next novel about?

KB: I'm not sure yet. I'm getting interested in mysticism and occult sciences as also in the importance of charity and giving back so it's likely going to be some combination of these ideas. But that's all I know right now. Before I begin writing another novel though, I think I need both silence and some new experiences to nurture the substance within. Otherwise I'll end up recycling the same ideas in a different story.